GARLANDS OF GOLD

17th-century Rotterdam.

Young Saskia is lady's maid to wealthy merchant's wife Vrouw Gibbons, but her talent for manufacturing beautifying face balms far exceeds her lowly status. When the Gibbons family returns to England, Saskia goes with them and sets up in business selling the beauty products which have earned her a devoted clientele, and hopes to win the heart of Grinling Gibbons, her employees' only son, a man whose interests lie elsewhere

Rosalind Laker titles available from
Severn House Large Print

Brilliance
To Dream of Snow

GARLANDS OF GOLD

Rosalind Laker

Severn House Large Print
London & New York

This first large print edition published 2010
in Great Britain and the USA by
SEVERN HOUSE PUBLISHERS LTD of
9-15 High Street, Sutton, Surrey, SM1 1DF.
First world regular print edition published 2008 by
Severn House Publishers Ltd., London and New York.

British Library Cataloguing in Publication Data

Laker, Rosalind.
　Garlands of gold.
　1. Women domestics--Fiction. 2. Rotterdam (Netherlands)--
　Social conditions--17th century--Fiction. 3. England--
　Social conditions--17th century--Fiction. 4. Love
　stories. 5. Large type books.
　I. Title
　823.9'14-dc22

　ISBN-13: 978-0-7278-7816-8

Printed and bound in Great Britain by
MPG Books Ltd, Bodmin, Cornwall.

To Mary Truy, who in 1611 signed her name in the newly published book of receipts that is now one of my most treasured possessions.

Author's Note

I have woven the events of Grinling Gibbons' life, including the fate of his house and that he lived on London's Bow Street until the end of his days, into my story, but apart from historical personages all the characters are fictional.

Grinling Gibbons, 1648–1721

One

Amid the cobbles the rain-pitted puddles were slivers of silver splashing up to soak the skirt-hems of the woman running heedlessly through them in her desperate haste. As she reached her destination, a tall old house in a long row that stretched along the street, she stumbled on the stone stoop and fell to her knees. Then, recovering her balance, she seized the heavy knocker and hammered without pause on the door. Rivulets of rain were running down her face, the hood of her crimson cloak having fallen back from her head, but she was oblivious to everything except her frantic need to be admitted.

'Open up!' she cried fiercely on a sob of exhaustion.

Upstairs in a simply furnished room on the sixth floor her fifteen-year-old daughter, Saskia, was writing down a beauty receipt in a red leather-bound book. She had already illustrated each stage of the procedure, partly because it added to her interest and also because she enjoyed drawing and had a flair for it. The receipt, a variation on a previous entry, she had entitled *Another way to make hair of a fair yellow or golden colour*. She had no need of such an artifice herself, for her hair beneath its plain, folded-back white cap was naturally of a rich bronze hue, but yellow was a fashionable hair colour and the aid to it had to be usefully recorded. Continuing in her neat hand, she wrote: *The last water that is drawn from honey, being a deep red colour, performs the same excellently, but the same has a strong smell and therefore must be sweetened by...*

Abruptly she raised her head from her task, hearing the commotion far below. Visitors did not usually do more than knock once politely, but perhaps drunken seamen from ships in the great harbour nearby were out to cause trouble again, frequently creating fights and brawls or smashing windows. Knowing how alarmed her foster mother had been on several previous occasions, she dropped her quill pen on to the table and darted across to the window. Throwing it wide into the night, she leaned out.

'Go away!' she called down fiercely. Then she saw that the street was deserted and whoever had banged the knocker so fiercely had apparently been admitted. Perhaps it was only someone wanting accommodation and desperate to get out of the rain, for her foster mother kept a respectable house and had regular lodgers in all her rooms.

She continued to rest her arms on the window sill, breathing in the damp air while the raindrops danced on the stone ledge. On a fine night the stars seemed close enough for her to seize a handful of them, for she felt nearer the sky here in her room than the street far below that was illumined by the sparse light from flickering

8

wall lamps. It seemed to her that these old Dutch houses, tall and narrow with their handsome, variegated gables, huddled together as if fearful of toppling down into the many byways that laced this vibrant, exciting city where shipping from all over the world was forever coming and going in its great harbour, bringing the mingled aromas of exotic spices, tarry ropes and storm-tested sails. She loved every salt-encrusted stick and stone of it.

Yet Rotterdam was not her birthplace. She had been born on Dutch soil when her French mother had just crossed into the United Provinces of the Netherlands and been forced to halt her travels to give birth in the back room of an inn. Diane Marchand did not move on again until she had taken her newborn to the local church to be baptized with a Dutch Christian name to please the child's absent father, a merchant dealing in cheeses from this land of many dykes and windmills. He and her mother had become lovers during their short acquaintance in the Parisian springtime, but he left without word or warning when she discovered that she was pregnant, all his promises of marriage having come to nothing.

Yet for all her frail, almost ethereal beauty, Diane had a will of steel. It was because he had once let slip that he had a house in Rotterdam that she had set out to find him, determined that he should accept his responsibilities. With dreams of the future she had studied the Dutch language during the time they were together and had gained enough fluency to make herself understood. In Rotterdam, after much searching, she had located his house only to find that it had become a place of mourning with a grieving widow and five children, for he had died following an accident only weeks before.

Although shocked and grief-stricken herself by the news, for she had loved him passionately, Diane did not reveal to the widow the true reason for her enquiry about him. Instead, sparing the woman further sorrow, she had made a plausible excuse for calling and left again as quickly as possible. Always practical and level-headed, she soon found a kindly Dutch widow, Cornelia van Beek, to foster her child. She also gained work for herself as a lady's maid, which was how she had previously earned her living.

Saskia closed the window again before turning once more to sit down and take up her quill pen to continue making the entry in her special record book with its fine red leather binding and brass clasp that needed a key. For some time her mother had been teaching her all the arts of a lady's personal maid and everything had to be written up and kept secure. It had been instilled in her never to reveal the secret ingredients that made up much of what was being handed down to her. Only thus, Diane insisted, could Saskia build up the necessary mystique surrounding her beautifying powers and thus ensure a secure reputation for herself and her skills.

Saskia was also kept busy making up to those same receipts the face balms and the pomades and powders and rouges that her mother needed in her work and also for selling on the side to private customers with Vrouw van Beek as her agent. It was an honest business, for Diane bought out of her own pocket all the necessary ingredients and the containers for the finished products while always gaining a little profit even after paying Vrouw van Beek a percentage.

Yet carrying out this pleasant work was not all that had to be done in Saskia's daily routine. Even before leaving school at the age of twelve, which was usual for girls, she had helped Vrouw van Beek in the house by carrying out various domestic chores.

Her daily tasks included scrubbing the stone stoop of the house and sweeping the pavement outside, for she was as diligent as any Dutch housewife in keeping the black and white tiled floors, common to most houses in Holland, spotless and shining. It was a general opinion upheld in this Calvinist society that cleanliness was next to godliness and therefore a way of keeping at bay the pestilence that swept the land from time to time.

In addition to all else and at her mother's whim, Saskia had English lessons from a retired governess addressed as Mistress Seymour, who was one of Vrouw van Beek's permanent lodgers. The elderly London-born woman had once been employed by a titled English family, who had taken her with them when they had fled from England into exile with Charles II after the royalist forces had finally been defeated by Cromwell's army at the Battle of Worcester. Although the King had since been restored to the English throne, loyal followers going home with him, Mistress Seymour's pupils had grown beyond her instruction and she had chosen to remain in Holland on a comfortable stipend allotted to her by the family. She liked to have her hair dressed by Saskia as did several other women tenants, which allowed the girl to earn a little money for herself. For relaxation Saskia passed time with friends from her schooldays, whom she met as often as possible, a highlight being a visit to one of the many chocolate houses when all were able to afford such a treat.

'Saskia!'

Vrouw van Beek's voice had come echoing up the stairs from the hall far below. Immediately Saskia left her chair again and darted out on to the landing at the head of the deep and twisting flight.

'Yes, Foster Mother?' she called down questioningly.

'Your mama is here! You are to put on your cloak and bring down your record book! Nothing else!'

Saskia's eyes widened. Although she saw her mother more frequently now than in the past, it was never at night and, because of her mother's delicate health, rarely in the rain. Within seconds she had snatched up her book and automatically locked its clasp. Grabbing her cloak off its peg, she threw it around her and with the book tucked safely under her arm she went on flying feet down the stairs that twisted and turned at every landing.

She experienced a sense of shock as soon as she saw her mother, pale-lipped and rain-soaked, sitting slumped in a chair.

'Mama! What's wrong?' Saskia, her green eyes dark with concern, rushed to put her arms about her mother's thin shoulders.

Diane managed a slight smile of reassurance and patted her daughter's anxious face. 'Nothing at all. I'm only out of breath.' She darted a warning glance at Vrouw van Beek in fear of a well-intentioned contradiction. 'I took too much haste to get here, but I have such great news to tell you. Just an hour ago Vrouw Gibbons finally agreed – on condition that you please her – for you to assist me in my attendance on her. Now we have to get back to the house as quickly as possible, because you are to dress her hair this evening for an informal supper at home.' She paused, caught for a few moments by a cough. 'There's no need to be nervous, because I shall supervise you.'

Saskia had become speechless with excitement and was not in the least apprehensive. It was what she wanted – the chance at last to start on a career for herself. This was just the beginning! A first step!

'Am I to live there too?' she asked eagerly.

'Yes, of course. Vrouw van Beek has kindly offered to pack up your belongings and we can send for them tomorrow. Now put on your clogs without any more delay.'

Taking off her indoor shoes, Saskia thrust them into the pocket of her cloak and turned to the rack by the door where she had left her clogs earlier in the day. She had been taught from a young age that no considerate person wore footwear indoors that would soil floors and when she was washing the tiles she was glad of it. Impulsively she turned and flung her arms about her foster mother in a loving hug. When she was a toddler she had begun to call the woman *Mama,* thinking she had two mothers, one of whom tucked her into bed at night, told her stories and sang to her, and also one whom she rarely saw and was usually irritable. But Diane, ever possessive, had soon put a stop to that, not knowing that the bond remained.

'I'll be back to see you whenever I can, dear Foster Mother!' Saskia declared emotionally, suddenly feeling wrenched apart by this unexpected break with the woman and her childhood home that were both dear to her. 'I'll still dress your hair when I come and buff your fingernails till they shine just as you like them.'

Cornelia van Beek doubted that Diane would allow it now she was getting the girl under her complete control at last. Yet the woman was ill, which was why after many requests her employer was finally allowing her to have her daughter's assistance. Nobody could begrudge the unfortunate Frenchwoman that blessing.

'We'll have to wait and see what spare time you have,' she answered. There were tears in her eyes at this abrupt parting from the child whom she had long since come to think of as her own. How empty the house was going to be without her lively presence. 'From what your mother has told me in the past,' she continued, 'I believe Vrouw Gibbons to be a very demanding English lady. You may find yourself running after her all

14

the time with not a minute to spare.'

'I'll always find time to come back and see you!'

Diane had struggled to her feet. 'We must go now,' she insisted. 'Come, Saskia.'

Cornelia van Beek cupped the girl's face in both hands and kissed her on the brow. 'Farewell, dear child. May life ever be good to you.'

After a final embrace Saskia turned to her mother, giving her a supporting arm, and together they bowed their hooded heads against the driving rain as they left the house. Cornelia van Beek stood in the candlelit doorway to watch them go, tears running down her face as fast as she dried them away with the edge of her apron. She had known the parting would come one day, but had never anticipated that it would be so abrupt. There would be the promised visits from the girl from time to time, but nothing would ever be the same again. She returned Saskia's last wave before they turned a corner out of sight.

More than once on their way, in spite of the shortage of time, Diane drew her daughter into the shelter of a doorway or under a lintel, needing a short rest before carrying on again. As she began gasping for breath, leaning her weight on her daughter's arm, Saskia became even more concerned.

'I can see that you are far from well, Mama,' Saskia said anxiously. 'Vrouw Gibbons has been working you too hard, but from now on you'll have me to take on all the tedious chores.'

Diane nodded, but could not speak.

15

As they continued slowly on their way they met a section of the Night Watch marching along to take up their posts of duty. They maintained law and order in the city, which was like any other in having its full share of crime. Saskia found the fully armed and disciplined men a comforting sight, for no villain would dare to appear while they were in the vicinity.

Soon the Gibbons' seven-storied house came into sight. Built of red brick with sandstone ornamentation, it had an imposing entrance with twin flights of steps leading from the street, the handrails delicately fashioned. Yet it was no wider than the average Dutch house as it stood nudging sides with its neighbours, for the old tax on the width of a building was restrictive. Yet Saskia knew that just as with Vrouw van Beek's home and most others it would be a labyrinth of rooms, some of them mezzanine, and would stretch back deeply to a courtyard or a garden at its rear. She also knew from all she had been told that Heer James Gibbons, a draper, and his wife, Bessie, were originally from England and he had become extremely prosperous dealing in exotic silks imported by the East India Company. They had three children, a married daughter and an elder son, both of whom lived away, and a younger son with the unusual Christian name of Grinling, which had been his mother's maiden name.

Grinling was born in Holland and when he had shown no inclination to follow his father into the drapery business his exceptional skill at carving had resulted in his being apprenticed in Amster-

16

dam to the renowned sculptor and woodcarver, Artus Quellen, who was responsible for statues and other grand decoration of the Town Hall presently being built there. Then, his apprenticeship at an end, Grinling had set off on a trip to Italy accompanied by a friend, who had been a fellow apprentice in Amsterdam, but had trained to be an architect. With them, as was customary, was a middle-aged tutor, whose duties included instructing them in the arts, taking them to see all the important historical sights and, most importantly, keeping them out of trouble.

'Follow me,' Diane said, going ahead down a narrow paved passageway incorporated into the side of the house to reach a doorway. There they entered a small hall where they changed their footwear, Saskia putting on her indoor shoes again. A delicious aroma of meat roasting on a spit drifted from the kitchen, but Diane turned instead to a flight of narrow stairs.

'Avoid going through the kitchen whenever you can,' she advised, holding on to the newel post while attempting to regain her breath and gather some strength before mounting the flight. 'There is always such a hot, greasy atmosphere when cooking is taking place and the smell can cling to your clothes. You must also remember that as a lady's maid you are a step above all the rest of the staff, even the housekeeper, because you alone will be privy to my lady's secrets in this or any other house in which you are employed.'

Saskia nodded. She had been instructed in all these matters by her mother many times before and had them written down in the early pages of her red leather book. She could only suppose that her memory was being refreshed now that all she had been taught was about to be put into practice at last. Putting her arm about her mother's waist Saskia supported her as they made slow progress up the stairs.

On the second floor Diane had her own small parlour and adjoining it was a bedchamber where a truckle bed had already been placed at the foot of her four-poster bed. It was there that her daughter would sleep. She sank down on to a chair to rest until she could draw breath again more easily and resume her responsibilities once more.

Saskia was dazzled by everything in her mother's abode, for it was the first time she had ever been there. She began examining it all with delight. There were some pretty little ornaments and the chairs, although worn, were upholstered in yellow silk while the bed-drapery, far from new, was wonderfully woven with a pattern of flowers and trimmed with gilt tassels. On a side table was her mother's Spanish strongbox, which she knew had been a gift from her Dutch father to Diane in the early days of their love affair. It was finely designed and had an intricate lock. Saskia supposed that he had picked it up somewhere on his travels. Without doubt her mother had expected it to hold love letters, but those never came. She had never seen it open, but supposed that Diane kept her savings in it. Fascinated, she traced her finger along the curlicues of its border pattern.

Then Diane ended abruptly her daughter's exploration of the room. 'Take off that damp cap now and tidy your hair,' she said sharply, rising to her feet. 'I'll find another one for you and also an apron to wear.'

The apron and the cap were both lace-edged and the girl felt as elegant as any lady as she regarded herself in a mirror. Diane had changed out of her mud-splashed skirts and also replaced her rain-soaked cap with a fresh one of linen that she had taken from a drawer. Now she looked her daughter critically up and down before giving a brusque nod.

'You'll do for now,' she said crisply, always sparing with praise. 'Remember that you must address our employer as *Mevrouw* Gibbons at all times.'

Turning abruptly on her heel, she led the way out of the room.

It was only a short distance along a corridor to Vrouw Gibbons' boudoir and there they entered into a flow of candlelight.

A mildly pretty woman in her late forties, her face bare of any cosmetics at the present time, was seated in readiness at her toilet-table, a silk robe over her petticoats, and her hair already unpinned. As an infant she had been baptized Elizabeth, but her late father had always called her Bessie and that pet name had stayed with her. As an adult she liked to think she had the same regal grace as England's good Queen Bess, who had reigned in England over a century ago, although she knew from the portraits she had seen of the royal lady that she herself was far

19

more comely.

With some surprise she viewed Saskia's reflection in her oval mirror, not having expected to see a girl on the brink of beauty. Diane's daughter was taller than average with a narrow waist, a taut and well-shaped young bosom, thick-lashed green eyes that were bright and sparkling, the cheekbones high and the chin determined, all with a vivacious look about her. She also had a creamy complexion and showing under the cap was gleaming hair full of reddish-gold lights that any woman would envy. Her mouth, full-lipped and well shaped, hinted at a passionate nature. Bessie Gibbons hoped it would not mean tantrums or, much worse, prove attractive to Grinling when he came home again from his travels. Young men were so susceptible and, from what she had observed, he was no different from all the rest. Neither was his English friend, Robert Harting, who was presently travelling with him.

'Good evening, Saskia,' she said in Dutch, inclining her head. 'So you are going to do your best to please me at all times.'

Saskia bobbed a curtsy. 'Yes, *mevrouw*,' she replied.

'Now I know that you and your mother speak French when you are together,' Vrouw Gibbons continued, 'but here in this house we speak only Dutch. My husband, Heer Gibbons, has always considered it our duty to be true Dutch citizens in every way ever since he and I made Holland our home not long after we were married.' Her voice flattened tonelessly. 'Perhaps never to return permanently to our roots.'

Saskia's immediate thought was that this Englishwoman suffered from bouts of homesickness, although Holland had been her place of abode for many years and she had even lived for some time with her English parents in Amsterdam before marrying James Gibbons. Yet for Saskia it was easy to recognize the signs, for there were times when she had seen Diane suffering despairing bouts of yearning for her homeland. Vrouw Gibbons obviously needed cheering up and nothing pleased a woman more than a complete change of coiffure that suited her. In her notebook Saskia had made many little drawings of coiffures that she had tried on herself as well as on Vrouw van Beek, all of them her own original variations on the current mode of a wide look to a coiffure with the back of the neck left exposed.

'I know how my mother usually dresses your hair, *mevrouw*, but if you would allow me,' she said, ignoring an anxious gesture from Diane, 'I should like to give you a completely new hairstyle this evening, but one that is also in fashion.'

The woman raised her eyebrows, taken aback by this show of initiative, but intrigued at the same time. 'Very well. But remember it is not for a grand occasion. Heer Gibbons and I are just dining at home with two close friends. Now let me see how you can apply cosmetics discreetly.'

All the little pots and powders needed were lined up on the toilet table in front of her. Saskia knew them all, for she had mixed the contents herself. Immediately she began to work, applying a delicate amount of cream to the woman's upturned face. Then a little colour was added to her fair eyebrows and lashes, followed by the softest bloom to her cheeks and a rosy hue to her lips. Finally powder was carefully applied, being pressed to her face by a pad without clouds of it flying about in the air. Now it was time for the woman's hair to be dressed.

Vrouw Gibbons indicated a wooden box that was on the toilet table. 'Some of my daily hair combs and ornaments are in there. Use whatever you need.'

Saskia paused before lifting the lid. It was exquisitely carved with a design of cherubs and ribbons, unlike anything she had ever seen before. 'This is beautiful!' she exclaimed, forgetting the golden rule never to comment on an employer's possessions without invitation.

'That is one of my son's apprentice pieces,' Vrouw Gibbons said casually, her thoughts centred on herself and her appearance at the present time, and then added almost automatically, 'He is extremely talented.'

'Yes, indeed! How proud you must be of him, *mevrouw*! These carved ribbons are so delicate that it looks as though the bows could be untied.' Then Saskia heard her mother's warning little cough in the background, reminding her not to make any more such comments. Hastily she raised the lid of the velvet lined box and took stock of the contents. Then she set to work, brushing the woman's hair until it fell smoothly down her back. Carefully she divided the hair into three strands, twisting the centre one into a

22

coil high on the back of the woman's head, exposing her neck as was fashionable. Then, taking two strings of tiny glass beads from the box, she began arranging the side hair into short loops layered over the ears, intertwining the beads at the same time. She worked swiftly and silently while watched by Vrouw Gibbons in the mirror and by her mother from a chair at the back of the room. When she had fastened the loops invisibly with a skilful use of hairpins the result was both charming and flattering with the necessary width to the coiffure and a discreet sparkle from the beads.

Taking up the hand-mirror, Saskia displayed the back and sides of the woman's head to her in the toilet table's looking-glass. Vrouw Gibbons turned her head critically to the left and to the right, touching the new coiffure with her finger-tips. Then, after what seemed an age to Diane, who was on the edge of her seat with anxiety, the woman smiled condescendingly.

'That's very pretty, Saskia. I like it. Now you shall assist me in dressing.'

As the girl helped her into a cinnamon-hued velvet gown Vrouw Gibbons continued to be pleased. There was no fumbling with the back lacing from these agile young fingers, and now the care with which the girl was smoothing down the fashionably wide lace collar over her shoulders showed an alert attention to detail. For choice she would never have taken on a fresh young beauty to be a constant reminder of her own fading looks, which no longer dazzled as much as in the past. Yet that was not the reason

23

why she had opposed for so long Diane's request for her to take the girl into the household. It was simply that she had always had a mature woman to wait on her and had feared that with Diane's daughter she would have to deal with inexperience and blundering incompetence. Even as late as this evening she had hesitated uncertainly before finally committing herself to giving Saskia a trial, although it was becoming apparent that Diane with her failing health would not be able to carry on alone much longer. It was no wonder that Diane had immediately rushed from the house to fetch the girl.

Looking across at Diane in the mirror, she gave a little nod that conveyed her approval of Saskia and saw relief flood into the sick woman's face. Now Diane could feel assured in the last months of her life that her daughter had a good home and perhaps even a secure future.

Immediately, Diane rose from her chair to come across the room and open a jewel-box from the toilet table. Then she held it as she had done so many times before for Vrouw Gibbons to make her choice. It also had a beautifully carved lid and she did not want her daughter making any more inappropriate remarks, but Saskia was gazing at it in wonder.

'Your son must have magic in his fingertips, *mevrouw*,' she said in awe.

'You have a vivid imagination,' Vrouw Gibbons replied on a cool note as she selected a pair of topaz earrings. She did not want this girl flattering Grinling with such praise, however innocently. 'I assure you that it is all done mun-

24

danely with skill and a chisel.'

She exchanged a meaningful look with Diane. Over the years they had come to understand each other completely. Diane nodded. The English-woman's message was clear. Saskia must be kept away from the son and heir. Then Vrouw Gibbons turned to the girl again. 'My husband and I have a very busy social life and from tonight you shall attend me when I retire, which will spare your mother from keeping any more late hours.'

Saskia bobbed. 'Yes, *mevrouw*,' she answered, glad that this woman seemed to have the same protective attitude towards her mother as she did herself.

As Vrouw Gibbons went from the room and the door closed behind her Saskia spun around on her toes to Diane in jubilation. 'I pleased her! Did you see that, Mama?'

'Yes, I did,' Diane said, her voice tired from the strain of the past hour, but then she added sharply, 'I should have been most displeased if it had been otherwise. Now I'll show you how to turn back her bed for tonight and where to place her night shift, robe and slippers.' In the adjoining dressing room, which contained a hip bath painted with flowers, she indicated the close stool. 'If she uses the close stool before going to bed or at any other time you ring the bell for a maidservant to come with a replacement container and the used one will be taken away.'

Together they made the bed ready and then left the room to have supper, which was served in Diane's own little parlour. Vrouw Gibbons was not late to bed and again was privately pleased with Saskia's careful attention. That night Saskia wore one of her mother's spare night shifts and slept well.

Next morning Diane was in a state of collapse after the exertion of the previous evening and fell when she attempted to leave her bed. Saskia helped her back into it and then rushed to tell their employer what had happened. Deeply concerned, Vrouw Gibbons sent at once for the doctor. He came, an elderly man handsomely dressed in black velvet, his grey periwig curling all over his shoulders. The housekeeper accompanied him into the patient's room, brusquely ordering Saskia out of the room to wait outside the door. When they emerged, the doctor, who looked grave, ignored the girl's frantic questioning and the housekeeper cruelly thrust her aside.

'Get out of the doctor's way, girl!'

He made his report to Vrouw Gibbons, who in her turn had to break the news to Saskia that her mother's days were numbered.

Diane never rose from her bed again. Everything possible was done for her comfort. She lingered for six weeks before she took her last breath, flickering out like a candle-flame. Bessie Gibbons shared Saskia's grief, for Diane had been both friend and confidante in times of joy and trouble, once even saving her from what would have been a dangerous indiscretion. Even her husband, James Gibbons, a thin-faced, middle-aged man with kindly brown eyes that by chance were the colour of his favourite periwig, showed his compassion with gentle words to the bereaved girl.

'This is a hard loss for you, Saskia, but time will heal and you will always know that you were blessed by having a good and caring mother.'

'I thank you, *mijnheer*,' she answered in little more than a strained whisper, bobbing to him while keeping tears at bay.

She was sobered by her mother's death. It was as if a cloak of responsibility had fallen on to her shoulders. Her first act was to inform the house-keeper that never again was she to be given orders as on the morning of her mother's collapse.

'In future I shall be the one giving instruction in everything relating to Vrouw Gibbons' *toilette*, her comfort and attire. Is that understood?'

The housekeeper turned a fiery red with anger, but tightened her lips and bobbed a curtsy. On her own again Saskia breathed a sigh of satisfaction at the bold step she had taken, but she had had to establish her authority in the hierarchy of the servants' world and show that she was no longer 'only Diane's daughter'.

Saskia was grateful that Vrouw Gibbons, showing the kindness of which she was capable at times, had given her two other adjoining rooms to have as her own on another floor. As it was, it was very distressing to sort out her mother's clothes and possessions, causing her to shed more tears.

She unlocked the Spanish strongbox in her

new accommodation. She found that it held a fitted tray in which lay a ruby pendant on a gold chain, which she had never seen her mother wear, and she wondered if it had been a gift from her errant father. If that were its origins, then maybe Diane had found it too painful a reminder ever to display on her bosom. Lifting out the tray, she found underneath her mother's small savings in a little leather drawstring pouch. There was also a large key, although there was no label on it to give any indication as to where it belonged. She replaced the tray and noted that there was just the right amount of space left to accommodate her red book of beauty receipts. She placed the volume in it and locked the box up again. Now it was doubly secure from any spying eye.

That same evening Vrouw Gibbons all unwittingly solved the mystery of the large key. 'I have just remembered, Saskia,' she said, 'when your mother came into my employ she brought a travelling chest with her. It was taken up to the top attic where she had access to it, for it would have taken up too much space in her rooms.'

'I believe I have found the key to it, *mevrouw*.'

'Then tomorrow go up there and see if it contains anything you want to keep.'

Next morning, as Saskia mounted the stairs to the top attic, she wondered what the travelling box would contain and why her mother had never mentioned it to her. Then on second thoughts she recalled that her mother had never really conversed with her on any matter, the few facts she knew about her father had been like

28

getting blood from a stone. But in any case she did not think the chest would hold anything of much importance or else Diane would have felt compelled to speak of it to her. Her guess was that it held books or perhaps some of her baby clothes, although her mother had never been in the least sentimental.

To her surprise it was a stout iron-bound wooden chest that awaited her. It had been placed under a circular window that gave her plenty of light as she knelt down and inserted the key. The lock turned easily and slowly she raised the lid.

To her astonishment it was packed full of tiny parcels, some wrapped in pieces of soft cloth, others in old French news-sheets or odd scraps of paper. Sitting back on her heels, she picked out one of the tiny parcels at random and removed the paper wrapping carefully. To her astonishment a beautiful little pot was revealed, suitable for containing any cosmetic cream or salve. The lid was delicately hand-painted with a spray of lilac. Putting it down on the floor beside her she opened another of the little parcels. This pot was slightly larger, but just as charming, although the rosebuds that covered it had obviously been painted by a different hand. Eagerly she uncovered yet another pot, which was of a rare fineness and from Japan, judging by the little figures with parasols standing together on a bridge. Holding it up to the light she saw that it was quite translucent and she marvelled that it had never been broken, which in itself was a tribute to her mother's careful packing. Then came a rose water bottle and some perfume flasks, two of which had slightly dented gold tops.

There was no doubt in her mind that most of the items were antique, although none was cracked. She took a guess that Diane had hunted for them among worthless second-hand goods on market stalls, in the corners of dusty shops, even perhaps in stinking rubbish. Had any of them been new their cost would have been beyond her mother's slender purse. The floor around her began to be covered by the pretty objects as if flowers were springing up all around her.

The striking of a clock in the distance forced her to halt in her discoveries, reminding her of her duties. A quick glance at a few of the news-sheets showed that some had been printed before her mother had left France. Others, wrapped around little pots of Delft china, were more recent, showing how her mother had continued the collection until her illness had begun to over-take her. It was impossible to estimate the number of items that were packed so closely together in the chest, but there were at least two hundred or perhaps even more.

Tears filled her eyes at the thought of her mother's sacrifice. How many hours of hard searching had gone into buying just one of the pots and how many cobbled streets trod to find yet another pretty item to be washed and dried and then carefully packed away. It showed how ambitious Diane had been originally for herself before a pregnancy had changed the course of her life, for these lovely goods could stock the shelves of a shop or be sold containing beauty products at a high price to those who could afford them. Then Diane, putting aside her own dream, had continued collecting for her daughter's future.

After Saskia had replaced all the pots and flasks that she had had time to examine she closed and locked the chest again, realizing at the same time that it held her true inheritance. It explained why her mother's savings had been so small, for Diane had invested all she could spare in increasing her collection, clinging to the hope that her daughter would benefit greatly one day from the contents of the chest. Feeling a little dazed by her discovery Saskia made her way downstairs again.

Later that day Vrouw Gibbons made a stipulation, which Saskia knew she must obey if she was to keep her employment.

'Your mother,' the woman said, 'had a sideline in selling her beauty preparations elsewhere. I ignored the matter simply because she had been with me so long and I never had any fault to find otherwise. But it has to stop now. Anything you make will be only for me. Is that understood?'

Saskia nodded. 'Yes, *mevrouw*.'

There was no other answer she could give.

Her book was so thick with pages that were yet to be filled that she doubted if she would ever reach the last one, for her handwriting was small and neat, enabling her to list a number of processes on a single page. Yet she continued to make fresh entries in her book whenever she experimented and found a variation that seemed to be an improvement on a previous receipt. She had also begun another section, which had come about through observing how meticulously Vrouw Gibbons arranged flowers, how she organized suppers and banquets when she always made a beautiful setting for the table. Yet often Saskia wished she could add a touch herself and visualized how she would have arranged the candles and the flowers and the napery. So, since she was only able to view the finished table, there was consolation in writing up her own ideas into her book and making little drawings to illustrate them.

Once when Saskia was seated with a sketch pad in the courtyard, being free for a little while from her duties, she was drawing sprigs of herbs plucked from the kitchen garden when Vrouw Gibbons came by. The woman stopped to look over Saskia's shoulder and was immediately full of admiration for the sketch in progress.

'How delicately and accurately you have captured your chosen specimens, Saskia,' she said. 'What else have you sketched?'

Saskia had risen to her feet and the woman held out her hand for the sketch pad, which was given to her. With genuine interest Vrouw Gibbons looked through the various drawings, for there had been a great flowering of art throughout the Dutch Republic in recent years and paintings were bought avidly by the rich from the acclaimed masters while those of lesser incomes purchased the work of struggling artists, who were thankful to get whatever monies they could for their efforts. Even the humblest dwelling had at least one or two pictures on the walls.

Vrouw Gibbons was proud that a number of fine paintings enhanced the rooms of her home. She was able to judge that Saskia's sketches were not of any great talent, but they were charming in their own way. There were market scenes done from memory, two drawings of the Gibbons' courtyard from different viewpoints, some of tulips and other blossoms, and several of the kitchen cat and her kittens.

After perusing the rest of the sketches with a nod of approval Vrouw Gibbons handed the sketch pad back to her.

'You are quite talented, Saskia. I should like you to make drawings of the house for me. Would you do that?'

'Yes, indeed, *mevrouw*,' Saskia replied gladly.

After that day she did several drawings of the house, all of which pleased both Vrouw Gibbons and her husband, he having one framed for his office wall at his business premises.

As the weeks went by Saskia's red leather-bound book contained more and more fresh entries as she continued to experiment. Yet she was beginning to know Vrouw Gibbons' every turn of mood and how to cope when the woman was tired or irritable. Vrouw Gibbons particularly liked a face mask that Saskia had devised from rose petals and was unaware that resting on the bed while it dried did her as much good as the refreshing effect on her features by the mask itself. She was totally unaware that new cosmetic methods were being tried out on her all the time, always with Saskia's aim for improvement and reliance on pure ingredients. All that mattered to Bessie Gibbons was that she was always well satisfied with her appearance after Saskia's ministrations.

Two

Although at first Saskia had not been aware that her relationship with her employer had started off on an uncertain footing, she had soon realized as time went by that there was something about her that the Englishwoman resented. Yet she could not think how or why she was failing in some way. Then one day she was enlightened as to the cause by the elderly Dutch nurse, who had stayed on in the house as one of the family after caring for the Gibbons children and then acting as lady's maid to Bessie Gibbons until her bones had started to creak. That was when, to her relief, Diane had replaced her. The Gibbons children when young had called her Nanny Bobbins, because she was like many of her fellow countrywomen in being an expert lacemaker and whenever she had a spare moment bobbins were forever dancing under her fingers. She was still known by her nickname to everybody in the house.

34

Fiercely proud of her birthplace in the province of Nord-Holland, Nanny Bobbins wore a plain starched cap for weekday wear, but always the stiffly starched lace cap of the region for churchgoing and festival days. It had lappets at the side, which were pinned up to give a square silhouette. In a land of beautiful regional caps it was one of the simplest designs, but most becoming, even for Nanny Bobbins' withered old face, and she was presently making one for Saskia, a friendship having sprung up between them. One of the reasons why Saskia liked going to the nurse's room, quite apart from her enjoyment of the old woman's company, was that on display were many of Grinling's very early pieces of carving from when he was a young boy. She loved looking at them and wished she could have a glimpse of his home workshop, which was a room near the kitchen quarters, but kept locked in his absence.

Nanny Bobbins' downstairs accommodation was off one of the many passageways that veined the tall house. She had been moved there from an upstairs room after her unsteady balance had caused her to fall on the stairs. One afternoon Saskia, coming there to mend a petticoat in her company, put down her sewing basket after entering to pick up one of Grinling's carvings that she particularly admired. It was a full-blown rose so finely fashioned in pale lime wood that there was even a tiny dewdrop on one of the petals. She cupped it in her hands as she studied it anew.

'How does he manage to give wood the
35

fragility of flowers?' she said in awe.

'That is the young master's God-given gift,' the old woman replied, glancing up over her spectacles as Saskia replaced it. 'But you had better watch out that you don't get kicked out when he comes home.' There was a warning note in her voice. 'His mother might decide to get rid of you if you start praising his work too much to his face. It's bad enough for Vrouw Gibbons that she has you flitting around her like a summer's morning while she looks in her mirror and sees the wrinkles deepen and her waist thickening.'

Saskia retorted indignantly. 'You're mistaken! I've no conceit about my looks and so that reason doesn't apply to me in any way. I know she is often sharp-tongued, but it must be some other matter that makes her lose patience with me. My mother was beautiful and she never said that Vrouw Gibbons was difficult with her.'

'That's because they were the same age and in any case Bessie Gibbons was just as lovely when she was younger.'

'With my creams and lotions I make her look beautiful all the time,' Saskia exclaimed in exasperation, sitting down and taking up her sewing. 'Even her teeth are much whiter since I made up that new dentifrice for her with the crushed rosemary to use twice daily. What's more, she does exactly as I have told her in rinsing afterwards with pure conduit water or white wine. She prefers the wine.' She sat back in her chair. 'So nobody would notice me in her shade if I were ever present at the soirées and parties that she and Heer Gibbons give so frequently. As for her son, I don't want him!'

The nurse chuckled. 'Wait till you see Grinling. He's a fine young man and not only talented with his wood carving, but in the sphere of music too. He plays several musical instruments and has a splendid singing voice, which you are sure to hear. But be wise and remember to keep away.'

'I will,' Saskia replied emphatically and put an end to that line of the conversation by looking across at what the nurse was sewing. 'That is not the cap you are making for me. Is mine nearly finished?'

The old woman gave a nod. 'Yes, you should have had it for your sixteenth natal day, but that date has come and gone, so now it will have to be a gift from St Nicholaes.'

'Oh, must I wait until the sixth day of December?' Saskia protested in amusement, knowing she was being teased. 'That is still three weeks away!'

Nanny Bobbins' eyes twinkled. 'Maybe I will reconsider. Who can tell?'

Two days later excitement rippled through the house as Heer and Vrouw Gibbons received a letter from their son that had been sent from the Italian border. It meant that allowing for the length of time it had taken to reach them he and his companions could be expected very shortly. Yet when he and his fellow travellers arrived home there was nobody to greet him, his father being at the Gibbons warehouse and his mother visiting a sick friend. Only Saskia, halfway down the stairs to the reception hall, witnessed their noisy arrival, which coincided with the first snowfall of winter.

They had flung the door open from the street in a blast of cold air. Snowflakes whirled about them as they came clomping into the house in their fashionable bucket-topped boots, taking no heed of the spotless floor in the pleasure of their arrival. Laughing and shouting, scarlet and purple plumes fluttering on their wide-brimmed black hats, they swirled off their cloaks, seeming to fill the whole generous space of the reception hall. Grinling was nineteen years old, his friend a year older, but with the experience of travel on them they would no longer be the same youths who had left Rotterdam some months ago. In their wake came the tutor, a tired look on his face and with a wearied stance, but he was already giving directions to the porters carrying in the first of several large travelling boxes.

'Where is everybody?' one of the young men shouted with all the authority of belonging there before happening to glance up and catch sight of Saskia standing motionless on the stairs. She was without a cap, being on her way down to try on the new one that Nanny Bobbins had ready for her. She was unaware that a hanging lamp, which had been lit to counteract the dullness of the day, was illumining her seductive, chisel-cheeked beauty and making a red-gold harvest of her hair against the shadows of the stairs. Long lashes deepened the shade of her alert green eyes.

'Your parents are out, *mijnheer*,' she said,

amazed to feel her heart lift joyously as she looked down into merry, very blue eyes in a face wide, well-boned and tanned with a broad and powerful nose, his chin strong, his grin wide and white-toothed, his hair dark brown and tumbling in curls about his shoulder. This then was Grinling Gibbons of the breathtaking skill with a chisel. 'But please allow me to welcome you home.'

'Indeed you may! We have never met before. Are you a cousin, friend or neighbour to be here in my parents' absence?'

'I'm *Juffrouw* Saskia Marchand, your mother's personal maid.'

He raised his eyebrows mischievously. 'How fortunate for my mother! Allow me to present my friend, Robert Harting, born a citizen of England, but temporarily of Rotterdam.'

She knew already from Nanny Bobbins that Robert Harting's late father had been among Charles II's most loyal army generals and had brought his young son with him when he had accompanied the king into exile. But that had been some years ago now and the boy had become a man.

With a curious shiver, almost of apprehension, she knew instinctively that from the first moment Robert Harting had been watching her closely from under the wide brim of his hat. His black-lashed dark eyes were narrowed in a burning stare of such intensity that she put a hand involuntarily to her throat. She was momentarily unnerved by it, feeling gauche and awkward, and deeply resenting the way in which he was regarding her, a compressed line to his well-cut, experienced mouth that clearly knew its way in the world. Obviously it did not suit his stiff English pride to be presented to a servant of the household. He was not truly handsome, but he had an energetic and virile presence as if he could master any sport in the field or in the saddle. Then he surprised and annoyed her still further by sweeping off his hat and giving her an exaggerated bow far beyond anything remotely suitable for a household employee.

'I'm honoured, *mejuffrouw*,' he said strongly.

She inclined her head stiffly and then turned quickly away to give a greeting to the harassed-looking tutor, not wanting him to feel left out. 'I bid you welcome back to Holland, *mijnheer*.'

He acknowledged her words with a wearied nod. By now the housekeeper had come rushing into the hall. It was clear she had been taking a nap, her cap slightly askew and strands of her hair awry. She had brought other servants with her and Grinling was greeting them all as the men among them began assisting with the boxes. Saskia darted quickly down the remaining stairs and slipped away to the nurse's room.

'So they're home,' the old woman greeted her. 'I heard the commotion.'

'You are right,' Saskia declared, throwing herself down into a chair where she swung her feet up and then down again in a rustle of petticoats. 'Grinling is a fine young man and I retract what I said before. I do wish he could be for me, but –' she added hastily, seeing the old woman's frown – 'he is out of my reach and I know it. I certainly would not want his friend, who clearly was offended by Master Grinling presenting me to him. He made a most mocking bow to me.'

'You mean young Robert Harting, do you? Remember that he's English and their ways are different from ours. Heer Gibbons thinks he keeps a thoroughly Dutch household here. Yet in the daily routine he has never let me take a place at his table whereas a Dutch master – unless it was a formal occasion – would happily sit down to eat with loyal servants and never think himself lowered by it.'

Saskia gave a nod. 'My English teacher, Mistress Seymour, told me all about life in a grand house in England. I don't think I should like it there.'

The old woman gave her a sharp look. 'But you must make the best of it when the time comes. I believe that sooner or later Heer and Vrouw Gibbons will return to England, even though they have lived here all their married lives.' She paused, seeing Saskia's startled expression. 'Why else do you think your mother wanted you to learn English? She knew all about Bessie Gibbons' bouts of homesickness and never underestimated the woman's ability to get her own way eventually about going home to settle again in her native land.'

'Where did the mistress and Heer Gibbons meet each other? Was it in England?'

'Yes. She grew up there, but then her late father moved here to become an importer of tobacco and brought her with him. It was surely the reason why Heer Gibbons followed to set up as a silk merchant here in the Dutch Republic, which was how he came to marry his sweetheart here in another land.'

'But she could always visit her birthplace. She has done it in the past. My mother accompanied her on two or three trips when she went to stay with relatives living there.'

'Yes, but think of all the great disasters that have kept Vrouw Gibbons away from her homeland for periods much longer than she would have wished. There was that terrible plague that knocked people down like ninepins and even reached our shores, although mercifully not to the same extent. Then there was the dreadful Great Fire of London when the house she had inherited from an aunt was among the thousands of homes destroyed. Worst of all for her was when our Dutch forces were twice engaged in war with England. Each time she was in terror that she would never get back to her homeland again.'

'I had not realized that her homesickness was so acute.'

'Love of one's own country is deep inside everyone, but for some it is more powerful than it is for others. In Bessie Gibbons' case it is most surely because she spent a happy childhood as well as her early, most impressionable years as a young girl in England. The result is that her heart has never left there.'

'So, in spite of living here all these years, she is still very much an Englishwoman?'

The old woman chuckled. 'Yes, but I'm proud to say that young Grinling is as Dutch as a windmill or a piece of Gouda cheese. He has been addressed as Master Grinling ever since he finished his apprenticeship and became a fully fledged craftsman. You must remember to address him always with respect.'

'Oh, I will indeed.'

Nurse Bobbins twisted in her chair as she turned to the little sewing-table at her side and pulled open its drawer. 'But we have something else to discuss now.' Carefully she took out the dainty lace cap she had finished and also the *oorijzer*, a metal brace to which it would be attached and kept in place. 'Let us try this on you now before Grinling comes in to see me, which I know he will.'

Saskia clasped her hands together in her excitement as she sprang to her feet and then dropped to her knees by the old woman's chair to make it easier to be fitted. First came the *oorijzer*, which settled comfortably on her head. Nanny Bobbins' old hands fumbled, but soon the cap was ready for the lappets to be fastened up at the sides with silver pins. With the task done Nanny Bobbins let her hands drop back into her lap.

'Now look at yourself, Saskia.'

The girl laughed in her joy, springing up to regard her reflection in a Florentine looking-glass on the wall, turning one way and then the other. 'It's the loveliest cap in all the world!' she exclaimed delightedly. 'Thank you a million times! I'll treasure it all my life!'

Then she spun around to take the old woman's soft hands into her own and kiss her on both cheeks. Nanny Bobbins, looking at the lovely young face framed in the lace, thought that she had never before seen such glowing joy in anyone's eyes. Gifts had not featured in this young woman's life, except from her foster mother in a sweetmeat-filled clog on St Nicholaes' Day and something useful, such as woollen stockings, on her natal days. As for Diane Marchand, she had never disclosed the secret of the wooden chest, which Nurse Bobbins now resented since being told by Saskia what it contained, but it did explain why the Frenchwoman had been so parsimonious towards her daughter, choosing instead to add to the hoarded contents of the chest that she had added to whenever she found something suitable. Saskia had made a full inventory of every item and brought some of the prettiest ones downstairs to show her, including some of Chinese and Japanese origins that must have come with ships of the East India Company in its earlier days. She had let the old nurse choose the one she liked best in memory of Diane and this now had a place of honour on a shelf.

As Saskia turned again to the mirror there came the thump of a fist on the door. 'That will be Master Grinling!' she exclaimed, making a move to leave the room, but Nanny Bobbins shook her head.

'Don't go.' Then as the knock came again she called out, 'Come in, you wicked lad!'

Immediately Grinling entered, exclaiming his greeting as he crossed the room swiftly to half lift her frail frame from the chair and give her a smacking kiss on each cheek. She protested with pleasure, flapping her hands at him, and as he set her back in her chair Saskia could see that she was as happy as if her own son had come home to her.

'Why am I a wicked lad?' he demanded, grinning widely at her as he stood back with his legs set apart and his hands resting on his hips. 'What are you accusing me of now?'

'Nothing that I know about,' she replied tartly, hiding her smile, 'but I doubt that you have kept to all my good advice on drinking, gambling and avoiding bad company during your travels in those nasty foreign lands.'

He raised his eyebrows in mock innocence. 'Would I ever disregard your wise words?'

'You always have done!' she retorted, clearly enjoying this sparring with him.

'You seem to have forgotten that I was there to study the arts and crafts of great masters just as Robert, being an architect, was there to study the marvellous Palladian buildings and other handsome architecture.' Then his tone sobered and his whole face shone with enthusiasm for what he had seen. 'There were carvings and sculptures in the churches and palaces that took my breath away, particularly in Florence and Rome, while in Venice it was Tintoretto's painting of the Crucifixion that kept me rooted to the spot! I lost all count of time as I stood gazing at it. I've brought an engraving of the Tintoretto masterpiece home with me and you can wonder at it yourself. All that I saw made my hands ache to start working again.'

45

'So you're ready to settle down, are you?'

'Yes, but not here. Robert is leaving for England in a few days' time and I'm going too. Since the Great Fire devastated such a vast area of London there will be work in plenty for newly trained architects like Robert and skilled craftsmen such as I.'

Nurse Bobbins gave a nod. 'You will not be the only young Dutch craftsman seeking his fortune there. I have heard of lads from the potteries taking the same step.'

'Yes, I was told that and those of other trades are going too.'

'Like a flock of migrant birds,' Nurse Bobbins commented crisply. 'I hope they never forget that it was their homeland that trained them and gave them the necessary skills. What are your friend's plans?'

'Robert wants to get back to England now without delay. There should be work to be had with the best of all English architects, Master Christopher Wren, who has been given the privileged task of drawing up the plans for the rebuilding of St Paul's Cathedral, which was destroyed in the Great Fire. He will also be responsible for the rest of the burned-out churches – eighty-seven of them! – that are still in ashes. But London will not be my first place of call, because I intend to go north to Yorkshire where I shall follow up some introductions that our tutor from the tour had promised me. I'll tell you more later.' He dived into one of his deep pockets and then handed her a little velvet-covered box. 'Here's a small gift for you from

46

Venice.'

From it the old nurse took out a crystal brooch set in silver and she exclaimed in delighted surprise that he had found something so pretty for her in a city that he said had more canals than Amsterdam. She thanked him, her pleasure mirrored on her wrinkled face, but as Saskia fastened the brooch on for her the old woman scolded him for his extravagance. He laughed, turning to make his way towards the door.

'I'll bring Robert in to see you later, but I wanted to be the first to greet you.' Then he gave Saskia an apologetic grin. 'I'm sorry I didn't have anything for you from abroad.'

She supposed he felt embarrassed through having given a gift to one person in the room and not to the other. She answered him happily. 'There is no need, *mijnheer*, because before you came into the room I had just received the gift of this lovely cap that I am wearing. Nanny Bobbins made it for me.'

He paused to study her appraisingly as she spun around for him to see the back of it where she knew the pattern of the lace would show up against the rich hue of her hair.

'Very pretty,' he said approvingly, throwing a dancing glance at the old nurse that told her it was not the cap he was admiring.

She clicked her tongue at him in annoyance. 'Be off with you now, boy. You can bring your stiff-necked friend to see me later.'

When he had gone Saskia removed the cap and held it carefully. 'There'll be feasting and celebrating this evening when Vrouw Gibbons

47

comes back home to find that the travellers have returned. For days she has been overseeing preparations for his homecoming. So after I've helped her change her gown and made her ready I'll take the opportunity to visit Vrouw van Beek for an hour or two. She can see my new cap at church on Sunday. How I shall love wearing it!'

'Take care when you go out. The streets can be dangerous at night.'

Saskia smiled, because the old nurse gave her the same warning every time she ventured out after dark. 'Have no fear for me. I shall not be late home.'

She spent two hours at her old home where she washed and dressed her former foster mother's hair while they exchanged news. Yet she did not mention the possibility of going to England one day in the future until they were having supper together as they had done so many times in the past. Cornelia van Beek showed no surprise.

'Yes, your mother was always sure that the time would come sooner or later,' she said with a nod, 'but you have no need to worry about it. Mistress Seymour told me more than once that you did very well during your English lessons with her.'

'She was an excellent teacher. But I don't know how Master Grinling will manage if he does go to England as he intends. Nanny Bobbins told me that he has hardly any knowledge of the language. That is because English was never used in the home when he was growing up and naturally only Dutch was spoken by his contemporaries throughout both his schooldays and his span of apprenticeship.'

'But you said he travelled with an English friend. Surely he has learned something of the language from him?'

'I doubt it. I've been told that Master Harting has been in Holland so long that he speaks Dutch fluently himself and, according to Nanny Bobbins, it is how they always converse. But they should talk English all the time.'

'Why don't you suggest it?'

Saskia threw up her hands expressively. 'I wouldn't dare! The Englishman would glower at me for my impudence! As Mistress Seymour once said to me, some people have an ear for languages and others don't.'

'I suppose that is true. Fortunately I've never been required to use anything except my mother tongue.'

Saskia glanced at the clock on the wall. 'It's getting late and I must go. Nurse Bobbins will start worrying about me.'

Cornelia van Beek was slightly jealous of the old nurse of whom Saskia seemed to be very fond, even though she knew the girl loved her like a second mother. 'But Mistress Seymour wants to see you before you leave and I promised the two old sisters on the third floor that you would call in to have a few words with them.'

The elderly women were all so glad to see her, for her visits were mostly fleeting with little time to spare. Now they seized the chance to chat with her and Mistress Seymour poured wine, which gave a party atmosphere. Others came

49

from their rooms to see her too, bringing more wine.

Cornelia van Beek was enjoying having Saskia under her roof so much that she indulged a little heavily in the wine, which was why she misread the clock, still thinking it was earlier than it was when Saskia departed.

Saskia had never before been so late getting back to the Gibbons' house. There had been a thaw and the snow was grey and wet, leaving the cobbles slippery and making her fearful of falling. Twice she skidded. She was desperately anxious to get home, not because she feared attack and it was most unlikely that the family celebrations would be over yet, but if it happened that Vrouw Gibbons had had need of her she knew her absence would put her into terrible trouble.

At first there were people about, but as she went into the quieter streets she was very much aware of being on her own. She had nothing of value on her that anyone would wish to steal, but it would be a great nuisance if she should have grabbed from her the cotton bag she was carrying with the cosmetic items she had taken for beautifying her former foster mother. She increased her pace, taking comfort from the fact that in her dark-blue cloak she would be virtually invisible in the darkness.

Here and there lighted windows threw golden patches across the wet snow and the occasional wall lantern gave a fitful glow. When some drunken seamen spilled out of a tavern just ahead of her she darted to the other side of the street in alarm. A backward glance over her shoulder showed her that they were busily engaged in fisticuffs, others shouting and urging them on. The city was always full of seamen from the ships that often filled the great harbour and they liked to drink and enjoy themselves after long months at sea.

She was only two streets away from the Gibbons' house when out of a passageway a burly man suddenly loomed up before her, blocking her way. Another fellow also emerged and was tying the cords of his trousers after relieving himself, the sound of another man doing the same in the darkness of the passage behind them. She would have darted past, but the first man sidestepped swiftly with arms outstretched while the other man rubbed his hands together as he anticipated some sport.

'Where are you going in such a hurry, girl?' the first one asked jovially, his speech slurred by alcohol as he waved the bottle he was holding.

'Home!' she replied fiercely. 'Now let me pass!'

'That's a lie for a start!' his companion declared aggressively, his mood having changed in a second, and he gripped her arm. 'You've a customer waiting somewhere who you think will pay you more than me and my shipmates.' He patted his pocket, lowering his head towards her like a great bull. 'Listen to me, girl. There'll be no limit if you give value for money, but a knife's blade where you least want it if you don't!'

She gasped, terrified that she would faint with

51

fright. 'Let me go!' She struggled to get her arm free, but his grip only tightened on her. That was when the third man appeared in the entrance to the passageway.

'Bring her in here,' he growled. 'I'm more than ready.'

Screaming, she hit out wildly, but this third man clamped his calloused hand over her mouth and his foul stench of sweat and ale filled her nostrils as he lifted her effortlessly into the dark passageway. There he thudded her back against the wall, causing her to hit her head hard. Her frantic struggles had no effect on his powerful strength. He let his breeches fall, intent on taking her swiftly. Totally panic-stricken, she tried to claw his face, but he grabbed her wrists in one hand while with the other he threw up her skirts. Then almost in the same instant he uttered a terrible roar, falling back from her as a flashing rapier pierced his ribs.

She shrieked hysterically, not knowing what was happening, for the darkness of the passageway seemed full of men and she feared that she was to be seized again by some rival gang from another ship ready to have their dreadful sport with her. Then there was a whiff of the fine perfume that gentlemen used as the swordsman, whoever he was, spun her about and the flat of his hand thrust her with such force towards the opening of the passageway that she fell through it to land sprawling in the mud-wet snow.

Without hesitation and still gripped by terror she scrambled up and set off at a run in the direction of the Gibbons' house, sobbing as she went.

On and on she ran until at last she threw herself through the entrance and slammed the door shut behind her, shooting home the bolts and leaning her forehead against the wooden panel. Her breathing was fast and she was shaking from head to foot. Then the inner door to the hallway opened and Nanny Bobbins' anxious voice penetrated her consciousness that she was safe.

'Oh, my dear child! I have been so worried about you.' Then as Saskia turned towards her the old woman's wrinkled face registered shock and dismay at the state of her. 'Merciful God! Whatever has happened to you?'

'I was attacked,' Saskia cried huskily, a shudder passing through her. 'Three men ambushed me!'

'Were you—?' In her distress the old woman was unable to utter what she needed to know.

Saskia shook her head and her voice was tremulous. 'I was not raped, although I pray that I'll never come as close to such horror ever again.' Then she gagged on the memory of the seaman's rough hands on her body.

The old woman hobbled forward and put a comforting arm about her. 'Thank Heaven that you were spared such violation! I came down to the hall bench to wait for the first sight of your return. You've never been this late back before. Come to my room now. I'll make you a cup of that delicious tea that Mistress Gibbons gave me on my seventy-fifth natal day. It will help to settle your distress.'

Over the cup of tea, the leaves of which had been spooned carefully from a tortoiseshell

53

caddy into a blue and white Delft teapot, Saskia told how and why she had stayed late at Vrouw van Beek's house and what had followed.

'I do not know who intervened to save me from rape,' she concluded, 'but I'll be eternally grateful.'

Nanny Bobbins, sitting back in her chair with her teacup, gave a satisfied smile. 'It was Grinling. He went to look for you.'

Saskia stared at her in astonishment, unaware that tears were still flowing down her cheeks. 'How did that happen?'

The old woman nodded. 'I became increasingly concerned when you failed to return. So then I told one of the servants, who was serving wine to the gathering – and goodness knows how many of Grinling's and Robert's friends have turned up to welcome them home! – to say that I wished to speak to him. He came out into the hall to hear what I wanted and when I told him how anxious I was about you he did not hesitate. He said the servants were busy waiting on the guests and he would go himself and look for you immediately.'

'He left his own party to search for me!'

There came a tap on the door at that moment and Nurse Bobbins indicated that Saskia should move to a high-backed wing chair where her dishevelled appearance could not be seen from the doorway. When this was done the old woman bid whoever it was to enter.

It was one of the maidservants that put her head round the door. 'Master Gibbons wanted you to know that he has followed *Juffrouw*

54

Marchand safely home.' Then she saw Saskia's hand resting on the chair arm. 'Oh, you know already, nurse.'

'Yes. I'm afraid of her catching cold from being out so late. I was about to ring for you. Prepare a hot bath in my bedchamber and take towels and a robe in there for her.'

It was not until Saskia undressed in Nanny Bobbins' bedchamber that she saw that the seaman's blood had splashed across her skirt and soaked into her petticoats, making a crimson stain. For a few moments she almost vomited. Then the sensation passed and thankfully she slipped into the warm water of the hip-bath. There she bent her knees to slide completely under the water to wash away entirely from her whole self the horror of the seaman's greedy hands and scratching fingernails. Emerging again, water streaming from her hair, she let her thoughts dwell on Grinling's timely intervention in rescuing her and for the first time since she was attacked a smile touched briefly the corners of her mouth and she closed her eyes in gratitude.

In her robe she went back to the old nurse's parlour to push all she had been wearing into the fire roaring in the tall Delft-tiled stove. Then, after a final comforting embrace from Nanny Bobbins, she made sure there was nobody to see her as she flitted across the hall to go upstairs. Then at the head of the first flight she paused to listen for a few moments. Grinling was singing and was most probably accompanying himself on the lute that was being played. Many times

Nanny Bobbins had spoken of how well he sang and also of his other musical talents. Now he was in full and glorious voice. She listened with quiet joy until the song ended to cheering and applause. This was followed by the tinkling notes of the clavichord and she guessed that Vrouw Gibbons was playing, which she did well, often entertaining guests with her music.

As Saskia dressed again in readiness for her final duties of the day she resigned herself to Vrouw Gibbons' fury at what would be considered her wilful folly in being late on the streets at night, especially since it was against the house rules and strictly forbidden. Even worse would be that she had caused Grinling to desert his guests, which was inexcusable in a host, especially when he could have detailed servants to look for her.

With a sigh she reached for a fresh pair of stockings and fastened them with their ribbons above her knees before sliding her feet into house shoes. Then she stood and shook her skirts into place before smoothing down her apron. Taking a deep breath, hoping that her dismissal was not in the offing, she went to Vrouw Gibbons' boudoir. There she sat waiting patiently as she did every night until her mistress came to bed. At first chance in the morning she would seek Grinling out and thank him for his kindness in saving her from what would have been a terrible happening if he had not come in the nick of time.

When she heard the approaching tap of his mother's heels, she rose from the chair, steeling herself for whatever was to come, certain it would be a searing tirade for her foolish behaviour that had caused Grinling to go looking for her. Then the door opened and to her surprise Vrouw Gibbons entered full of smiles.

'What a delightful evening it has been, Saskia!' the woman declared, flushed and happy. 'It is wonderful that my dear son is safely home from his travels.'

She talked only of the party and the gift of a fine Italian painting he had brought her. Saskia soon realized that in the general jollifications Vrouw Gibbons had not been aware of her son's short absence. When finally Saskia left the room she felt that she had had a double escape from trouble that evening.

Three

Saskia did not get a chance to thank her rescuer until several days after the event, but she had heard him singing again. It was not only in the evenings when company had gathered, but now and again he was in full song or whistling musically as he went about the house. He and Robert were coming and going all the time, being invited to the homes of friends, meeting them in alehouses, making preparations for journeying to England and generally occupying every minute of their time. Twice she would have passed Robert, but she did not want to meet those vivid dark eyes and it was easy to make a detour with so many stairs and passageways in a Dutch house.

It was frustrating for her to be under the same roof as Grinling and still miss the chance to speak to him on his own. She would look down from a gallery just in time to see him crossing the hall with Robert Harting on their way out. At other times he entered a room, closing the door after him before she could get there. More than once his mother descended on him with a swish of full skirts like a silken bat and the chance to thank him was lost once again.

She had made up her mind to make him a pomander as a small gift of appreciation for his kindly act. The perfume of a pomander, quickly inhaled, counteracted any foul odours suddenly encountered. She believed Dutch towns to be cleaner than most in Europe, but nevertheless Rotterdam had plenty of pungent places and there would be many more in England.

She had made a number of pomanders for Vrouw Gibbons, using pretty glass balls with outlets for the perfume, which were specially purchased. When they were filled she decorated them with ribbons as well as small silk flowers or other trimmings, making them a charming accessory to hang at a convenient length from the wrist.

A few days later Saskia had time to go to the market place where she purchased a medium-sized orange from a fruit stall. Then at home again she set to work, making holes in it with a pin and inserting a clove into each one until the whole fruit was fully covered without a space anywhere. Then, using a receipt from her red leather book, she took a grain of civit and two of musk, which she ground up with a little rose water. Then she worked the resulting paste into the clove-studded orange and left it to dry on a table in her room where it began to emit a fine fragrance.

It amazed Saskia that Vrouw Gibbons showed no distress over her son's forthcoming departure, although his going away again might prove to be a permanent move. Then she began to suspect that his leaving was being used as a weapon against the woman's own husband to persuade him to move back to England. A snatch of conversation inadvertently overheard just before a door closed confirmed Saskia's opinion.

'But Grinling will need an anchor in England,' Vrouw Gibbons was saying to her husband, 'and what better than we should be there to open a family home for him.'

'Are you out of your mind?' he growled impatiently. 'Grinling is a man now – not a boy. He will want his own place and total independence.'

The door closed, but Saskia had heard enough to wonder if indeed her own time in Holland was strictly limited and travel to a foreign land awaited her. It all depended on whether Vrouw Gibbons had her way.

Later that day the opportunity to speak to Grinling came at last. Saskia was on her way to see Nurse Bobbins and caught a glimpse of him entering his workshop. She darted after him.

'May I speak to you for one moment, Master Grinling?' she requested eagerly from the doorway.

He grinned at her. 'Of course. Come in.'

She entered the workshop and stood gazing about her. It had a tiled floor and a window above a long workbench that gave plenty of light with a view of the rear courtyard. The walls were covered with rows of tools, either hanging from nails or on shelves, all as neat as if forming a pattern in themselves. There were many chisels and gouges in every size and other tools that she did not recognize. Some short planks of wood were stacked in a corner. He noticed her interest as he opened up a travelling toolbox on the bench in readiness to take down the tools from the walls and pack them away for his forth-coming departure for England.

'Yes?' he prompted kindly, seeing how absorb-ed she was in looking at everything.

'What a wonderful collection of tools!' she exclaimed. 'Are you taking them all with you?'

'Yes. There are some I use most of the time and others I could not do without for various intricate tasks.'

'You have had a splendid atelier in which to work at home whenever you wished,' she said, still looking about her.

'It started as a hobby room for me after my mother had become as tired of wood shavings and sawdust floating about the house as she was of binding up my cut fingers. So my father called in a wood carver to give me basic instructions and that really set me on the path I knew I wanted to follow.' He folded his arms as he leaned back against the bench. 'After I've left here I think you should have this room for making and mixing your beauty preparations.'

'I should like it very much,' she admitted, thinking how advantageous it would be to have space and shelves instead of trying to manage in the cramped quarters of her own small rooms, 'but your mother may have other plans for it.'

'I'll speak to her about it later today.' He moved away from the bench. 'It's most opportune that you've come here now, because I've made a little gift for you to compensate for not having anything from my travels on the day of my return.' He opened a cupboard door and for a matter of seconds in the brightness of the sunshine pouring through the window she saw an oval wooden plaque, known as a portrait medallion, with her own face carved on it in profile. Almost immediately he thrust it out of sight, taking out instead a little round looking-glass surrounded by carved foliage inset with tiny flowers and berries. She was wide-eyed as he handed it to her.

'It's beautiful!' she breathed. It reflected her awed and delighted face as she held it in front of her. 'How very kind of you! I'll keep it always.'

'I had started it before I left for Italy,' he said, pleased by her bright-eyed pleasure in his gift. 'So it was simply a matter of a little more work and a final polishing.'

'But how do you do that?' she asked wonderingly. 'The wood shines like silk.'

'I use *equisetum hyemale*,' he replied, his eyes amused.

'Whatever is that?' she exclaimed in bewilderment.

'You'll know it better as "horsetail" perhaps?'

'But that's a weed! It's called "scouring rush" as well, which is the best name for it, because I've used its stalks bound together for scouring pots. When I was at school my friends and I made whistles from the hollow stalks.'

'That's what it is.'

'But perhaps it does not grow in England?'

'Yes, it does. England has plenty of watersides and other damp places where it can be found just as it is in most of Europe, but it is also sold in markets as it is here in Holland, because it can be used for so many purposes.'

She looked at him keenly. 'I believe you have just divulged your own secret method of the finishing touch to me.'

He laughed. 'Maybe and maybe not. At least I can be sure that you are not going to set up in competition against me.'

'Yes, you are right,' she answered, amused. Then she added seriously, 'I should not think anyone could compete with your skills.'

He shook his head. 'You would not say that if you had seen the wonderful carvings that I saw on my travels. But I hope for my work to reach the highest possible standards in the future. That is when I'll have my own workshop with assistant carvers working for me. Naturally I don't expect that to happen overnight.'

'Nevertheless, I hope it comes about quickly

for you.' There were many questions that she wanted to ask him out of a natural curiosity, but most of all she would like to ask about the portrait medallion she had glimpsed in the cupboard. Did it mean that he found her pretty enough to want to capture her looks to keep for himself? Was it possible that he was as attracted to her just as she knew she was to him? But since he had chosen to keep that symbol of his admiration out of her sight she could not ask him about it.

'I'll certainly do my best.' He saw that she had wandered over to his stack of planks. 'I'm taking those woods too. They will get me started.'

She looked over her shoulder at him. 'Is there anything special about them?'

He came across to her and tapped the planks in turn. 'These are box wood. It's from a tree that doesn't grow very tall or very big, which means that two planks and sometimes several more have to be fastened together before work can be started on a task of any size.' He indicated a paler wood. 'That is called lime wood, but it is from the Linden tree, which I like to work on best of all. It is a very pale wood, but how that will be received in England I don't know. Oak is that country's favourite wood for carving of all kinds.'

Turning away from the planks, he reached for a roll of thick paper on a shelf and began to unroll it into three separate sheets on to a clear space on the bench, putting small tools on the corners to keep them flat.

'I remember that you wanted to see this

63

Tintoretto etching that I brought home.'

She stood by his side to gaze down at the spread scene, moving slowly to examine it from one end to the other. Christ was depicted on the cross, looking down on the grieving women huddled below, while one of the thieves was being raised up on another cross and the second thief was being nailed to a third. It was all amid busy crowds of spectators, including some in authority on horseback, seeming to be controlling all that was happening. The vitality of movement combined with the compassion and the torment revealed in the masterpiece seemed almost tangible from the force with which it had been created. She could not begin to guess how much more compelling the original painting would be.

'It is magnificent,' she breathed. 'I can see why you were rooted to the spot when you saw this masterpiece in Venice.' When they had studied it together a little longer, she noting every vibrant detail, she spoke again. 'I'm very grateful that you have let me see this image of it.'

He gave her one of his smiling glances as he began rolling up the etching again. 'It was a pleasure.'

As she stepped away from the workbench she remembered the reason why she was there. 'This is the first chance I have had to thank you fully for coming to find me on the very night of your homecoming.'

He raised his brows in surprise. 'Didn't you know? Robert was ahead of me in fetching his

64

rapier as soon as Nurse Bobbins' message was conveyed to us. He would have gone alone to search for you, not wanting me to leave my guests, but naturally I would not let him go alone when it was possible that your safe-keeping was at stake.' His mouth spread into a wide grin. 'I think he hoped for some sport. It would not have been the first time he and I used rapiers to end a troublesome incident. We had quite a few adventures on our travels.'

She was taken aback by the news that Robert would have been the first to come for her. 'I should express my appreciation to him too. Do you know where I could find him now?'

'I think he's in the library.' He gave her a smiling glance. 'I'll tell you something else. It was Robert who nicked your assailant and I followed suit with the other rogue.'

'I'm grateful to you both.'

She left the workshop, but before going to the library she took a few minutes to show Nanny Bobbins the gift she had received. The old woman admired it, holding it between her wrinkled hands, and then she eyed the excited girl keenly.

'You haven't forgotten my warning?'

Saskia laughed light-heartedly. 'Indeed not! It's just that I have never owned anything so beautiful before.' Then she grimaced at what lay ahead of her. 'Now I'm going to see Robert Harting in the library. I've only just heard that he would have set out alone to find me on that horrible night.'

'Then it is right that you should express your

thanks.' Nanny Bobbins handed back the looking-glass, noticing with some misgivings that Saskia immediately held it close again as if against her heart.

On her way to the library Saskia steeled herself for coming face to face with the Englishman again. When she reached it the door was open and Robert Harting was standing with his back towards her as he looked through a book that he had taken down from one of the shelves. He must have sensed her presence, because he glanced back sharply over his shoulder as she crossed the threshold.

'How are you, *juffrouw*?' he asked at once, his dark eyes boring into her just as at their first meeting. 'I should have asked you before now, but I was advised not to remind you of an extremely unpleasant experience.'

'That must have been Nanny Bobbins who instructed you.'

A smile touched the corners of his handsome mouth. 'You guessed correctly. I was also re-assured that you were totally recovered from any fright you sustained.'

'Again by Nanny Bobbins?'

'Of course.' He put the book back on the shelf and came across to her. Then he noticed the little looking-glass that she was holding. 'What is that?'

She displayed it proudly. 'A gift from Master Grinling. Just look at those tiny flowers and berries and leaves! Isn't it quite beautiful?'

He thought to himself that its real beauty lay in the face it would reflect, but he duly admired the carved frame that was giving her so much pleasure. 'Did you come specially to show this gift to me?'

She was still unaware how she held it against her breasts as she came to the point of her visit. 'No, that did not bring me here. I should have thanked you fully long before this moment for what you did for me the other evening, but it was not until a few minutes ago that I learned that you were ahead of Master Grinling when you both came to my rescue.'

'Your rescue?' he echoed with raised eyebrows. 'That's a grand way to describe finding you in the dark.'

'But you did save me when I had never before needed such help.'

He shrugged carelessly, dismissing the matter, and she wished he would not stare at her in such a way. It was as if he were absorbing her into himself with his fierce gaze. Yet she decided that in spite of her earlier misgivings this was an opportunity to speak of her concern for Grinling in the forthcoming change in his life.

'Would you be offended if I made a suggestion as to how you could help Master Grinling when he goes to live in England?'

'Not at all. Please sit down.' Robert pushed a chair forward for her and when she was seated he swung another around for himself. 'Tell me what you have in mind.'

'I think from this moment on you should talk only English to him. Unless he has some command of the language he will be at such a disadvantage in a country where everything will be

67

new to him.'

To her surprise he smiled with a shake of his head, his eyes amused. 'Do you think I haven't tried that? Most of the time on our tour I refused to speak anything but English and, when necessary, Italian. Our tutor did the same, but although Grinling did his best he has a Dutch accent as thick as berries on a cherry tree and sometimes when he does speak English you would still suppose he was speaking his own tongue.'

She was surprised. 'I didn't know.'

'How could you?' He shrugged his shoulders. 'But you must not worry about him. He can read English well, although he writes it phonetically, which is somewhat strange at times. Yet usually he can make his meaning clear.'

She relaxed, sitting back. 'You have reassured me. I didn't want him to be cheated by some unscrupulous master when starting work in your country.'

'Do you think we are all villains there?'

'No, no,' she said hastily, rising to her feet. 'I was just concerned for him.'

He left his chair to walk with her to the door, but blocked her leaving by stretching an arm across to hold on to it. They were close and he was looking down into her upturned face. 'I'm sure he would be charmed by your interest.'

Then, taking her totally by surprise, he leaned forward and for a startled moment she thought he was going to kiss her. But he was only pushing the door wider for her and she turned quickly to leave his presence. With all the dignity she could muster she made for the staircase, plagued

68

by the terrible conviction that she had actually swayed towards him when she had thought a kiss imminent. She could feel her cheeks flushing hotly and placed the cool back of her hand against her face as she hurried away. He had been teasing her and she was furious with him for causing her such embarrassment.

He watched her go and heard the last rustle of her petticoats as she took a hasty turn in the stairs. Then he laughed, quite softly, before turning back into the library.

In her room she shut the door swiftly behind her and went to the window, still holding the looking-glass to her like a small shield. Robert had played a subtle trick on her. Looking out unseeingly at the falling snow she reminded herself that men in any household, whatever their age, so often considered maids and other young servants to be fair game. Robert in his English arrogance had shown previously that he was more than aware of the social gap between them and for a moment or two he had taken advantage of her being on her own. She had no intention of complaining to Vrouw Gibbons, for there was nothing she could complain about in that slight encounter. He had not touched her or actually kissed her, and if she even hinted at her disquiet she would most surely be accused of coquettishness or otherwise enticing him in some way.

She straightened her shoulders, able to see that she had her own way of retaliating! He should not receive a pomander from her when he left for England! When he saw her give one to Grinling he would know that it was his outrageous trick

69

that had forfeited a gift.

Yet in the morning Saskia reconsidered the situation. He had dealt with those rogues that had attacked her and she should be grateful enough to pardon the liberty he had taken with her. After all, nothing had happened that she could set down in black and white. Quite often in merry gatherings the youths she knew as friends from schooldays had sometimes managed the briefest of contact with her lips even as she had turned her face away with laughter. Now in the cold light of morning she decided that in acknowledgement of Robert Harting's kind act she was obliged to make him a pomander too.

Later that day Saskia took advantage of a free afternoon to meet a friend, Anna, and go skating with her. As they went through the market she was relieved to see that under a cloth protecting the fruit from the icy air there were still some oranges for sale. Ships coming in from all parts of the world kept Rotterdam well stocked with supplies and what were exotic fruits in other lands were common fare on Dutch tables. After purchasing an orange of the size that she wanted she put it in her pocket, promising herself that she would start work on it that same evening.

'How long are you free today?' Anna asked as they went along. She was a pretty girl, her round cheeks rosy in the cold air.

'Two hours. Vrouw Gibbons is playing cards at another lady's house this afternoon, but I must be back in good time before she returns.'

'Is she still being an old harridan towards you?' Anna asked pityingly. She worked in her

70

father's bakery and he was lenient in letting her have time off whenever she wanted it.

'She is never easy to please these days,' Saskia admitted, 'but I'm content to work for her until such time when I'm ready for a change.' Then she looked up blissfully as the pale winter sunshine broke through the clouds. 'Let's hurry! I want to skate before the sun disappears again.'

Rotterdam lacked the many canals that were to be found in Amsterdam where important skating races and other winter sports took place annually on the ice, but there were still some good skating areas and local people took advantage of them. The girls arrived to find the ice quite busy and they gave a wave to those skaters whom they knew. Although there was a man hiring out skates they had their own and tied them on to their shoes with leather thongs. Then, hand in hand, they began to skim across the ice before parting to skate individually. In her enjoyment Saskia did not notice that someone else had joined a little group of spectators and was watching her.

Yet Grinling did not watch for long. Instead, he hired a pair of skates and seconds later swept an arm about her waist to skate on with her.

'I thought you needed a partner!' he declared merrily. She laughed with pleasure at the surprise he had given her and felt again that special inner joy at his presence, which was increased still more by his embrace. Anna, passing them, raised her eyebrows in amused surprise.

Grinling and Saskia talked as they skated, laughing helplessly when they both fell after

71

swerving to avoid an unsteady skater. He looked merrily into her eyes as he helped her up and supported her briefly before they skated on again. When it was time for her to return to the Gibbons house Anna had tactfully disappeared, and Saskia was happy to have Grinling to herself as they walked home together. She asked him about his travels and he in his turn wanted to know more about her and how she of French descent had a Dutch name and came to be living in Holland. She answered him truthfully, only keeping back her late father's name in case the family should be known to him.

Vrouw Gibbons arrived home shortly after their return and as was usual she found Saskia waiting to attend her. The woman never knew of the afternoon her son and her personal maid had spent together.

On the day Grinling and Robert were to sail for England they were in the hall on the point of departure when Saskia gave them each a pomander. Both realized the reason for the gifts and looked at her in understanding as they thanked her. Then she drew back behind the other domestic staff, who had gathered as bidden by Vrouw Gibbons to see the young men leave. All the travelling baggage had already been transported to the ship and only farewells were left to be said. Grinling had a few words for everyone. When he came to Saskia he gave her a warm smile as she bobbed a curtsy to him.

'I wish you well,' he said gently.

'As I do you, *mijnheer*,' she replied evenly, although the parting was tearing her heart to shreds and her voice no more than a choked whisper.

He turned back to his parents for a final farewell. His mother was full of tears, which suggested to Saskia that the woman had given up hope of seeing him again in the near future. Then, just as Robert was leaving, he appeared to change his mind. The servants parted for him as he came over to Saskia.

'I'll do my best for Grinling,' he said in a low voice. 'Have no fear for him.'

Saskia met his eyes. 'I thank you, *mijnheer*.'

Then he swung away and left the house, Grinling following him. Vrouw Gibbons hurried out in their wake to stand on the steps with her husband at her side and wave them on their way.

Saskia, helping Nanny Bobbins back to her room, happened to notice as she glanced down one of the passages that the workshop door had been left open. As soon as the old woman was settled in her chair Saskia left her and hurried to the workshop. Swiftly she opened the cupboard that had held the portrait medallion carved with her image, but it was gone. Grinling had taken it with him! She felt her cheeks colour up with pleasure.

The next day the workshop was swept and scrubbed and whitewashed until it no longer held the aroma of wood. But it was not for Saskia, even though Grinling had spoken on her behalf. Instead it became a room for Vrouw Gibbons' seamstress and assistants when they came to make gowns for her out of her choice of her husband's latest import of silks and brocades. So

Saskia's small apartment remained the only source of delicate aromas, the scents of rose water and oil of lavender, rosemary and musk wafting pleasantly into the house whenever her door was opened.

Four

Six months went by during which Vrouw Gibbons became increasingly ill-tempered and difficult to please. It was very clear both to Saskia and Nanny Bobbins that she was still not getting her own way about a move back home to England. Her husband had obviously dug in his heels, which was understandable in that it was generally known that a great deal of new business had come his way.

In the meantime Grinling's letters told that he had established himself in Yorkshire where he had been introduced to a number of important people in the local community, resulting in some commissions. Yet it was not what he wanted on a permanent basis, although it had provided a good insight into English customs and ways. He would soon move on to London where Robert was established already, having bought himself a house with monies invested by his late father before the flight into exile. As architects were in great demand he had plenty of work to keep him busy. He was presently designing an elaborate terrace for a newly built house that had replaced some burned-out property.

Grinling also mentioned his pleasure in that there were an amazing number of pretty girls in England, which made his mother roll up her eyes and express the hope to his father that he would not be too foolish. By now she had become more or less resigned to her husband's obstinacy and life in the household had evened out again.

Occasionally a letter came from Grinling to Nanny Bobbins. Saskia would read it for her as the old woman's eyesight was deteriorating. Afterwards they would discuss it together, for he would tell what he had been carving and they tried to picture how each piece would look. Every time he sent greetings to Saskia, which made her blush with pleasure.

She knew that he would have no idea how the short period of knowing him had set a pattern on her life. Although she could have had no shortage of beaux if she had wished it, sometimes having a liking for one or another of the young men that crossed her path, none measured up to the memory she had of Grinling. At least she knew he could not forget her when he had her carved image on the portrait medallion, which she liked to picture hanging on his workshop wall.

Yet with the passing of time her memory of him might have faded if after being six months away he had not sent his parents a small oil painting of himself that a friend had done for him. It was a remarkable likeness and Saskia, looking into those smiling blue eyes again, felt the same deep pull on her heart.

He was no longer in York, but had moved to Deptford, which was five miles downriver from London. It was the site of the Royal dockyard where ships for the Royal Navy were built as well as grand and elaborately decorated river-barges for the rich, many of whom lived in the great houses along the banks of the Thames. His work involved decorative carving for the vessels and he had recently finished a figurehead for a great ship that bore the likeness of a young lady he knew well.

Saskia's immediate thought was that he was telling her she was his inspiration and she hugged this secret joy to herself. He had written something similar to his mother in a letter that had come at the same time and immediately she drew an entirely different conclusion.

'He has become involved with someone unsuitable!' she exclaimed in dismay, shaking the letter at her husband, who was writing at his desk. 'No respectable young woman would agree to being portrayed as a ship's figurehead! The female ones are usually bare-breasted!' She gave a deep groan of despair, clasping her forehead on the thought. 'Who can this brazen girl be? How did she get her claws into him?'

Her husband rested his quill pen and answered her patiently. 'Don't jump to conclusions, Bessie, my dear. If the young woman is not a passing fancy I'm sure that we shall hear more about her in future letters.' He wanted an end to this interruption of his work.

'She's not a passing fancy! I feel it in my bones! It's the thin edge of the wedge! In his next letter he will tell us that he is betrothed!'

'Indeed? So you have the gift of foresight, my dear?' he commented drily.

She stamped her foot in her impatience. 'Are you not concerned?'

'No, I am not. You seem to have forgotten that Grinling is a man and no longer a boy. He has travelled and seen enough of the world to know the good from the bad. I choose to rely on his wise judgement.'

She threw up her hands in despair. 'Be sensible, James! People in love forget how to think properly. When you were courting me I was in such a whirl that I did not know whether I was on my head or my heels! You were the same!'

'Er ... not quite, my dear. I was thirty years old and knew my own mind.'

She was pacing up and down, not listening. 'We must go to England on a visit and see this young woman for ourselves.' She was careful not to make him think she had anything permanent in mind. 'We can stay with Cousin Henrietta in London. Just long enough to find out how serious the matter is and for you to put your foot down if the young woman is not suitable.'

His patience had reached its limit. 'From what I have observed so far in my lifetime,' he stated sternly, 'it is parental opposition that can draw a young couple in love even closer together. As for staying with Henrietta, that is out of the question. Her sojourn here with us lasted six months instead of six weeks and it seemed like for ever.'

'But she had lost the love of her life and it was natural that she needed the comfort of family.'

'The man had gone back to his wife!' he exclaimed in exasperation, thumping his fist on the desk in emphasis. 'She had no right to him in the first place.' Then, seeing his wife was ready to continue the argument, he sat back in his chair in wearied resignation. 'Oh, very well, Bessie,' he said in a tired voice. 'Leave me out of this matter, but go to England if you must. I can see that is what you want to do. All I ask is that you try not to alienate our son too much through your interference!'

'As if I would!' she exclaimed indignantly, but her eyes shone with triumph. With a soft swirl of her velvet skirt she swept out of the room and he heard her calling for Saskia.

With a sigh he pinched the bridge of his nose between finger and thumb for a minute or two, keeping his eyes closed for a short respite. He was very much aware that the scene with his wife had brought on a bout of the indigestion that plagued him at times. He knew he would have to retire before too long, for his health was not all it should be, but first of all he had to draw his elder son back into the fold. He needed to hand over the business to Dinely, who had settled down since his marriage, having an import business of his own in Antwerp, but that could be amalgamated into the Gibbons silk business.

Yet James had always expected to retire in Holland. It was such a long time since he had left England when he had been intent on marrying

Bessie and starting his own business. He was mentally and physically comfortable in this flat green land where windmills rotated with a hiss of sails to their own steady rhythm and sturdy wooden bridges, deceptively delicate in design, crossed canals that rippled iridescently with the colours of the sky. Most of all he liked the people and he and Bessie had many good friends. Moreover there were almost none of the sharp divisions of class so prevalent in his own country The Dutch could be formal enough when occasions demanded, but otherwise they had an ease of manner that he much admired. He would have run his household more on Dutch lines if Bessie would have tolerated it, but she never forgot that she had distant aristocratic cousins in England and, figuratively speaking, had taken on their mantle.

After adjusting his spectacles, the ribbons of which had slipped slightly at the back of his periwig, he dipped his quill pen into the inkwell and carried on with his work.

When Saskia had a few minutes to spare during the packing for Vrouw Gibbons, which had had to be commenced immediately, she ran to break the news to Nanny Bobbins.

'I'm going to England!' she exclaimed delightedly, the thought of seeing Grinling again having eliminated all her previous doubts about leaving her own country. 'Have you heard? Vrouw Gibbons plans to visit her son.'

'Yes, she was here to tell me about it and to see if I have finished the lace collar for one of the new silk gowns that now she will be taking with her. Fortunately I have.'

'I'm so looking forward to seeing him,' Saskia's voice throbbed with excitement.

The old woman regarded her fondly. 'I'm sure he will be pleased to see you. But you must remember that he is living another life now and, according to his mother, has written about a young woman he admires.'

'I know,' Saskia answered blissfully. 'She is the one who inspired the figurehead.'

Just for a moment the thought crossed the old woman's mind that Saskia imagined the young woman in question to be herself, but he had been far too long away to have held an image of her in his mind. Unknown to her Saskia was remembering the portrait medallion and her conviction remained unchanged.

Before departure Vrouw Gibbons gave Saskia strict instructions. 'We shall talk only in English from the moment we step on board the vessel that will be taking us to England. There you shall speak of me as "Mistress Gibbons" and address me as "madam" in the English way.'

The crossing of the North Sea to England was quite smooth, but Vrouw Gibbons kept to her bunk in the cabin the whole time, which allowed Saskia to wander freely on board during the day unless needed to produce a lavender-scented handkerchief, a cup of weak tea or to perform some other small task. When they landed in the port of Harwich on a bright sunny morning a four-horse coach, which was Cousin Henrietta's own equipage, was waiting for them.

Saskia enjoyed every moment of the journey to London, interested to see that everything was so different from her own country and she marvelled that a stretch of sea could create such a contrast. Instead of a flat horizon there were gentle undulating hills. Although the coach took them across bridges over flowing rivers there were no canals that she could see, and even the thatched roofs in England were all of a yellowish hue whereas those in Holland were as sleek and dark as the fur of a cat. There were windmills, but nothing like the number she was used to seeing at home where sometimes there were as many as six or seven in a row and, according to Mistress Gibbons, the English ones ground corn for flour and were not regulating the water level as so many did at home.

Nobody wore clogs, although many of the ragged children, who ran begging to the coach whenever it stopped, were barefoot. She thought how the poorest Dutch fathers would carve clogs for their offspring, and that could have been done here, for there were plenty of suitable lumps of wood to be gathered from under the trees that frequently shaded the road to London. In fact everything was as beautifully green here as in the Dutch countryside and people seemed to share the same love of flowers, for even the humblest cottage had some blossoms by its door.

When passing through towns Saskia took note of the fashions, which followed the same trends as in Holland. Men of style wore enormous curled periwigs that flowed to their shoulders, their knee-length, full-skirted silk or velvet coats swirled as they walked, and their tubular breeches met high bucket boots that flapped over at the top, often with a trimming of lace or a flurry of ribbons. The women wore wide-brimmed hats like the men, but in softer colours, and overskirts were drawn back to reveal handsome underskirts over abundant petticoats. As it was a warm summer day, a light wrap of lace or silk completed their attire. As for the poor – and those she thought of as everyday folk – they were no different from their Dutch counterparts.

When eventually London was reached the coach had to pass through one of the areas that had been destroyed by the Great Fire and the devastation was terrible to see. Street after street, although swept clear of ash and debris for traffic, was lined with blackened ruins, for the old houses of London, many of them Tudor and earlier, had blazed like torches, the flames leaping from one building to the next. Pathetically, here and there, attempts had been made by destitute families to reconstruct shelter out of whatever could be found to house them while the great task of rebuilding the city took place, signs of it in progress. There were wide gaps where firebreaks had finally controlled the spread of the flames. Soon the borderline of the conflagration was reached and then streets, shops and houses showed no sign of what had happened to the rest of the city during those terrible days and nights.

Rushmere House, Cousin Henrietta's grand grey stone residence, was set beyond iron gates in a formal garden with everything planted in squares with paths between in the current fashion. As the coach went up the drive to come to a halt at the steps up to the entrance a man-servant opened the door and Henrietta Rushmere herself blossomed forth like a colourful flower in silken shades of rose and crimson. In a flutter of lace cuffs, she clasped her hands together in delight at her cousin's arrival.

'My dear Bessie! Welcome!'

The two women, who were the same age all but three months between, embraced joyfully.

'How wonderful to see you again, Henrietta! I had begun to fear this day would never come!'

With arms linked as if they were girls again they went into the house. Bessie was scarcely over the threshold when she came to a halt to face her cousin and ask the question that had been churning inside her all the way there.

'Henrietta! I just have to know! Is there a young woman with whom Grinling might be in love?'

Henrietta looked completely bewildered. 'He has never asked to bring a young lady here and neither has he ever spoken of having a sweet-heart. I'm sure I would have seen signs of a romance.'

It should have been reassuring, but Bessie was unconvinced. If Henrietta knew nothing it could mean that the young woman in question was as unsuitable as she had feared. She would just have to keep an alert eye open for any female that made soft glances at her son and then judge for herself.

Saskia had watched the meeting of the two cousins with interest. There was no doubt that

Mistress Henrietta had been a great beauty in her youth. She had very intense, almost brittle good looks that time had only managed to pluck at over the years and her cosmetics had been most discreetly applied. As for her hair, it had been coloured to a pleasing tawny hue and was exquisitely dressed with side-ringlets that Saskia guessed were supported by wires skilfully hidden from sight. It was a new quirk of fashion that she had yet to try on her mistress. She looked forward to meeting Mistress Henrietta's personal maid, sure that some helpful hints could be exchanged.

It came as a great surprise to find her counterpart was a Dutchwoman, named Amalia Visser, who was from Amsterdam. She was fifty years old, a long, lean woman with quite beautiful hands and, although her features were pleasant enough, her face was marred by a sad look in her eyes.

Amalia waited until Saskia had supervised the unpacking of her employer's travelling boxes and then invited her to a cup of tea in her own little parlour, which was very comfortable and had a view of the end of the formal garden. Together they chatted in Dutch.

'It is such a treat for me to have someone from home to talk to in my native tongue,' Amalia confided, 'and I knew your mother. We met some years ago through a mutual acquaintance.'

'You knew her!' Saskia felt a warm wave of emotion sweep over her in finding this unexpected link with the past.

'Yes, but I don't remember ever seeing you,

although I knew of your existence.'

'Work and parentage were two different roles for my mother and one did not overlap the other.'

'I realized that. Now tell me how things are in Holland and all that is happening. I'm starved for news.'

Saskia thought to herself that here again was someone who was homesick. So she did her best, telling that there was no slump in the demand for fine paintings from artists that were making their names known in the great flourishing of art throughout the Netherlands and how the bulbs of beautiful tulips were increasing in price, more and more being grown for exportation as well as for the home market. All she knew of politics and other national affairs was what she had gathered from the news-sheets that James Gibbons discarded when he had read them. If he had come across some political item that had enraged him he always denounced it in an angry voice that could be heard all over the house. Saskia had always found his comments interesting and sometimes enlightening.

Amalia listened intently to Saskia's every word and then heaved a deep sigh. 'You make me wish I were back home again more than ever. I've no complaints about how I am treated here and I'm paid well enough, but England isn't Holland and my heart is there.'

'Does Master Grinling ever visit here?' Saskia guarded against her question coming in a rush, but it was what she had wanted to ask from the start.

Amalia, as Saskia had anticipated, mistook the reason for her interest. 'Yes, I know he's Dutch by birth, but I don't have any conversation with him if that's what you're thinking. His mother and Mistress Henrietta are first cousins, as you will know, and so he comes to dine occasionally when she invites friends to her table. He is always an asset as a guest, because he is musical and will often sing and accompany himself on a viol or a lute to please her and her other guests. There are times when he plays a fiddle beautifully and I've heard him on a flute too.'

'Yes, I have heard him sing and play.' Saskia had an eager question on her mind. 'Does he come on his own to visit?'

'Sometimes alone, at other times with a friend or two, because Mistress Henrietta often includes people more of his age, although – from what she has said to me – he is a young man at ease in any gathering, whatever the age group. Why do you ask?'

'I'm just interested,' Saskia replied and quickly changed to another question on safer ground. 'How is it that you're working here in England?'

'It was your mother that contacted me when I was living in Rotterdam. Mistress Gibbons wanted her cousin to have her own lady's maid while visiting in Holland and as my own lady had just died I was glad to obtain another position so quickly. I stayed on with Mistress Henrietta when she returned to England. It's pleasant enough living here and for a while I had a follower, as servants' suitors are called here. He was a dear man and was very good to me. He

86

made my life worth living, but since he passed away a few months ago I've become very unsettled.'

They talked on for a while, their conversation turning inevitably to beauty preparations. Saskia was cautious, remembering her mother's warning never to betray to others the secrets of her skills and explained her reticence.

Amalia understood and nodded her approval. 'I want you to keep your knowledge to yourself. That was wise advice that your mother gave you, because if you have exceptional talents you can rise high in our particular field, even to the Palace itself.'

'You are very understanding,' Saskia said thankfully.

'I have always been moderately skilled,' Amalia confessed easily, 'but anything I know to be good I'll gladly pass on to you.'

'There are two things I should most like to know. How do you wire Mistress Henrietta's hair in that pretty way and what is the special dye that you use to colour it that is so pleasing?'

'Get out that red book you've told me about and then you can write it down.'

Saskia, who had already unpacked, went eagerly to fetch her red leather book out of the Spanish strongbox. Then she took pen and ink, ready to record what was needed to achieve the pleasing colour that dyed Henrietta's otherwise grey hair. But when Amalia began to list the ingredients Saskia sat back in surprise, putting down her pen.

'You use oil of vitriol?' she queried, frowning.

87

'Even though you dilute it I know that it can cause a painful rash and much else if it comes in contact with the scalp.'

'There is a way around that problem,' Amalia replied. 'Mistress Henrietta's hair is very fine and needs hair supplements at all times. So I buy strands of fair hair and dye them in the oil until they become that tawny colour. Then, when they are ready and have become the hue I require, I brush them out and weave them into her hair, creating the glossy coiffure that you admired.'

Saskia had often used strands on the heads of her foster mother's tenants, but had only used safe dyes in the colouring of them. Yet she wrote the receipt down in case she should ever require it, but she made a special note that it should be used with special care.

As they talked on they found it interesting that they were both of the same mind, just as Saskia's mother had been in her day, in regarding the popular use of lead in cosmetics as the most dangerous of ingredients. Both had seen on older women – and on men too – the ravages that it could wreak on complexions over a period of time.

That same evening of arrival, after a message had been sent to Grinling that his mother had arrived, he came to the house to see her. Saskia, knowing she would have no chance to speak to him, waited on the gallery above the hall to see him arrive. At the clang of the doorbell she gasped with happy anticipation and then there he was, smiling as his mother came hastening across the hall to greet him in English.

'My dear son! How well you look! Your father sends his most cordial greetings!'

'I'm delighted to see you, Mother,' he replied genuinely in the same language, his Dutch accent totally unrelieved by the time he had already spent in England. Saskia was amazed that there was no sign of any improvement. 'What a pity Father was too busy to come with you. Is he in good health?'

'No, he is not. He has never been the same since he had that heart trouble. It is high time he retired, but nothing exists that will drag him away from his three loves – the office, the shop and his warehouse.'

Grinling grinned. 'Just as I am with my tools and my woods.'

For a matter of moments Saskia had the chance to see that in the time that had passed since his departure from Holland he had lost his boyish looks and matured to a splendid masculine handsomeness. It made her yearn for him more than ever and enviously she watched him disappear with his mother into the room known as the Blue Drawing Room and heard Mistress Henrietta welcome him before the door closed.

Before he left at the end of the evening his mother drew him into the neighbouring music room to speak to him on his own.

'Now,' she said as soon as she was seated while her son wandered over to the clavichord. 'I want you to tell me the identity of the young woman who has captured your admiration and perhaps your heart?'

He raised the lid of the instrument and ran the

fingers of one hand along the ivory keys. 'I have nothing to tell you,' he replied easily.

'But whose likeness did you capture in the ship's figurehead?'

He compressed his lips in sudden understanding of his mother's probing. He waited for a moment or two before he closed the lid again and turned to face her. 'So that is why you made this visit!'

'I knew the young woman must be someone special to have inspired you. So naturally I was eager to meet a future daughter-in-law.'

He shook his head. 'Then your visit is in vain, Mother. There is a lovely girl well known to me, but she is out of my reach. Somebody else is pursuing her with every chance of winning her. So that is the situation and now this discussion is closed.'

She knew him well enough not to attempt to question him any further. He had the same stern expression now as his father when a limit had been reached.

'Very well, dear son.' She rose from the chair in a rustle of silk. 'I'll say no more, except I shall hope that one day you will meet a well-born young lady and win your heart's desire.'

'I thank you, Mother.'

Saskia did not see him leave that evening, but two days later she was informed that an arrangement had been made by Grinling for his mother and Mistress Henrietta to view some of his latest work on a day when he would not be at the Royal docks. He was renting a small cottage in order to have a workshop for private commissions away from the industrial site.

'You shall come with us, Saskia,' Mistress Gibbons said to her. 'You make excellent little drawings and I want you to draw my son's workshop and copy whatever we shall be viewing today. The drawings will enable my husband to see what Master Grinling is achieving here in England. It will also be a splendid record to have when we are back in Rotterdam again.'

Saskia did not think that anything she put down on paper would do justice to Grinling's work or his surroundings, but she kept silent, not wanting to risk this unexpected opportunity to spend some time in his presence. Inwardly she was filled with excitement, but she kept her composure and Mistress Gibbons did not notice the flush in her cheeks.

In the coach Saskia sat opposite the two ladies, a straw basket containing her sketching materials on her lap, and they set off through the city streets into the countryside. It was no more than two miles to Grinling's thatched cottage, which was situated at the edge of a wooded glade and in the middle of a grassy stretch of meadow. The remains of a pebbled path curved to the door from the road, a little stream flowing gently nearby.

The cottage itself was old, a wattle and daub building covered with once-white plaster and it had a slightly crooked chimney stack at one end. Its state of disrepair caused Mistress Gibbons to frown disapprovingly before she had even alighted from the coach. Yet Saskia saw that the cottage had an unusually high and wide window that showed signs on the plaster of having replaced a much smaller one. Remembering how Grinling had told her it was essential that he had good light for his work, she saw that in spite of the window's small panes it would give him what he needed. The view that he had from it was of the road and more woods beyond.

There was a glimpse of movement in the cottage and then he was at the door, holding it wide with a smile to match. He was in his shirt-sleeves with a leather apron that looped around his neck and tied behind his back.

'Good day to you, ladies,' he greeted the arrivals, giving them a bow. 'Come in!' Then, spotting Saskia, who was following his mother and her cousin, he bowed again, his eyes holding hers as they exchanged smiles. 'You are most welcome too, Saskia. I believe your coming to England will fulfil your destiny.'

His mother glanced at him impatiently and compelled his attention again. 'What nonsense are you talking?'

Unnoticed by either of the two ladies Saskia had caught her breath at his words, for in his mention of destiny surely he meant that he believed as she did that their futures were linked. Indoors she glanced quickly around, but there was no sign of her carved likeness. Perhaps it had been put out of sight again, but this time it would have been to avoid any confrontation with his mother during her visit, for she most surely would have questioned him about it and objected strongly to a display of her maid's profile.

'As I arranged with you, Grinling,' Mistress

Gibbons was saying, 'Saskia will make as many drawings as I shall need to show your father all aspects of your work. Not only here in this place, but in the workshop at the Royal docks where you are employed.'

He raised an amused eyebrow. 'I'll have to see what can be arranged. The workshops there are not under my jurisdiction.'

'Of course it can be arranged. Cousin Henrietta knows one of the top officials in charge. Nobody will notice Saskia sitting quietly in a corner.'

'I wouldn't wager on that,' he remarked drily. 'Pretty girls are scarce there.'

Saskia smiled to herself at Grinling's compliment. It was clear that he had become totally fluent in English, but again she thought it was strange that his Dutch accent should remain so thick upon his tongue. Yet in her opinion, it could only add to his attractiveness to women.

His mother was not listening. She stood looking around with a disparaging air. 'Couldn't you have found something better than this awful place?'

Saskia wondered why often the most devoted of mothers could alienate themselves from their children by forever finding fault. Yet Grinling seemed remarkably tolerant.

'I needed somewhere quiet and peaceful that was within the limits of what I could afford,' he replied, 'and, apart from enlarging the window, I haven't had to spend anything on it. So now let me take you on a grand tour of my property.' His eyes were twinkling. 'We'll begin here in my place of commissioned and non-commissioned work, mostly the latter.'

What had once been the cottage's living room was well set out with a work-surface fitted sturdily under the window for maximum light. Lying on it and securely fastened was a large rectangular slab of wood, its gouged surface showing that it was a relief carving currently being worked on from the back. The walls held neat rows of even more tools than had been in his home workshop in Rotterdam and two old chairs offered seating. The only other furniture was a narrow table.

A door led into a tiny kitchen and Mistress Gibbons swept through it, even her skirts seeming to rustle with disapproval, and her cousin followed her with Saskia close behind. There was an open hearth where a small cauldron was suspended over some cold ashes on the hearth and an ancient table stood against the wall with a few shelves above it on which was some assorted crockery, a couple of tankards and several knives, forks and spoons sticking upright in a jar.

Saskia, looking out of the kitchen window, saw there was a pump nearby and the back door, which stood open, had a porch to it. At the end of a grassy patch was a stable with one stall that housed Grinling's horse and she guessed that a door at the side of it led to a privy.

Upstairs there was just one large attic bedroom taking up the whole space under the eaves. His mother climbed the flight of stairs just high enough to be able to see into the room that had a small-paned window looking towards the road and another that faced the stables behind the cottage. There was a single bed, a chair and a cupboard as well as a stack of woods, some partly carved, which he said he was preparing for a future project. A finished carving, propped against the wall, was of the stoning of St Stephen, which Bessie herself would not have wanted, but she supposed there was always a market for religious themes. Most of all she was aghast that he should be occupying such miserable premises.

'You don't sleep in this ramshackle place, do you?' she demanded in disbelief.

He helped her descend again. 'Only if I have been working here until very late, otherwise I'm at my lodgings near the docks.'

'Nevertheless I still want Saskia to include sketches of this place. Its wretched state will enable your father to see how you are living without a proper home for you to enjoy whenever you are at leisure. Now let us see what you have been making.'

Henrietta opened her mouth, about to remind her cousin that he was for ever welcome at her house whenever he was free from work, but she closed it again, for Bessie would not listen in her present disagreeable mood.

The most important commissioned piece Grinling had to show them was a recently finished overmantel enhanced dramatically by a decorative carving of fish, dolphins, lobsters, oysters and other sea-creatures with a ship in full sail at the top in a handsome swirl of waves, all of

95

which were fashioned in pale lime wood and seemed almost luminous against the much darker oak of the design's setting.

At the sight of it his mother's attitude changed completely and she threw up her hands in delight. 'That would make the perfect gift for me to take back to your father!' she exclaimed, going forward to examine it closely. 'I must take him something he will like very much to compensate for my absence. Naturally I'll reimburse you, Grinling. We can get it shipped home and it can be installed in his office where he receives the East India shipowners and the captains of the silk-bearing vessels and all other businessmen.'

Grinling shook his head firmly. 'I'm sorry to disappoint you, Mother, but I cannot let it go. It is a specially commissioned piece.'

'So who is the person that is so important that he or she comes before your own parents?' his mother demanded dangerously.

'Robert Harting commissioned it.'

Involuntarily Saskia jerked up her chin. She had not heard Robert's name for a long time, and had not realized until this moment that the memory of her encounter with him in the library was still very vivid in her mind. In contrast Mistress Gibbons received her son's information with a happy smile and a flick of her gloved hand.

'Oh, he is an agreeable young man. He will stand aside to allow you to please me.'

'No, Mother,' Grinling replied on a sterner note. 'It's been designed for a new house that Robert is building for a gentleman, who is as

96

much involved in shipping as my father. It is as I told you in one of my letters. Robert is getting plenty of work.'

'Then if this gentleman's house is still being built you could carve another for him,' Mistress Gibbons insisted, still with a smile on her lips. 'I simply must have this one for your father.'

Grinling gave a disbelieving laugh and shook his head. 'Have you no idea how long it takes to carve a piece like this, Mother? Even when several carvers are involved? Remember that I have been working on it by myself. The measurements were fixed in Robert's architectural plan for the house before a single brick was laid! That's how it has to be when a special feature with such intricate carving in this size is required. It is to be collected in a day or two as the grand drawing room where it is to be installed has been ready long since, the building of the house having taken as long as the carving itself.'

She regarded him coolly, thinking that he had turned out to be as stubborn as his father. She hated to be crossed in anything, which lay at the root of many clashes she had had with her husband throughout the turbulent years of their marriage.

'Are you saying that Robert's wishes come before those of your own mother, who bore you in the midst of indescribable physical suffering?'

'In this case, yes.'

Her eyes flashed, but although she pursed her lips in suppressed fury she said no more on the subject. Once again she had recognized that intractable Gibbons streak of pig-headedness that she had failed to crush out of his father and she would not humiliate herself any further. With a show of indifference that hid her burning anger she looked at some religious portrait medallions of the saints that he had taken from a shelf to show Cousin Henrietta.

'Are these portrait medallions a Catholic commission?' she asked coldly, being fiercely Protestant to the core.

'Yes,' he replied easily. 'They're for a cardinal who lives in one of the grand mansions along the river.'

'They are quite splendid!' Cousin Henrietta enthused, her admiration genuine. She was afraid she was sounding too effusive, but it was only because she was embarrassed by her cousin's attitude towards Grinling. She thought Bessie should be grateful for such a fine and talented son, a blessing that had been denied her in her childless marriage. But she had a goddaughter, whom she loved dearly and who filled the gap in her life whenever she came to stay.

'And what is that?' Mistress Gibbons was asking as she pointed to the large rectangular piece of wood on the bench that was in the process of being carved from the reverse side.

'It is another of the religious carvings that I'm presently working on in the hope of a sale one day.'

Mistress Gibbons was no longer interested. She was too annoyed with him for being so stubborn and denying her wish.

'We'll go now,' she said crisply, 'or else we shall have little time for shopping.' Then she

98

seemed to remember that Saskia was present and turned to her. 'You have brought all you need for your sketching?'

'Yes, madam. I shall start work straight away.'

'Good. Then do your best, but you must not chatter and disturb my son's concentration in any way. We shall pass by here later this afternoon for you to ride back with us, but on other days you must walk. Be sure to make a very detailed drawing of the overmantel,' she said before adding on a hint of sarcasm, 'however long it may take.'

It was a veiled barb directed at her son for what she saw as an excuse for refusing her what she had wanted so much. As she and her cousin left the cottage he saw them to the coach before returning to Saskia with a mischievous grin.

'I have drawings in plenty of everything I carve,' he said, lapsing into Dutch, 'and could have given my mother all she wanted, but I thought that I'd do you a good turn by giving you an excuse to get away on your own sometimes. It cannot be easy to be at someone's beck and call every minute of the day.'

He is, she thought, the dearest of men in every way. 'Yet that is what I am paid for and your mother is very good to me. However,' she admitted honestly, 'it will be wonderful to have the chance to draw and to be out for a while by myself without a strict time limit.'

She could have added that most marvellous of all was the prospect of being alone with him and she saw his kindly intervention as yet another sign of the depth of his feelings towards her. She wondered how soon she might ask him about the portrait medallion of herself and decided that she must be patient.

'I want you to see what I'm working on now before you start your sketching,' he said, crossing to the workbench where he unfastened the reversed carving. He lifted it and as he turned it around for her to see she recognized it instantly with a little gasp of mingled surprise and admiration. It was the Tintoretto etching transformed into a relief carving, fully three-dimensional and pulsating with its original drama and astonishing beauty.

'That is wonderful!' she breathed.

'It is not finished yet and I don't get a lot of time to work on it with all my other commitments, so I do what I can whenever I have a spare hour or two.'

'I'm so pleased you have shown it to me.'

'I remember how fascinated you were by the etching, which was why I wanted you to see this work.' He replaced it on the bench. 'Now where are you going to start your sketching?'

She glanced up from taking a drawing pad, charcoal and writing-sticks from the basket she carried. 'As it is such a pleasant day I thought I'd start by sketching the cottage outside from across the lane.'

'That's a good idea. I'll take a chair across for you.'

When she was settled he went back indoors. The afternoon sun shone full on him through the window as he worked on the Tintoretto carving and she caught glimpses of him whenever she glanced up from her sketching pad. She did not spare the cottage in her drawing, making the thatch as ragged as it was, the weeds thick around the walls and the fallen bricks on a corner showed its need of repair. Yet all the time she thought what a wise choice he had made in selecting this south-facing cottage as his workshop, for she could see that its enlarged window would not only capture the maximum amount of light, but would catch whatever sun there was at various times of the day to assist him immeasurably in his intricate work.

It was not such a quiet site as might have been expected in the countryside, for although the cottage lay well back from the road it was on a route in and out of London and traffic of every kind passed along it. There were private equip-ages with coachmen in livery, public vehicles with noisy passengers, and riders on horseback and people on foot, including pedlars, some of whom left the road to try to persuade her to buy some trinket from their trays. Local farming folk also went by, sometimes with a herd of cows or a flock of sheep. Although she glanced up from her sketching now and again she did not see the approach of a man on horseback as he rode across the grass in her direction.

Robert Harting thought with satisfaction that his time of waiting was over at last. He had been unable to forget her, even though he was never short of female company. He had been on the point of returning to Rotterdam specially to see her, but Grinling had dissuaded him.

'You'll make no progress if you do that. Saskia

doesn't know you except as a friend of mine. She will not have forgotten that you were first to reach her on the night of the assault on her or that you had that short conversation with her in the library, but that would be the end of it. I'm certain it would never occur to her to see more into such a short acquaintance. I admit that the few occasions when I talked to her I thought her an intelligent girl and that means that she would have no illusions about the difficulties of an association with you. She would most certainly know you were attempting to seduce her.'

'What makes you think that should be the limit of what I would desire from her?'

Grinling had narrowed his eyes and drawn a deep breath. 'Do you mean that with time you would consider a more serious move?'

Robert shrugged. 'All I can say is that I have not been able to put her from my mind.'

Grinling gave a deep sigh, shaking his head. 'Then the advice I give you is to be patient. Sooner or later my mother will be unable to stay away any longer from attempting to interfere in my life, whether it is where I work, what I eat or even whom I bed if she can possibly find out! And when she comes you can wager that she will bring Saskia with her.'

'How can you be so sure?'

'Simply because she has never gone anywhere without a personal maid in tow and it will be the same when she comes to England.'

Now, as Robert brought his horse to a standstill, his gaze was fixed on the girl seated with her sketch pad. She made a picture herself in her blue-grey gown, her apron as white as the Nordland lace cap that she wore on her neatly dressed, wheat-bronze hair. He knew of a very tranquil painting by a Delft artist, named Vermeer, which was of a young woman standing in rays of sunshine pouring in through a window. Now he thought how perfectly that artist's brush would have captured the similar scene of beauty with the girl who sat on a chair ahead of him now, her lace-capped head bowed over her task.

He dismounted and began to lead his horse the rest of the way towards her. She was so absorbed in her task that she was taken by surprise when his shadow fell across her work.

Startled, she looked up. Even though he was standing against the sun she knew him instantly, every nerve becoming tense. His masculine presence seemed to overwhelm her as it had that day in the library.

'Master Harting,' she said almost inaudibly.

'Good day to you, *Juffrouw* Saskia,' he said in Dutch, doffing his hat as he bowed to her. 'It is a pleasure to meet you again.'

She answered firmly in English. 'I'm instructed to speak only the language of this kingdom while I am here.'

He thought her Dutch accent charming and, as he looked down into her lovely, upturned face as he had done once before, he knew she still had that extraordinary power to dazzle him with her unusual beauty.

'Grinling told me you would be coming here to make some sketches for his mother,' he said, speaking in English as she had directed. 'May I see what you have done?'

But Grinling had sighted him and came to the door to wave them in. 'It's time the artist has a rest from work,' he called out, 'and I've an excellent bottle of wine here that we can share.'

But it was too late. The Rushmere coach had come into view along the road. In any case, Saskia thought, she would have not dared to risk even a sip of wine in case it lingered on her breath, for then his mother would most surely have barred her from coming to the cottage again. So she put her drawing materials back in the basket and went to stand ready at the road-side.

'It is Robert, I do declare!' Mistress Gibbons exclaimed as the coach drew up and he fore-stalled the coachman by opening the door. They did not alight, but when greetings had been ex-changed Mistress Henrietta issued an invitation for him to join Grinling in dining with them that evening. He accepted at once, often being invited with Grinling to what was always a pleasant evening with plenty of intellectual and stimulating conversation, for Mistress Henrietta was an excellent hostess and knew how to gather guests that would enjoy one another's company.

Saskia had taken her seat in the coach and did not look in Robert's direction. As the equipage rolled forward on its way the two ladies returned Grinling's wave as he collected Saskia's chair and went back indoors with it, Robert following him.

'Let me see what you have drawn this after-noon, Saskia,' Mistress Gibbons said, holding out her hand.

'It's not finished yet,' Saskia said as she produced her sketch pad.

The drawing was carefully studied by both women and Mistress Gibbons gave an approving nod. 'You have captured the cottage's dilapidated state most accurately.' She turned to look at her cousin. 'This sketch alone should shame James into the realization that he must buy a fine house that Grinling could use until such time as he and I come home again.'

Cousin Henrietta made no reply. She believed that if there should be such a house Grinling would still prefer his cottage workshop and wish to be left alone to make his own way in the world.

That evening quite a number of guests came to dine and Saskia judged by the laughter and lively buzz of conversation that the evening was a success. Yet when Mistress Gibbons came to bed she was in a dangerous mood. Not a word was said, but Saskia guessed that she had spoken to Robert about the overmantel and had failed to persuade him that it should be hers.

A week later Mistress Gibbons found a house in Deptford to replace the property she had lost in the Great Fire and which would be ideal for her and her husband's comfort in their old age. It was in the same pleasant residential area as Rushmere House with a formal garden and graced by trees. She was bitterly disappointed when Grinling refused to take up residence there.

'No, Mother,' he said sternly. 'When I move I

105

intend to be in the heart of the city and its commerce. Not in a fancy house away from everything.'

Yet the house would not be left empty, for it was owned by one of Cousin Henrietta's widowed friends, who had her own plans to move nearer her daughter living in the county of Berkshire, but was willing to remain as a tenant until such time as the new owner wished to move in.

Bessie Gibbons had not informed her husband of her intention to purchase. The deal went through and contracts were signed. Saskia had been instructed to make a drawing of the exterior of the house. Some interior redecoration had to be carried out, but when Bessie returned to Holland she knew that she could rely on Henrietta and Grinling to see that it was all done satisfactorily. In the meantime she would continue to enjoy her visit, her pleasure increased now that she had a house that James would like as soon as he saw Saskia's drawing of it, for her mind was made up that before long he should return to their homeland with her.

Five

Saskia did not go every day to sketch, for there were times when she had to be on hand to perform various duties for Mistress Gibbons and most days Grinling was busy at the workshops of the Royal docks. Fortunately Bessie Gibbons was taking such savage satisfaction in gathering drawings of her son's working conditions that she spared Saskia for her sketching more than she might otherwise have done. She did not really care for the drawings the girl made at the workshops of the Royal docks, for they showed Grinling as just one caver amongst many others as if he had no special talent to make him stand out from the rest.

Yet Saskia knew that was not the case, for she soon noticed how often he alone worked on an intricate piece, even though he kept to the same workbench alongside all the rest of the carvers.

Henrietta's friend, Sir Arthur Garner, had been surprised by her request that a young female artist should be allowed access to the workshops. He warned of bad language and coarse talk that the girl would inevitably overhear, quite apart from the likelihood of being subject to unwelcome overtures. In her own mind Henrietta supported all his reasons why Saskia should not be there, but once her cousin had her mind set on something there would be no peace until it was fulfilled. In the end an agreement was reached whereby Saskia would have a chaperone with her at all times and Henrietta herself hired a reliable woman, named Dolly Hoskins, to keep guard.

Dolly was sharp-nosed and sharp-tongued, plump-bosomed and wide-hipped. She took her duties seriously and sat knitting at Saskia's side all the time.

'Clear off!' she would snarl at the lecherous men that came too near. To those who swore within hearing she would roar at them to keep their filthy traps shut, often forgetting that her own language was little better.

Grinling always came for a word or two with Saskia and sometimes he sat with her and Dolly while the three of them ate their noontime bread and cheese or whatever else they had brought with them. One day Saskia asked him where in the docks she could see the ship with the figure-head that he had carved, thinking that her viewing of her likeness would have to bring whatever he felt for her out into the open, but he shook his head regretfully.

'That ship sailed from here a couple of months ago. I believe she is docked at Plymouth at the present time.'

She thought to herself that it might as well be docked on the moon for all the chance she would have of viewing it. Slowly she was coming to believe that Grinling would never speak of his innermost feelings for her. She should have remembered from what she had first learned about England in her English lessons that social gulfs were far wider and deeper in this country than in bourgeois Holland and could never be bridged. Clearly Grinling had taken on English views now that he was living here. Sadly and with agonizing heartache she began to resign herself to going back to Rotterdam with all her hopes crushed and her love for Grinling stronger than ever.

Yet it pleased her that all the time she was gaining knowledge about his skill at carving. It was from the talk of other carvers that she learned he had brought tools from Holland that had not been seen before in England, some of which had been made to his own specifications. It was with these tools that he was able to bring a fresh and entirely new approach to the ancient craft of English carving.

The day came when Bessie Gibbons decided she had enough drawings with which to convince her husband that Grinling was suffering hardship, and she should return to Rotterdam in good time for St Nicholaes day, for there were parties to arrange and much to do. Sadly Saskia began to supervise the packing. Yet unbeknown to her the course of her life was about to be changed. Henrietta knew that her maid, Amalia, yearned to go home to Holland again and it seemed only fair to let her go, but on condition that a secure future would be ensured for her. So she put forward her idea to her cousin one evening when they had just finished a card game together.

'What would you say, Bessie,' she began, 'if I suggested that we exchange our personal maids? My Amalia longs so much to go home again and I like Saskia, who I've seen to be a quick and willing girl.'

Bessie Gibbons sat back in surprise. 'Well, exchange is no robbery as the old adage goes, and although Saskia is very clever arranging my hair it looks so much better when I've asked Amalia to wire it sometimes. I believe Saskia prefers a softer look, but,' she added firmly, 'no maid is going to dictate her wishes to me!'

'Then you would be agreeable to my suggestion?'

'Well, I have to admit that I should much prefer a more mature woman like Amalia to attend me. I find Saskia's youth and beauty quite galling at times when my looking-glass shows yet another wrinkle and my neck is no longer as smooth as I would wish.' She let her fingertips trail down her throat. 'Wouldn't you feel the same if she were hovering about you?'

In spite of having been beautiful since childhood Henrietta was not vain. Like many handsome people, she had been secure in her own good looks, which had given her the self-confidence and social presence that guaranteed attention and respect at all times.

'No,' she answered. 'It is Saskia's youth and smiling ways that I find most agreeable. I would be willing to make the exchange if you and James would guarantee Amalia's care into her old age, which is what I was prepared to do.'

Bessie Gibbons gave a reassuring nod. 'We

already have Nanny Bobbins and will do the same for Amalia as we have arranged for her.'

Henrietta nodded. 'Then it is settled subject to our personal maids being willing to adopt this arrangement.'

When the proposal was put to Amalia and Saskia it would have been impossible to say which of them was the most pleased. Amalia wept with joy that she was to return to her homeland and Saskia thought only of how Grinling would remain in her life and that with time he must surely speak one day of his feelings for her. For days it was as if her feet did not touch the floor, for she was buoyed up by happiness. She had been dreading leaving England, not knowing if she would ever see Grinling again. Now her immediate concern was for her mother's chest left in the attic at the Rotterdam house.

'Do not worry, Saskia,' Mistress Gibbons replied. 'It shall be sent on to you together with some boxes of mine in the direct charge of a guard employed for his honesty.'

She gave Saskia a little rope of pearls from a trinket-box before leaving with Amalia. Saskia was delighted with them. She drew from her savings and had the rope shortened so that it fitted closely around the base of her neck in the fashionable style and had two of the spare ones made into drop-earrings.

On the day that Bessie Gibbons departed with Amalia, a wad of drawings going with her, Saskia became resigned to the end of visits to the cottage and the docks.

It was not long after her cousin's departure before Henrietta discovered that her cousin had boasted to others about Saskia's beautifying skills and what a sacrifice it was to be leaving her behind. It was not unusual for servants to be gossiped about, although it was usually to decry the standard of their work generally, but Bessie had intrigued her listeners, who admired her very fine complexion and she had always enjoyed being the centre of attention, especially since she knew she did not look her age.

At first Henrietta ignored hints dropped by friends that they wished they had a clever girl like Saskia to make their beauty preparations. She tried to pacify their keenness by getting Saskia to make up little pots of various creams to be given as gifts, but their praise and their demands only grew. A hand cream was better than any other ever tried, complexions were enhanced to a glow by another concoction, which had also cured an unsightly rash on one lady's face, and all agreed fingernails had never shone better than when polished by a buffer of the Dutch girl's invention.

Finally Henrietta, feeling that her generosity had been tried to its limits, asked Saskia if she would like to make extra beauty preparations to sell to this circle of ladies.

'It would be a favour to me if you would use some of your spare time to produce whatever is requested,' she said, her annoyance with Bessie and all the ladies concerned reflected in the strength of her tone. 'I should expect you to meet all costs yourself, but I would give you per-

112

mission to consult and deliver everything personally, because –' here her voice rose to an almost hysterical pitch – 'I do not want my house to be treated as a shop!'

'I should be very pleased to do it, madam,' Saskia answered quickly. 'Please do not concern yourself. Nothing shall interfere with what I do for you.'

'I am very relieved to hear you give me your word on this matter.'

Within a few weeks Saskia had a regular delivery of her beauty aids, always having to enter a house by way of the servants' entrance, although she was usually received in the boudoir where her advice was solemnly taken. Complexions did improve and hands unquestionably became more beautiful, simply because she did not use any harmful ingredients in her preparations, but it reflected well on her reputation.

Winter had set in and Saskia's sightings of Grinling became rare, usually only a glimpse of him when he arrived at Rushmere House for a social occasion. One afternoon in her free time she walked as far as the cottage, but it was closed and shuttered that day. She returned to Rushmere House to find that her chest of pots had arrived from Rotterdam and had been taken up to a storage room where it would be easily accessible.

To Saskia's joy the following week she met Grinling entirely by chance. It was a bitterly cold December day and she had been into an apothecary's shop on Russell Street where she had bought some oil for her beauty creams. As she set off again she passed the windows of the popular Wills coffee house on the corner of Bow Street and did not know she had been sighted until Grinling called her name from its doorway.

'Saskia!'

She turned quickly at the sound of his voice. 'Master Grinling!' she exclaimed on a note of delighted surprise.

'I glimpsed you going past. Are you in a hurry or do you have time to take a cup of coffee?'

'I have time,' she answered quickly. She would risk being late getting back to Rushmere House. In fact, she would risk anything to be in his company.

He held the door for her as she entered and the delicious aroma of ground coffee-beans competed with the more pungent odour of tobacco from a large number of long-stemmed pipes being puffed on all sides. Apart from the pleasure of drinking coffee, men gathered in coffee houses to talk business and there were alcoves against the walls that gave some privacy. Yet it was not a male preserve, for there were also business women engaged in deep discussions, for it was not unusual for an intelligent widow to carry on her late husband's shop or workshop and make a success of it. Other tables were taken by casual customers of both sexes who were there only to chat or gossip.

As Grinling led her to one of the alcoves Saskia saw with a sense of disappointment that Robert was seated there, for she had expected Grinling to be on his own. He stood as she approached and she hoped he was leaving, but he was only being polite and sat down again as soon as she had taken her seat.

'I can see you are well,' he said, for her cheeks had been nipped to a rosy colour by the cold weather and her eyes were bright with excitement.

'Yes, indeed,' she answered as a waiter poured coffee into the fresh cup that had been placed in front of her, but she turned eagerly to Grinling. 'Is the Tintoretto carving finished?'

'Almost. Just a final polishing. After Christmas I'll let you know when I'll be at the cottage. Then you can come and see it.'

'I will indeed!'

There was no lack of talk and laughter with Grinling present, but after a short while and to Saskia's intense disappointment, he glanced at the wall clock and said that he had to leave.

'My apologies, Saskia,' he said to her as he rose to his feet. 'I have an appointment that I must not miss.' He put her hand to his lips in farewell, something he had never done before. 'But I leave you in good company.'

Then with a swirl of his coat-tails he left. Robert rested his forearms on the table as he regarded Saskia steadily.

'Now you are left with me,' he said drily with an eyebrow raised, which made her wonder uncomfortably if he had guessed at her feelings for Grinling even though she was sure she had never given herself away. 'It gives me the chance to say something to you that is long overdue.'

'Whatever can that be?' she inquired cautiously.

'It comes in the range of apologies for indiscretions,' he said, his eyes holding hers. 'There is one I owe you that is long overdue from when we were still in Holland. Somehow there has never been the right moment to voice it, but now is a golden opportunity.'

Momentarily she was puzzled, but then she remembered the incident in the library and she looked sharply at him. He spoke quietly.

'I took a liberty with you when you came to see me that day in the Gibbons' library,' he said evenly. Then amusement began to dance in his eyes and the corners of his lips curled upwards. 'I was truly about to kiss you and I saw that you knew it, but would not have been pleased. So I beg your pardon most humbly and trust that I'm forgiven.'

Having been in Grinling's company she was still in an exceptionally happy and benevolent mood. 'I accept your apology, Master Harting,' she replied, wondering why she had ever been alarmed by him. He was just a flirtatious man who happened to be better-looking in a dangerous sort of way than most men.

'So I'm forgiven?' he queried softly.

'Most certainly,' she declared willingly. 'Before I left Holland I already knew from Master Grinling's letters received by Nanny Bobbins that you did look after him when he was first in England. Just as you had promised me.'

He shook his head on a smile. 'I did what I could, but it was virtually nothing. Grinling has only to enter a room with that generous interest in all he surveys and everybody wants to know him. Soon commissions for his work came along without any of it being through me.'

'I'm hoping that he can soon be a success in his own right without working for others,' she confided. 'I know he wants his own important workshop one day.'

'That day will come, I'm sure of it.'

Feeling relaxed in his company for the first time, she decided to risk asking him the question that was constantly uppermost in her mind.

'When we were still in Holland,' she began, 'I happen to know that he carved a portrait medallion of me. Do you know where it is?'

He nodded. 'I know exactly where it is.'

'I should like so much to see it.'

He shook his head. 'I don't think either Grinling or Mistress Rushmere would approve of your entering a gentleman's rooms in order to view it.'

'I'm sure they wouldn't,' she agreed regretfully, but she was full of glee. So Grinling did have the medallion where he could see it daily. Somehow she managed to concentrate on Robert's next words.

'Recently I have drawn up plans for a new theatre that is to be built in London and some very large pieces of carving will be needed for the proscenium arch. I have already put forward Grinling's name to Thomas Betterton, who is sponsoring the venture.'

'Do you mean the famous actor?' she asked, her interest gripped. Then, when he gave a nod, she added, 'I have heard Mistress Rushmere speak of him. She has seen him in many plays.'

'He is a great actor. Perhaps the greatest of all time.'

'I've never been to a performance in a theatre,' she said, 'but in Holland I often watched bands of strolling players perform in the market place. It doesn't surprise me that in spite of all the rebuilding of churches and houses and municipal buildings that a new theatre should be considered equally important. People need to enjoy themselves.'

'I agree. As you know, throughout Cromwell's strict regime every theatre throughout the land was closed. Travelling players were thrown into prison if they dared to perform and even dancing around a maypole and every other kind of harmless entertainment was banned. All hymn-singing in church was forbidden too.'

'What a dreary place England must have been during those years of Cromwell's rule. Nurse Bobbins told me once that although Master Grinling's father liked to have everything Dutch in his Rotterdam house there was always a traditional plum pudding on Christmas Day. It was a patriotic English gesture of defiance, because Cromwell had banned it as a frivolous indulgence in England.'

'That's true. Those of us who were with the royal exile were lucky to be out of it and it gave me the opportunity to train to be an architect with an exceptionally brilliant tutor. Now we have a King in his rightful place, a man that truly enjoys all the good things in life. In a way he is the patron of all theatres since nobody enjoys a well-performed play and other entertainments

118

more than he.'

She thought to herself that indeed the King was a friend of the theatre, for it was well known that he had even taken a mistress from its ranks, a copper-haired actress, named Nell Gwyn.

'So now with the Restoration fully established it is as if Cromwell had never been,' he added with a smile. 'We can all sing our hearts out in the market place or on the stage or in church and anywhere else we fancy.'

'I intend to do the same in the new St Paul's Cathedral one day,' she said confidently. 'They say it is going to be beautiful beyond belief.'

'That will be a long while yet,' he answered seriously. 'The final plan has not yet been approved by either the King or the clergy. I was at the site recently. It is still being cleared of the burned-out ruins, but of course nothing remains of the priceless library it housed or its beautiful altar silver and tapestries. So many treasures of every kind were lost during the Great Fire that can never be replaced.'

'It was a tragedy in many ways,' she said with a nod. 'Did you see Master Wren there?'

'Yes, he stood in the middle of the site in discussion with one of his assistants when something caught his eyes. I saw him pick up a piece of stone from the old cathedral and it was marked with the Latin inscription *Resurgam*, which means "I shall rise again". He held it up for those of us around him to see as he declared that the cathedral would indeed rise again and these words of hope would be engraved at a selected place in the new cathedral where it

119

could always be seen.'

'I find that quite moving,' she said thought-fully. 'What sort of man is Master Wren?'

'He is a quiet man and deeply religious, which is why he has a strict rule for those working for him, whether they be assistant architects or humble bricklayers.'

'What is the rule?'

'It is that foul oaths of even a minor nature are strictly forbidden under the pain of instant dismissal if uttered on a holy site during the rebuilding of the cathedral or any of the churches.'

She thought it commendable, but judging from what she had heard in the dockyard she thought it would be far from easy for those to whom rough speech was normal.

'How do you know that?' she asked.

'It came up in a conversation I had with him, and in any case it is a well-known fact in building spheres.' He did not intend to divulge what else Wren had said to him, but it had been a pious man's fierce rebuke for a young man's way of life that did not match his own.

'Mend your ways, Harting,' the architect had said. 'Less wine, women and song and then I'll consider your application to assist me, because I need skills such as yours for this vast project. But tainted hands have no place in the planning or the supervision of the church rebuilding that I would delegate in all the time ahead.'

Robert was unaware that he frowned as he recalled the damning nature of those words. It still galled him that he was being denied the work he wanted above all else, even though he was busy enough with other commissions. Architects were in great demand during this present housing crisis in the aftermath of the Great Fire.

'Do you think the King will visit this new theatre when it opens?' Saskia was asking.

Robert mentally dismissed the unpleasant interview and smiled at her. 'Yes, I'm sure he will. Probably on the opening night, because Mr Betterton intends to appear in the first performance and he is an actor well liked by His Majesty.'

'If there is a royal visit,' she declared merrily, 'somehow I shall be there to give the King a cheer when he goes inside.'

'I have a better suggestion,' Robert said, his eyes amused. 'After our Merry Monarch has been seated in the royal box I'll arrange that you have the next best seat in the house!'

She laughed, not taking him seriously. 'If that were possible, I should think it a dream come true.'

'Then that shall be fulfilled on the opening night.'

She drew back in her chair, suddenly realizing that their conversation was going along lines that were not of her choosing. 'It has been fun to daydream, but real life is very different. Now I must go.'

He rose to his feet with her. 'I always keep my word.'

For a matter of seconds she met his serious gaze and felt her mood change. How had she managed to forget for a short time that she saw him as a dangerous shadow on her life? She believed that almost from the start she had seen him as a barrier standing between her and the man she would always love.

'Good day, Master Harting. I thank you for the coffee,' she said, suddenly anxious to get away.

He went outside with her and wished her well. As she hurried on her way he watched her disappear down the street. He was well aware that there had been fear in her eyes during those last few seconds before she had swung away and the reason puzzled him. Then he promised himself that one day he would see passion in her gaze, for he believed that when loved she would ignite like tinder to a flame.

Saskia had just finished colouring the roots of Mistress Henrietta's hair when there was a knock on the boudoir door. Wiping her hands, she opened it to take a silver salver, bearing a letter, from the manservant presenting it. Mistress Henrietta recognized the handwriting immediately. 'It is from my darling god-daughter, Elizabeth! Now I shall hear when she will be coming to live with me or whether,' she added anxiously, holding the letter briefly to her chest, 'she has decided otherwise!'

'I hope it is good news, madam,' Saskia said sincerely.

Mistress Henrietta broke the seal on the letter and almost at once gave an exclamation of joy. 'She's coming!'

Saskia wiped away a trickle of colour running down the side of her mistress's happy face. She had heard talk of the girl, whose mother had been Mistress Henrietta's best friend from childhood. Sadly the woman had died when her daughter was only twelve years old, and her father had soon married again. His second wife had had no interest in children and least of all in her stepdaughter, whose presence she had bitterly resented.

'After Elizabeth's father passed away two years ago,' Mistress Henrietta explained after she had read the letter through a second time, 'I invited his widow to bring my god-daughter and stay for a while. I had thought to give them both some comfort in their grief. Elizabeth did benefit from being with me, but her wretched stepmother treated her so badly that I lost my temper and ordered the woman to depart, intending to keep the girl with me. But she would not allow it and I had no authority to go against her will.'

'So how is the young woman able to come now?' Saskia asked with interest.

'Because her stepmother is marrying again, a wealthy alderman with a grand house full of servants, which means that in her jealous hatred of Elizabeth's charm and vitality she does not want to be outshone in her new social circle. The girl has had a most ardent suitor herself, a young man with looks and money, but she has not accepted him.'

Saskia began to look forward to Elizabeth's coming almost as much as Mistress Henrietta, for it would be enjoyable to have someone else young in the house, even though it would mean a change of routine.

'You shall wait on her, Saskia,' Mistress Henrietta had said. 'She has had no personal maid herself, simply because her disagreeable stepmother was so miserly with her. It is right that she should have someone as young as herself in attendance. I happen to know of an experienced lady's maid in need of employment, who has been highly recommended and she will do me very nicely.'

'But, madam,' Saskia had protested, 'I could wait on you both.'

'No, that would never work.' Mistress Henrietta made a dismissive gesture. 'So often both Elizabeth and I would need you at the same time.'

The new personal maid moved in next morning. She had served a minor member of the Royal family and had given herself airs ever since. Her name was Martha Cooper, her age forty and her attitude condescending towards Saskia, whose youth and beauty she immediately resented.

'I suggest that we start as we mean to go on, Saskia,' she announced. 'You shall not borrow or otherwise interfere with any of my beauty powders, creams and so forth while I shall treat yours with the same respect. Neither shall you voice any criticism of my methods if they differ from yours, and I will keep equally silent for the same reason. We shall always keep to the realms of our ladies' individual boudoirs unless there is a crisis when we might need each other's help. Do you agree?'

'Wholeheartedly,' Saskia replied, wary of this

124

woman's attitude, but wanting to keep on agree-able terms. Remembering how Amalia had welcomed her on her first day she made the same offer. 'Would you care to join me for a cup of tea?'

Martha gave a gracious nod that a certain duchess, whom she had once served, might have envied. She was satisfied that she had put this girl in her place. 'Yes, you may make me one, but I'll drink it in my own room.'

Saskia raised an eyebrow as she turned away and went down to the kitchen for hot water. She hoped that the new young mistress, whom she awaited, would not have such airs and graces when she came.

Six

Christmas was over and the holly and other greenery had been taken down on Twelfth Night when Elizabeth arrived. As a last spiteful act her stepmother had denied her the joy of the merry time she would have had at Rushmere House. All the servants immediately lined up in the hall as soon as the Rushmere coach, which had been sent to collect her, was seen coming through the gates. A few flakes of snow had begun to fall.

Saskia was wearing her Nordland lace cap, which she was allowed to do on special occasions or in her free time. She tried to peer forward to see the new arrival as Mistress Henrietta swept out on to the steps to embrace her guest, but it was not until the girl entered the hall that Saskia had a full view of her.

Elizabeth was fair-haired and of average height with a hand-span waist comparable to Saskia's own. She was not pretty in the conventional sense, for her face was narrow with high cheekbones and her nose, although well formed with delicate nostrils, was long, but she had an impish look about her and her eyes were a hazelnut brown, thickly lashed under fine brows. Saskia knew already that the new arrival was her own age, their natal days only two months apart.

'So you are to wait on me,' Elizabeth said happily when Saskia was presented to her. 'You are as pretty as your unusual Christian name. I'm sure I shall be very content in your care.'

It was a good beginning. Saskia gave a silent sigh of relief as she bobbed a curtsy in acknowledgement.

While Elizabeth took tea with Mistress Henrietta in the green drawing room Saskia unpacked the single travelling box that had been taken up to the guest's boudoir. She was surprised at how little the young woman had brought with her. Carefully packed on top of the garments were two little Chelsea figurines of a shepherd and a shepherdess, which Saskia placed on the polished rosewood surface of a clothes press. A small jewel box went on the dressing table and a satin handkerchief sachet showed that it contained a slim packet of letters tied with a pink ribbon. Saskia smiled as she put the sachet beside the silver-backed hairbrush, comb and hand-mirror. It seemed as if Elizabeth had a sweetheart.

She turned to face the door as she heard Elizabeth approaching and bobbed the customary curtsy as the girl entered.

'You've put everything away already,' the girl said with pleasure, glancing about the room.

'There was only one travelling box. Have you more to be delivered?'

Elizabeth shook her head. 'No. In any case, I didn't have very much in my wardrobe to bring with me.' She wandered across to the clothes closet. 'These figurines were a gift to me from my late mother and my stepmother thought them worthless, which was why she allowed me to keep them. Everything else that belonged to Mama was tossed out by her long ago, except valuable things, which she sold for her own benefit.' She adjusted very slightly the position of the shepherdess. 'I like them to look directly at each other, because I believe that they are in love.'

'I'm sure you are right,' Saskia agreed, liking the little fantasy.

Elizabeth looked around again with a little sigh of satisfaction. 'I stayed in this room when I was here a year ago. I had no idea then that within such a short time this dear house would become my home. In my early childhood I used to come with my mother on visits. We always had such a happy time. Now Godmother Henrietta wants me to make my arrival here today into the begin-

127

ning of a new life for me.'

'I'm sure it will be,' Saskia said, smiling.

Elizabeth clasped her hands together excitedly. 'It is already arranged that tomorrow a seamstress will come with patterns and fashion-dolls for me to choose a whole new wardrobe! So I want you to advise me on what you think would suit me best.'

Saskia raised her eyebrows in surprise. 'But surely Mistress Henrietta, who is a lady of fashion, would wish to help you choose?'

Elizabeth shook her head firmly. 'No, it is she who told me to discuss this matter with you. After all, although you are Dutch-born you have Parisian blood in your veins and therefore have a distinctive flair where clothes are concerned. My godmother said over tea that you even wear your apron like a fashion accessory. She thought you could advise me very well.'

Saskia smiled and shook her head almost in bewilderment. 'You have given me an alarming task, but also a very enjoyable one.'

'Then I'm sure we shall do well together in this and everything else.'

The seamstress and her two assistants arrived next morning. Saskia, remembering the fine silks that Mistress Gibbons had always worn, was pleased to find some of equal quality and beauty among those that were displayed with a rippling flourish. Henrietta had told Elizabeth to totally replenish her wardrobe with garments for every occasion, but the girl, unused to being allowed whatever she wanted and wary of the cost, would have chosen several times from a cheaper range if Saskia had not tossed those swatches aside.

'Those would not drape so well!' Lost in the pleasure of the task in hand, Saskia became equally dictatorial when it came to the choice of colours. 'Not the orange patterned silk! Nor that harsh blue! Neither would suit your fine complexion, Mistress Elizabeth. This soft pink will enhance your colouring and so will this ivory silk.'

The seamstress was displeased that her advice was not being sought, but she endorsed the various choices being made.

As well as the silks there were also samples of delicate lace on display, for styles of the new gowns had also to be decided. It was fashionable to have wide necklines, which were cut low to expose the shoulders for evening, and most often were trimmed with a fall of beautiful and expensive lace. It was a good time for lacemakers, for their products had probably never been in such demand by both men and women in the fashionable world, and Saskia thought often of Nanny Bobbins whose beautiful work had graced Bessie Gibbons' gowns and her husband's cravats.

By the time everything was decided Mistress Henrietta came to approve all that had been chosen and Elizabeth was still in a daze of excitement.

'I thank you with all my heart, dear Godmother!' she exclaimed, kissing her on both cheeks. 'Saskia has been such a help as you said she would be. May I tell her now what her reward is to be?' As the woman nodded with a smile, Elizabeth spun around to face Saskia. 'I saw you holding one length of silk against yourself – not once, but twice! – and I could also see how it would suit you.' She turned to the seamstress, who stood waiting while her assistants packed away all they had brought with them. 'Now you may measure Saskia for a gown of the turquoise silk and another from the velvet swatch that my godmother selected earlier.'

Saskia, scarcely able to believe what she had heard, flushed delightedly and curtsied deeply to Mistress Henrietta. 'I scarcely know how to thank you, madam. You are most kind.'

Saskia had had silk gowns in the past and still had two brought from Holland, but they had all been hand-me-downs from Mistress Gibbons, who had only worn silk or silk velvet, and every one of them had had to be taken to pieces to be recut and altered in order for the garment to fit her. Usually she had made a purse or a jacket from the surplus material, but this one would be to her exact measurements.

'There is a reason,' Mistress Henrietta replied. 'I intend that you should chaperone Elizabeth at times when I choose to remain at home or I am otherwise engaged, and you will have to be suitably dressed. All I ask in return is that you put my god-daughter's interests and welfare before all else in your attendance on her.'

'I give my word gladly, madam.'

Within a week the fittings took place. Saskia's two gowns, one for formal day wear and the other for evening occasions, had no extra fripperies, but it would not have been seemly for her garment to outshine any of Elizabeth's new gowns. In her unassuming way, Elizabeth rejoiced as much in Saskia's new garments as in her own. Fittings took place within the week and the finished garments were delivered soon afterwards. Mistress Henrietta had already sent out invitations to a ball at which Elizabeth could renew acquaintances from past visits.

Saskia found Elizabeth a pleasure to look after, for she was level-headed and undemanding, appreciative of everything done for her. An intelligent girl and a happy one, she seemed to glow from within at this new turn her life had taken.

One afternoon, when Elizabeth had given Saskia a letter to post, it was also the chance to set out on a brisk walk. She had a letter to send herself, for she wrote jointly to Nanny Bobbins and Vrouw van Beek, who had formed a friendship after her departure. Her foster mother, guessing how much she would be missed, had begun calling on the old nurse and they enjoyed each other's company.

After dispatching the letters Saskia set off on her walk. It was a crisp, cold January day and the sky very cloudy as if snow might be in the offing, but she had a warm, hooded wrap and a muff for her hands that Mistress Henrietta had given her at Christmas. She had not seen Grinling since the day they had drunk coffee together with Robert and, inevitably, she turned her steps in the direction of the cottage, hoping he would be there.

It was as Saskia approached the cottage that

131

she saw a gentleman, cloaked and wearing a wide-brimmed hat, following the road that went past it. She recognized him, for he was a familiar tall, thin figure in the neighbourhood. He was Master John Evelyn, a distinguished gentleman who lived in a great mansion not far away. Quite often she had seen him striding along while she was on her own walks and she was sure that he believed as she did that clean fresh air was good for the lungs.

When he came level with the cottage he would have passed it without a glance as no doubt he had done many times before, but at that moment the clouds broke and some pale winter sunshine shone through to pierce the window and show movement within. As Saskia watched she saw that he glanced involuntarily towards the sudden illumining of the interior and then he halted abruptly to stand staring at whatever he had glimpsed happening within. Then with a sudden spurt of speed he approached the cottage door and knocked on it briskly with the head of his cane.

Saskia came to a standstill. She saw Grinling open the door to Master Evelyn, who entered almost deferentially. The door closed after him and Saskia, hoping that the wealthy man wanted some carving done at his home, resigned herself to waiting until he left again. It was too cold to stand still and she walked up and down for at least half an hour before the visitor departed. He was smiling as he went. Grinling, about to close the door again, spotted her and, grinning widely, waved for her to come in. She saw as soon as she entered that it was the Tintoretto carving that lay on the workbench and a final polishing had been taking place.

'Saskia! You could not have come at a better time!' He picked her up and swung her around joyously before setting her on her feet again.

'What has happened?' she asked, laughing with him.

'John Evelyn was here! Did you see him?'

'Yes. He was going past the cottage, but whatever you were doing caught his eye.'

'He said that as he glanced through my window he happened to see me at work on my Tintoretto carving. He recognized the subject matter instantly, having seen the original painting in Venice just as I did. He seemed extremely impressed, saying he had never thought to see that masterpiece come alive in wood.'

'What a fine compliment!'

'And there's more to tell. He holds some position of importance at Court and is going to arrange for me to show my carving to the King! He is certain that His Majesty will want to purchase it!'

As she exclaimed with delighted surprise he in his own mind was recalling how surprised John Evelyn had looked when hearing that the purchase price would be a hundred pounds. It was a tremendous sum at any time, but even more audacious for work done by an unknown carver working in poor conditions. Yet Grinling was resolved that his work should never be undervalued. He knew the quality of it and for a long time had believed that it was only a question of time before his skills were truly appreciated and fetched the price they deserved. Now that conviction showed every sign of coming to fruition.

'How long will it be before you go to the Palace of Whitehall?' she was asking eagerly.

'According to Master Evelyn it should only be a matter of two or three weeks.'

'What an exciting day that will be!'

'It will indeed, but I ask a favour of you, Saskia. Do not mention this matter when you go back to Rushmere House. I should like to choose my own moment to speak of it.'

She nodded. 'Of course I'll respect your wishes.'

On her way home she rejoiced that from a distance she had viewed a meeting that showed every sign of being a turning point in Grinling's life.

Seven

It was at the ball at Rushmere House a week later when Saskia saw Grinling again. He was much on her mind as she dressed Elizabeth's hair for the evening, drawing it back from her face in the new turn of fashion that was banishing curls from the sides of the face to fall down the nape of the neck. The trouble was that Elizabeth was so excited and nervous that she fidgeted and fussed. It was the first social occasion since her arrival, for her godmother had not wanted to present her officially before she had a wardrobe that would encompass everything to which she would be invited.

'Are you sure I should change my hairstyle this evening?' Elizabeth asked anxiously for the third time. 'I do so want to look my very best.'

'So you shall,' Saskia reassured her. 'You have a lovely neck and the beautiful earrings that Mistress Rushmere has given you will enhance it. Now if you could sit still for a few more moments I'll fasten these little flowers in your hair.'

When that was done and Elizabeth was ready to go downstairs she did look very pretty in her pink silk gown, its overskirt drawn back to show the rose-patterned underskirt. Saskia took the fan, which lay ready, and handed it to her.

'I hope this will be the happiest evening of your life so far,' Saskia said sincerely.

'Thank you, dear Saskia! You have done your best for me.'

She left the room in a swirl of silk and Saskia followed after her. Her attendance duties for the evening, which she would share with Martha, were the same as she had carried out so often in the past for Mistress Gibbons' lady guests. She had to be on hand for any of them wanting replacement hairpins or feeling faint or needing guidance to the room where the close-stool was to be found. She had just returned to the ball-room from such an errand, passing Martha who was standing nearby, when Grinling arrived. He looked very fine in a blue silk coat, his cravat a fall of lace and in honour of the formality of the occasion he was wearing a fine curling wig that flowed over his broad shoulders. He had already greeted his hostess and was searching the room with an eager gaze.

For a few blissful seconds Saskia thought he was looking for her. Then everything seemed to crash about her as she saw him sight Elizabeth, who turned as if sensing his arrival and there passed between them a look of such intense joy that it was almost tangible.

A dance had just finished and Saskia, gripped by shock, all colour draining painfully from her face, watched as he strode swiftly across the shining floor to take Elizabeth's hand into his. The girl's expression was radiant and their eyes held even as he bowed low to her and put her hand to his lips.

Saskia in her wretchedness saw that he did not release it afterwards. Instead they kept their clasped fingers hidden by the folds of her skirt and his coat. As they gazed at each other, smiling and speaking softly, not wanting their private conversation overheard, it was easy to guess that he was caressing her palm, conveying all the secret messages that the touch of lovers can pass to each other in total understanding. There flashed through Saskia's mind the packet of letters tied with pink ribbons that she had unpacked from Elizabeth's travelling box upon her arrival at Rushmere House and the inner glow in Elizabeth's eyes that she had not recognized as love. Then this evening there was the girl's

136

trembling excitement when getting ready, understandable now since she was soon to meet the
man who loved her and whom she loved in
return.

Saskia was unaware that she was standing as if
turned to ice until suddenly Robert spoke softly
in her ear. 'Do you want them to see how devastated you are? Where is your pride, Saskia? He
was never for you.'

'How did they meet?' she asked brokenly,
somehow absorbing his advice and trying to
conceal the anguish she was feeling.

'On her last visit about a year ago when she
was here with her stepmother.' He put his hand
on her arm and drew her away until they were by
a window and out of the earshot of others. 'They
have written to each other ever since.'

'I didn't know,' she whispered, feeling that her
whole life had shattered.

'They loved each other on sight,' Robert continued, not sparing her. 'Grinling has already
gained her godmother's consent to the marriage.
He told me that he knew instantly when he first
set eyes on Elizabeth that he had met the woman
he would marry. It can happen like that more
often than most people realize.'

She lowered her head and spoke in a choked
voice. 'I'll love him till the end of my days.'

He showed no sympathy. 'You probably will,
but you can slot the memory away and get on
with your life.'

Her head shot up. 'You are heartless!' she
exclaimed furiously.

He looked amused, enraging her still further,

137

and took her firmly by the wrist. 'Come along and dance with me.'

'No!' she protested, aghast. 'I mustn't mix with the guests!' She was fearful of breaking down in tears and desperate to get away to the solitude of her own room.

He continued to be merciless. 'What do you have to lose? Surely you won't remain in this house to wait on someone betrothed to the man you wanted for yourself?'

He had not relinquished his grip and, ignoring her hissing protest, he proceeded to draw her relentlessly towards the dancing. Although she hung back she was helpless in his grasp, betrayed by her shoes sliding on the polished floor. Then abruptly he swept her into the parading measure being danced to a merry tune struck up by the orchestra and they followed the couples ahead around the floor. Yet the truth of his cruel words had knifed her through. She could not stay on in Rushmere House to witness the joyous celebrations of the betrothal, the preparation of a trousseau and then, hardest of all, preparing the bride for her wedding night.

Grinling and Elizabeth were several couples ahead in the dance and Mistress Rushmere beamed on them as they passed her, but she snapped her fan shut in outrage, her face colouring up, as she saw her god-daughter's personal maid go dancing by. She did not know that Saskia's hand was still being held in a vice-like hold and it was either to dance or make an exhibition of herself by sitting down on the floor and being skimmed along.

At the end of the measure Robert did release her and she fled away out of the ballroom, only to meet Martha, who had been watching all that had taken place.

'You'll be getting the boot tomorrow for prancing about the floor, Saskia,' she sneered.

Saskia knew that would be the outcome, but as she intended to go by her own will the jeer meant nothing to her. Upstairs she did not take refuge in her room as she had originally intended. Instead she went to sit and wait stoically in Elizabeth's boudoir, having reminded herself that her duties must be carried out until her departure tomorrow. She was beyond weeping, the wound she had suffered was too deep for the release of tears. Those would come when the shock of losing Grinling for ever gave way inevitably to despair.

When the guests had departed Elizabeth came to bed in a whirlwind of joyous excitement, totally unaware of anything else that had happened that evening.

'Grinling proposed to me!' she exclaimed, her eyes sparkling as she thrust her hand forward to display the very fine ruby and gold ring. 'We stole away on our own into the library and he went down on one knee! He told me he had adored me from the moment we first met, and he has been so afraid that my stepmother would pressure me into marrying the suitor who wanted me. But I would never have done that! Then we returned to the ballroom and my godmother asked Sir Arthur to announce our betrothal after the supper dance.' She flung out her arms. 'Oh,

I'm so happy, Saskia! I hope so much that you will know such joy one day!'

Saskia thought to herself as she helped the girl to undress that her chance of such happiness had crumbled away for ever this evening, for she would never love another man as much as she still loved Grinling.

Elizabeth chatted on excitedly. 'He told me some good news about his career. The King has agreed to see an example of his work! Isn't that wonderful?'

Saskia agreed that it was indeed a stroke of good fortune for him. She also knew now why he had asked her not to say anything about this showing of his Tintoretto carving to the King. He had wanted Elizabeth to be the first to know.

When eventually Elizabeth, still ecstatic, was in bed Saskia was able to go to her own room, but not to sleep. Instead, moving like an automaton, she packed her clothes and belongings into a travelling bag ready for her departure. She had her hooded cape lying in readiness on a chair when she answered Mistress Rushmere's summons next morning and found her alone in her boudoir.

She was not yet dressed and sitting in a filmy robe before her dressing table, but she put aside a hand-mirror as Saskia entered. 'Now this is about yesterday evening, Saskia,' she began sternly. 'You should not have allowed Master Harting to take you on to the ballroom floor—'

'I know, madam,' Saskia said quickly, 'and I offer my sincere apologies. May I hope that you are not too angry to give me a letter of recommendation for another post?'

Mistress Rushmere's eyebrows shot up. 'Yes, I am more than angry with you! In fact I am furious! Quite a number of my guests recognized you and expressed their shock. But,' she added, holding up a hand to stem any reply from Saskia, 'I also absolve you from most of the blame. Master Harting explained to me that he was responsible for bringing you against your will on to the ballroom floor. I told him it was a silly caper unbefitting for a gentleman and I believe he took my reprimand to heart.'

Saskia could have replied that, as she had told him in her anger, she did not believe he had a heart. 'Yet it is right that I should accept my part in the folly and leave,' she replied.

The woman gasped with exasperation and thumped her fists on her lap. 'Leave? Indeed not! My god-daughter will need your assistance in many things more than ever now that she is betrothed! She has come to rely on you and with her marriage ahead she would not want a stranger to take over from you at this time. Now go along and find her. You can also send Martha in to me.'

As Saskia left the room she saw Martha slipping away and realized the woman had been listening at the door.

'Did you not hear, Martha?' she questioned crisply, causing the woman to pause and turn to face her. 'Mistress Henrietta requires your presence.'

The woman glared, but went with a swish of her petticoats to obey the summons. She was not surprised that some people in the company had recognized Saskia, although normally servants were faceless for guests, becoming only helpful hands. It was the Dutch girl's beauty that was memorable. She had seen how both men and women gave her a second look. As for that Master Harting, his heavy-lidded, handsome eyes followed Saskia relentlessly whenever she was present. It could only be that he had seduction in mind. That should bring the wretched girl crashing down from her high and mighty attitude.

Jealousy and envy made Martha bite her lip as she went into Mistress Rushmere's boudoir.

Eight

It was a fine sunny day when Grinling arrived at the Palace of Whitehall with his Tintoretto carving wrapped in linen and weighing heavily under his arm. He had been to London many times and, in the company of friends, had enjoyed its alehouses and theatres and its pleasure gardens where there was music and dancing. He had often gazed at the palace from various vantage points, for it covered an area the size of a small town and was said to be the largest building in the world, but today he had the authority to enter, knowing that John Evelyn would be waiting for him.

He was not in the least nervous, secure in the knowledge that indeed his carving was fit for a king, and he looked forward to displaying it. He had decided to move to London as soon as he and Elizabeth were married. Through Robert's introduction he had met the great actor, Thomas Betterton, who had commissioned him to carry out an exceptional amount of work for the new London theatre that was to be known as the Dorset Garden Theatre. He believed his future was assured and royal acceptance of his work would be an open door to many choice commissions.

John Evelyn greeted him in the grand reception hall. 'Good day to you, Master Gibbons! You are in good time as I expected. There are two very distinguished gentlemen on business in the Palace this morning and I'm hoping that after you have been received by His Majesty that I may present you to them. They are Master Christopher Wren and Master Samuel Pepys!'

Grinling's optimism soared. The former could give him enough splendid work for churches and palaces to last the rest of his life and the latter was highly influential in naval and court circles. 'I'd be honoured to meet them,' he said.

It was quite a long walk to the royal apartments. They followed seemingly endless enfilades that took them through many fine rooms of gracious proportions as well as innumerable anterooms. On the way they met Master Wren and then Master Pepys, both of whom were bound for the royal apartment. Grinling was presented to each in turn and Sir John was quick to divulge the purpose of Grinling's visit. Both gentlemen expressed polite interest and the four of them proceeded together to the King's apartment.

There the double doors were flanked by two soldiers in the scarlet coats, shining breastplates and plumed helmets of the trusted First Guards, a regiment that the King had raised abroad during his exile. As the doors were opened wide John Evelyn led the way into the royal presence.

Charles was not alone in the crimson and gold room. There were several gentlemen present, some with a fashionably tall cane that was an elegant accessory and all heavily bewigged as was Charles himself, his strong features accentuated by his eyebrows and lashes, which were as black as soot. When young he had been known as 'the black boy', many coaching inns and alehouses taking that nickname for their swinging inn signs, all because of his jet-dark hair and olive skin.

Grinling and John Evelyn bowed low. Then both straightened up as the King came towards them, more than six feet tall and with a smile full of the charm that made him so irresistible to women. Scurrying around his feet were several of the little spaniels of whom he was very fond.

'I bid you welcome, gentlemen,' he said genially.

'I thank you, sire,' John Evelyn replied, bowing low. 'Pray allow me to present the talented woodcarver, Master Grinling Gibbons.'

Now Grinling bowed deeply. 'I'm greatly honoured, sire.'

Charles knew all about him, having previously been primed by John Evelyn. He also knew the price of the carving, which had already set him against it, however good it might prove to be. His demanding mistresses and his own extravagance had made an impact on the royal coffers and there were hostile murmurs against his lavish spending by a number of government ministers. Yet he had been intrigued by John Evelyn's lavish praise of the young Dutchman's extraordinary talent, which had made him curious to see this Tintoretto copy in wood. Sir John, drawing back to allow Grinling to stand alone to present his work, noticed with satisfaction that both Wren and Pepys were among the gentlemen that had come forward to view what was about to be displayed.

'So show me your work, Master Gibbons,' the King said, lowering his tall frame into a chair with its back to one of the many windows. 'The light will show it up well if you stand before me.'

Grinling whipped off the linen covering and the carving was revealed in all its glory. The King's face did not change expression as he studied the work of art, but inwardly he marvelled at the carver's exceptional skills that had replicated so wonderfully the passion and power of such a great masterpiece into the beauty of wood. Several of the courtiers voiced their praise and there was a spontaneous patter of applause.

Charles put his fingertips together as he continued to scrutinize the carving. He felt intense regret that he had to decide against purchasing it, but apart from the price there were those who would say that his leaning towards Catholicism was revealed yet again in the buying of such a piece more fit for a Roman Catholic church than a secular palace. As a Protestant king he had to be wary and keep whatever his private religious inclinations were to himself. He was aware of silence in the room as everyone waited for his decision, but he had a perfect way by which to get out of this tricky situation.

'I should like the Queen to see this splendid carving,' he said, rising to his feet. If his wife bought it, which he fully expected since she was of the Catholic faith and deeply devout, he would be absolved from any accusation of further extravagance. She would know how and where such a carving should be displayed for it to have full honour.'

It was a dismissal with promise, although John Evelyn would have preferred the King to be the outright purchaser. As he and Grinling bowed themselves out of the room he had the uncomfortable feeling that Wren would not be following up any passing interest in what had been shown, which probably meant that he had more than enough carvers to work for him and preferred to deal with those whom he already knew. As for Pepys, although he had viewed the carving, he had returned to continue talking deeply with one of the gentlemen, who in his turn had shown no interest in the exhibit at all.

It was a brisk walk along another route through the palace, passing through one gilded doorway after another, to reach Queen Catherine's apartment. She received them graciously, having been informed in advance of a remarkable carving being brought to the palace that morning. She was small and her face quite plain, her hair drawn back from her face into curls falling from the back of her head, and her gown was of yellow patterned silk. As it had been with the King, she was not alone. There were several ladies present, including Madame de Bordes d'Assigny, a Frenchwoman, who was Queen Catherine's most favoured lady-in-waiting. At the arrival of John Evelyn and Grinling she had moved to stand by the royal chair.

The carving had been carried in by a footman, who now rested it on a table in order that the queen, seated in her chair, could study it at the right height. Catherine smiled in high approval of the work.

'It is a very handsome carving, Master Gibbons,' she said, her Portuguese accent very pronounced, 'and you have treated the subject matter most powerfully and reverently. I think it is a beautiful masterpiece in itself.'

'I thank you, your Majesty,' Grinling replied, well pleased.

'But, madam,' the Frenchwoman intervened with a frown, always liking to emphasize her own importance among the queen's ladies, 'it is not to be compared in any way to the original.'

Catherine glanced up at her in surprise. 'Have you been to Venice?'

'No, but I have seen an etching of the masterpiece and this carving has neither the strength

147

nor the purity that guided Tintoretto's hand.'

'The only difference,' John Evelyn said firmly, 'is that between wood and paint. Nothing more.'

Yet Catherine had turned her head to look again, more critically this time, at the carving while Madame de Bordes d'Assigny continued to point out what she saw as defects and inaccuracies, complaining that nothing was exactly as Tintoretto had painted the scene.

John Evelyn breathed deeply in annoyance. This wretched woman knew no more about art than a toad! How could she when her only expertise was in choosing for the Queen the best of fripperies from France. Yet he saw that Catherine had taken notice of what had been said as she turned with a smile that encompassed both Grinling and himself.

'I thank you, gentlemen, for bringing this work of art for me to see. It has given me great pleasure. I bid you good day.'

Outside the apartment doors John Evelyn thumped his tall cane in angry frustration, fluttering its ribbons. 'How dare that woman influence the Queen in such a manner! I could see that Her Majesty wanted it! She would have bought it if she had been allowed to make up her own mind without that detestable woman interfering!' He drew in a deep breath to calm himself. 'But don't despair, Master Gibbons. Your day will come.'

Grinling had no intention of despairing, although naturally he was intensely disappointed that he had not sold his carving to either the King or the Queen. Yet he considered it to be

148

their loss that they had not acquired his work of art when they had had the chance. It was an attitude he was to maintain all his life. He truly believed, and with every right, that there was not a carver anywhere who could match the skills in his fingers. It was to his advantage that his self-confidence was such that setbacks did not daunt him, for he foresaw a time not too far ahead when people would clamour for his work.

In the meantime he had his marriage to look forward to and the thought of possessing Elizabeth made him almost dizzy with desire and love. Yet before the wedding took place he must find a house in London where there would be a room with plenty of light for his workshop. The problem of housing was acute. So many residences had been destroyed in the Great Fire that it was a sellers' market with exorbitant prices being asked for quite humble dwellings and there was constant competition to buy from plans before even a brick was laid.

A while ago Grinling had already started carving the proscenium arch for Mr Betterton's theatre and had finished other decorative carvings that the actor had also commissioned for the auditorium and foyer. To carve flamboyantly for the playhouse was an entirely new experience. It was a complete contrast to the diminutive scale of much of his carving, a skill that seemed to be beyond the ability of even the best carvers that he had met. But this new venture for the theatre appealed to his sense of fun and it had been a great joy to him at his first meeting with Elizabeth to discover that in spite of her outwardly

149

reserved appearance she shared his merry sense of humour. So he had known from the start that they would never be without a personal joy in each other to enhance their lives together.

He whistled cheerfully the next day as he put the Tintoretto in a cupboard. The right purchaser would come along one day.

Three weeks later he received the news that his parents were coming for the wedding. His mother hinted that she and his father were most likely to stay on indefinitely in the recently purchased house as he had not been well again. Grinling read with interest that his elder brother, Dinely, had returned to Rotterdam at their father's request.

Fortunately – his mother wrote – *Dinely has made up his differences with your father and is willing to amalgamate his business with ours. He is already here arranging matters, which is a great joy to me as you will realize.*

It had been Dinely's refusal to follow in their father's footsteps into the drapery business that had resulted in the rift within the family, and Grinling believed it was also the reason why his parents had been more tolerant towards his choice of career than they might otherwise have been. He knew that neither his father nor his mother could have endured having both sons estranged from them, especially with their daughter so far away across the sea. He could excuse his mother's maternal interference at times, for he was aware that being the youngest of her offspring he was also her favourite child, but he did not intend to let her start dictating to him as to where he and Elizabeth should make their first home together.

With time running out and any good available property well beyond anything he could afford he rented a suite of rooms on the top floor at *La Belle Sauvage*, a large coaching inn on Ludgate Hill in the heart of London where there was already a workshop next to the stables, which he had rented after moving out of the cottage. He had already found that travellers and regular customers at the inn with money in their pockets had taken an interest in the work of a carver on the premises. Several commissions had resulted from their calling in out of curiosity to see what he was producing. Elizabeth, wanting only to be with him, happily accepted the prospect of living in an inn for the time being, especially as there was a certain prestige in occupying the suite normally kept for travellers of rank and importance. In addition, the prospect of being in London with all its entertainments and many shops was thrilling for her, for after the dull and repressive years she had endured she longed for excitement and London was there to oblige her.

When she went to see her future home, chaperoned by Mistress Henrietta, she was amazed to find that the rooms were larger than she had expected and finely decorated, the chandeliers of crystal. But it was the views from the windows that appealed to her most of all. Some looked down into the courtyard where there was such a coming and going of coaches and riders and passengers, a cheerful din arising from it all. But she liked best the windows that gave her the sights and sounds of the busy street stretching up Ludgate Hill. London was in her blood and she had never known that it had been waiting for her.

Nine

During the dark hours of one long night Saskia shed her tears. When morning came it was as if she had condensed a lifetime of grief into those heartbreaking hours. Leaving her bed, she went to look at her tired face and red-rimmed eyes in the looking-glass. She was resolved that from now on there should be no more tears. She had to get on with her life, no matter that it was as if the sun had gone from it. Her love for Grinling had somehow enslaved her, filling her with useless yearnings. Now she was resolved never to let that happen again, even though the love she had felt for him would linger all her life through. It was time now to follow an idea that had been in her head ever since she had first seen the contents of the chest that her mother had bequeathed her.

She bathed her eyes and applied a touch of her own cosmetics to hide the effects of her weeping. Fortunately Elizabeth did not notice anything amiss, except to ask with concern if Saskia

152

had caught a cold.

'No,' Saskia replied in what sounded to her ears as an unnaturally bright tone. 'I think some dust blew into my eyes when I was out yesterday.'

Elizabeth accepted the harmless little deception without question. She was to choose the design and fabric for her wedding gown that morning and although the marriage date was still three months ahead she could think of nothing else. She would have married Grinling on the day he had proposed if that had been possible, but her godmother wanted to give James Gibbons plenty of time to organize his business affairs in Rotterdam before he and his wife journeyed to England for the wedding.

At a suitable moment Saskia broached the subject to Elizabeth of leaving her service. Since Mistress Rushmere had refused to consider it Saskia felt that her only chance of release was to speak to Elizabeth herself.

'Why?' Elizabeth asked in distress. 'Have you wearied of attending me? Or is it that you don't want to live in London after my betrothed and I are married?'

'The truth is that I want to make a different life for myself,' Saskia answered frankly. 'I believe I have the means to make a living from the sale of my cosmetics.' She did not add that she no longer wanted to be at anyone else's beck and call, for that would have been hurtful to Elizabeth, who had tried never to be too demanding.

The girl looked bewildered. 'How shall I manage without you?'

153

'Very well indeed,' Saskia replied confidently. 'If you and Mistress Henrietta will permit it I know of someone I think would be suitable to take my place. I would train her right up to your wedding day and then she could take over from me.'

'Very well,' Elizabeth agreed with great reluctance. 'I can see that your mind is made up. But the girl you choose must be pleasant by nature. Where shall you live?'

'I hope to find accommodation at a reasonable rent and I shall start selling at a stall in one of the markets.'

'None of the ladies who presently buy your products would ever purchase anything from a market stall!' Elizabeth declared.

'I'm aware of that. If they are agreeable I shall continue to call on them at home for orders, but I must have another outlet through which I can increase my sales.'

Elizabeth tapped a finger thoughtfully against her cheek. 'Why not have Grinling's cottage after he moves out?' she suggested, wanting to help in any way possible this girl whom she thought of as a friend more than servant. 'It stood empty for a long time before Grinling rented it as a temporary workshop and I'm sure the landlord would be glad of another reliable tenant to follow on.'

Saskia had drawn in her breath delightedly, her thoughts racing ahead. 'It faces the road into London and coaches and other traffic pass that way all the time. I could have a display of my wares at the roadside!' She gasped again as another thought struck her. 'I could even have my own herb garden there!'

'You would be a pretty sight for travellers,' Elizabeth endorsed, clapping her hands together. 'I'll ask Grinling to get everything arranged for you without delay.'

After Elizabeth had spoken persuasively to Mistress Henrietta on Saskia's behalf it was agreed that she could leave, but it was stipulated that it must not be until after the wedding. The woman made her displeasure very obvious.

'You have disappointed me, Saskia,' she said sharply. 'I had hoped you would be a loyal servant to Elizabeth until the end of your days.' It did not occur to her that anyone born into the position of servant might wish for more in life. 'Do you have anyone already in mind that you could train?'

'Yes, madam,' Saskia replied. 'Her name is Lucy Townsend. She is the daughter of a ribbon-seller from whom I have bought items on your behalf. I have observed her several times in the ribbon shop. She is fifteen years old, quick and willing as well as being artistic in blending colours. Her mother is most anxious to put her into elevated service with a good family.'

'Then you may bring her here and Elizabeth shall decide if she is agreeable.'

Luckily the interview went well. Lucy, pixie-faced and slim as a stem, was a naturally smiling person, which pleased Elizabeth, who liked con-viviality at all times after the unhappiness she had known in the past. Saskia forced herself to accept that it was why Elizabeth would be the

155

perfect partner for Grinling with his good-tempered nature and enjoyment of life.

'I want to learn everything,' Lucy said eagerly to Saskia as soon as they were on their own again. 'I aim to be the best lady's maid in the land!'

'That's a splendid ambition,' Saskia said approvingly.

She started the girl's training by giving her a leather-bound book in which to write down all the beauty tips that she collected. Saskia only withheld the secrets of her own special preparations, remembering her mother's insistence that such precious knowledge should only be handed down to a daughter or a responsible daughter-in-law. There were plenty of aids known to all personal maids, such as little bags of oatmeal softening water for the face and the belief, although neither Saskia nor Diane had held to it, that dew gathered on the first day of May guaranteed a good complexion.

As the days went by Saskia saw that Lucy took a pride in each new entry, which reminded her of her own eagerness in the early days. It was not important that Lucy wrote phonetically, much as Grinling still did, for she was as quick to learn as Saskia had hoped she would be and her nimble fingers soon became adept at dressing hair. Fortunately Martha, whose jealousy had poisoned her relationship with Saskia, was more agreeably disposed towards the young newcomer, seeing no rivalry in her.

Yet Martha's bitter dislike of Saskia grew increasingly towards unremitting hatred that was frequently exacerbated all unwittingly by Mistress Henrietta saying irritably that Saskia had carried out various tasks more efficiently and why did Martha not follow the French girl's beauty receipts exactly instead of making her own concoctions? The final straw came when the colouring of Mistress Henrietta's hair went awry. Quite uncharacteristically she shrieked her outrage at Martha and sent her to fetch Saskia to put matters right again.

As a result Martha began to fear dismissal, and she blamed Saskia entirely. She began to watch and wait for some opportunity for revenge that would also put herself in a better light with her employer, but nothing seemed to present itself. She did not realize that much of Henrietta Rushmere's impatience with her was that the woman bitterly regretted assigning Saskia to Elizabeth, certain that the Dutch girl would never have thought of leaving if she had remained with her.

A few days before Grinling moved the last of his carvings, tools and materials into the workshop situated at courtyard level below his new London address, Saskia went to measure the cottage windows for curtains in what was to be her new home. The landlord, a local farmer, had accepted her tenancy. Most importantly of all she wanted the portrait medallion of herself and planned to ask Grinling for it at the first opportunity. She was sure that Elizabeth would not want the likeness of a former servant on display and she did not want it to be disposed of elsewhere.

As she approached the cottage from along the

road she saw there was a horse and cart outside and Grinling was helping the carter load up a variety of wooden planks for transport to the new workshop. He greeted her over his shoulder as he shoved a last plank on board before turning towards her.

'If you have come to help with the loading up for the city you are too late,' he teased, pulling down his rolled up shirtsleeves and then picking up his coat where it lay on the grass verge. Behind him the carter had taken the reins and was already driving away.

'I've come to ask a favour from you,' she began hesitantly.

'What could that be?' he asked cheerily, guiding her into the cottage.

The walls were now bare of his many tools and the racks had been removed. The two old chairs were still there and she sat down on one, guessing that he was leaving them for her tenancy as well as the ancient table and cupboard. Elizabeth had already promised her that he would also leave his wooden-slatted bed and had persuaded her godmother to give Saskia a feather bed from Rushmere House's well-stocked linen closet. There was evidence of the flagstone floor having been swept, although a few wood shavings had been overlooked in one of the corners.

She took a deep breath. 'I'm hoping that you will let me have a carving that you will not want to have in your new home.'

'I do not know what that would be. So, Saskia, enlighten me,' he answered amicably, folding his arms as he stood leaning against the only

158

remaining workbench, which at her request he had left in place. The sunshine through the window panes rimmed him with light and cast his shadow across the stone-flagged floor.

'It's the portrait medallion of me that you carved in your workshop before you came to England. I saw it when you opened a cupboard door the day I was in there.'

'Ah,' he said slowly with a nod of understanding. There was a long pause before he spoke again. 'That was a commissioned piece and I enjoyed doing it, but I made it as a gift.'

'You don't have it?' she asked incredulously. 'Then who—?'

Her voice trailed away as comprehension dawned. He saw that she had guessed the answer to her half-spoken question. 'That's right,' he said. 'Robert has it.'

She bowed her head, hating Robert for having torn away her final belief that Grinling had always cared for her enough to keep her likeness, even though it had never been love.

Grinling crossed the floor to put his fingertips under her chin and raise it to look down into her expressive eyes. 'Put away the past, Saskia,' he said gently. 'You are about to make a new beginning in this cottage. Let it open the world wide for you.'

She nodded. Then, unable to stop herself, she sprang swiftly up from the chair and clung to him, her face buried in his shoulder. His arms hovered about her before enclosing her for a few moments just because she was young and lovely and in distress that he loved someone else. Then

159

he released her.

He spoke her name, but without looking at him she sped away through the door and made for the road, her cloak flowing out behind her. She knew in her heart that in those few moments of embrace he had only felt pity for her. Pity! She wanted to scream out at the pain of her heart exploding within her.

Preparations for the wedding went ahead. Numbness had settled on Saskia, for it was the only way she could deal with all the joyous happenings and the general excitement in the house as the day drew near.

When the wedding morning dawned Lucy would have liked to be the one to dress the bride's hair, but Saskia did everything for Elizabeth, determined that the girl should be as beautiful as a bride deserved to be on her special day. She did not see it as a task, but as her own marriage gift to bring joy to Grinling.

Leaving Lucy to assist the bride into the coach Saskia went ahead to the church to await Elizabeth's arrival. She saw that Robert stood at Grinling's side as his swordsman, but she kept out of his view. Then Elizabeth arrived and Saskia knelt to arrange the folds of the silver and blue brocade bridal gown.

'I thank you, dear Saskia,' Elizabeth whispered before she turned to go gracefully up the aisle on the arm of Mistress Henrietta's friend, Sir Arthur Garner. Elizabeth was so radiantly happy that she dazzled, her face a joy to see beneath the circlet of roses on her fair head.

That night after the music and the feasting

there was the usual riotous ceremony of escorting the groom to the bride, the male guests well inebriated. Elizabeth, clad in a white nightgown, her hair brushed flowing to her shoulders, sat upright in bed against the lace-trimmed pillows while Saskia and Lucy folded the bed clothes neatly across her. Then at the sound of the approaching commotion Elizabeth was seized by total panic. She clutched Saskia's hand in both her own.

'I'm afraid!'

Saskia thought to herself how eagerly she would have been awaiting Grinling's arms, but she managed to smile reassuringly. 'I arranged with the menservants that none of the guests are to be allowed in. It will only be your bridegroom coming to you with a heart full of love.'

She was aware of Lucy looking curiously at her, for her voice had trembled, but Elizabeth had not noticed, reassured by Saskia's words. She became serene as she folded her hands in front of her on the sheet, her wedding band gleaming gold on her finger.

It was as Saskia had promised. Although Grinling was thrust by many hands into the room as though catapulted, his dressing-robe billowing back from his nightshirt, none of the guests managed to follow him. Saskia glimpsed his adoring smile at his bride in the few seconds before she and Lucy slipped through a door into the dressing room and away from the bridal chamber.

In her room a candle-lamp showed everything ready and packed for her departure. She had fulfilled her duty by staying until after the wedding and seeing the bride to bed. Elizabeth had been told that it would be Lucy who would attend her in the morning.

While Saskia put on her cloak for departure and gathered a last few things into her purse, Lucy went downstairs to summon the strong-shouldered lad waiting with a handcart to move Saskia's possessions to her new home, including the iron-bound chest.

When she went downstairs chandeliers and candelabra glowed everywhere. All the servants were still about, for the merriment would continue until dawn, and there would be much to clear up afterwards. They all bade her a jocular farewell, for bottles had been opened in the kitchen too.

Outside there was a full moon and a sky full of stars, the air mild after the sunny wedding day. There was little need of the lantern that swung at the front of the handcart as its wheels bumped along the rough surface of the dusty road. When the cottage was reached Saskia was pleased to see that the roof had been partly re-thatched to make it watertight and the lopsided shutters had been straightened. When she turned the key in the new lock on the door she entered to the smell of fresh whitewash and scrubbed floors. The landlord had kept his word to Grinling that he would make the place more habitable for his new tenant.

When she had lit a candle and paid the lad she bolted the door after him. Throwing back her head with a smile on her lips, she hugged her arms with satisfaction. She had her own home at last and, most precious of all, her independence with none ever to bid her come and go again. Grinling had advised her to let the world into her life and that was how it should be from now on.

Ten

It took a few days for Saskia to get the cottage exactly as she wanted it to be within the limits of her purse. Prior to moving in, and in addition to making curtains for the windows, she had gone to a market place and bought the crockery, cutlery and cooking utensils that she would need as well as two rugs, one for the flagstones and the other for the wooden floor of the bedchamber upstairs. Before leaving the market she bought a selection of all the available plants and seedlings that she needed for her herb garden and three clumps of different lavenders, which she hoped would grow well. Then, having hired the same lad that had moved her belongings from Rushmere House, she had her purchases transported to the cottage.

She had already prepared the ground for her herb garden and did all her planting that same day, putting in mint and rosemary, rue and tansy and others that she would be using in time to come. Soon she would plant more. An elderberry tree near the stable would supply her with the berries that she would need for one of her dyes.

Then, sitting back on her heels, she smiled with pleasure at the neat rows she had created before rising to fetch water from the pump and give the herbs a good shower.

When all was in order in the cottage she scrubbed anew the table in the kitchen and set out all the items she needed to make up a good stock of her products. She would have liked to work by the window as Grinling had done, but her ingredients would have dried up if exposed to too much sun. Last of all she hung Grinling's looking-glass with its foliaged frame on the wall facing the entrance where it could be seen and admired by anyone entering the cottage. She associated it with the happiness she had experienced on the day he had given it to her or else it would have been too painful ever to look at her reflection in it again.

She was mixing some face powders and had filled some of the ordinary pots she had purchased with some of her creams when her landlord, Ted Robinson, came to see her at the end of her first week to collect his rent. He was a broadbuilt and large-bellied, stern-looking man with heavy jowls. His sharp eyes took in everything.

'I wanted to see for myself what you're doing to the old place, mistress,' he said, 'but in future my wife will call weekly for the money. She will also sell you eggs, butter, cheese and a chicken now and again from our farm if you should wish to buy.'

'That could be very helpful to me,' Saskia replied.

'My son, George, is my right hand on the farm,

but I have a youngster, Joe, who can run errands for you and perform chores for a bit of money. He's fourteen, but ain't much for farm work. Master Gibbons found him helpful from time to time.' Then he turned to leave. 'I wish you well, mistress. Good day to you.'

Mistress Robinson called the next day, bringing a house-warming gift of a dozen eggs, which she set down on the kitchen table. She was almost as rotund as her husband, but much shorter, her pretty face round and dimpled and heavily freckled, her hair under its frilled cap was brown brindled with grey. Her smile was partly toothless, but wide and welcoming.

'I'm Kate,' she announced, dispensing with all formality, 'and I'm glad to know you're going to be living here. My great-grandma lived under this roof once, not that I remember her.'

'Now it has become a home again,' Saskia replied, interested to know something of the cottage's history. 'My name is Saskia.'

Kate's eyes widened. 'That ain't an English name and you speak in a pretty way.'

'I'm from Holland.'

Kate clapped her hands together in surprise. 'I knew from what Ted told me that you were a foreigner, but I didn't know that you came from the same country as Master Gibbons. Your speech is easy to understand, but I was often befuddled trying to grasp what he was saying to me. Sometimes I thought he was talking in his own language.' All the time she had been speaking her eyes were taking in everything around her, including the little containers on a shelf.

'You've some nice knick-knacks there.'

'They contain my products.'

'Ted told me you make lotions to beautify. I could do with something for my hands. They get so rough and dry with all I have to do.' She displayed her scarred, calloused hands.

Immediately Saskia turned to the shelf where she selected a pot and then handed it to Kate. 'Accept this salve with my good wishes. Rub it into your hands at night. It will help.'

Kate was shyly delighted. She took off the lid to examine and smell the contents and then took some on a fingertip to rub it into the back of her hand. 'I thank you!'

She stayed a little longer to chat, telling Saskia about the farm, how long she and Ted had been married, and that after having George no other babies had survived more than a few weeks until Joe was born twelve years later. 'There's a row of five little crosses in the churchyard,' she said sadly, 'but I go every Sunday after church to talk to my babies.'

Saskia put a compassionate hand on the woman's arm and there was no need for words. Kate smiled at her and it was the birth of friendship.

Grinling had recommended a potter, named Rufus, who was a young man with a small pottery of his own and was as ambitious as Saskia was herself. He was eager to make the containers she would need, each well glazed with a simple and colourful design, for she intended to keep the pretty little pots in the chest for a more expensive range later on. Meanwhile she was having a display stall made for the roadside with a green and white striped canvas awning that would give shade on sunny days as well as protection from the rain when the weather changed. It had all been a severe drain on her savings, but she considered it to be a sound investment.

She was busy mixing a carmine rouge when there came a hearty knock on the door. Expecting to see Rufus with the first delivery of his pots, she opened it wide to find Robert looming in front of her, seeming to fill the narrow doorway.

'I've come to wish you well with your new venture,' he announced.

'That is very kind of you, Master Harting,' she replied, wishing he had not come.

'I'm sure you are very busy,' he said, seeing she was wiping her pink-stained fingers with a cloth, 'but I trust you can spare me five minutes.'

'Yes, of course,' she replied as politeness demanded.

Then, as he entered, he produced from behind his back a nosegay set in lace and tied with flowing ribbons, which he presented to her. In his other hand he held a bottle and she recognized it as being that of a very special French wine known as champagne, although she had never tasted it.

She inhaled the perfume of the blossoms. 'These are lovely flowers,' she said appreciatively, not denying him the thanks he deserved. 'I'll get a jar to put them in.'

As she went into the kitchen to take a glass jar

from a shelf he followed her, glancing around.

'Everything looks very different from the last time I was here,' he commented, clearly taking a professional interest in the renovations that had been carried out.

She glanced over her shoulder. 'Remember that Grinling used it solely as a workshop, but now it is my home.' Taking a ladle from a hook on the wall, she scooped some water from a bucket into the jar and put the nosegay in it, thinking how beautiful it looked. Then she saw that he was about to open the champagne. 'I haven't any wine glasses.'

'That's not important today. It is the occasion that matters.'

She produced two of the thick glasses that she did possess. He took them from her and she carried the nosegay into the main room where she set it down on the cupboard and arranged its pastel-hued ribbons around the base of the jar. Then she turned to watch Robert pour the sparkling wine. It was like liquid sunshine.

'My mother told me once that it is a royal wine in France,' she said, taking a glass from him as she settled herself in one of the chairs, 'because King Louis XIV never drinks anything else.'

'Clearly a man of excellent taste,' Robert replied easily, still standing. 'As a matter of fact I bought this champagne when I was in France a while ago and I've been keeping it for a special occasion.'

'You were there?' she exclaimed, unaware that there was a note of yearning in her voice, for she had always wanted to visit the land of her mother's birth.

'Yes, I'll tell you why in a moment, but first we must have a toast.' He held his glass out towards her. 'May success be yours.'

'I echo that toast to you in return,' she replied, inclining her head as he sat down opposite her, crossing one long leg over the other. As she sipped the champagne it ran golden down her throat. Momentarily she closed her eyes blissfully. 'No wonder the Sun King enjoys this wine so much.'

'When do you intend to start selling your wares?' he asked.

'Next Saturday and I shall be ready at dawn, because that is one of the busiest days for traffic into town. Market days are always busy too, but nobody would have time to look at my stall in the early morning. I know from the time when I was sketching here that the farm women and girls are usually in charge of geese or goats or helping their men with cows or sheep and having no time to think of anything else. There would be no trade either with the women selling butter and eggs and other home produce, because they ride by in wagons, all wanting to get to market ahead of their competitors.'

'But they will return by the same route with money in their pockets from the sales they have made,' he said with amusement, foreseeing her strategy.

She gave a nod, her eyes dancing. 'That is when I shall have my stall displaying its full glory for them. My two chairs set by the stall will tempt those who are wearied to rest as they choose from my products.'

He narrowed his eyes at her. 'Where did you learn to be such an astute saleswoman?'

She laughed. 'I grew up in a houseful of women, which taught me a great deal. I know that every female, whatever her age or circumstances, wishes to look younger or more beautiful and most of them want to be more attractive to the opposite sex. Even the loveliest of women can be discontented with their appearance, aiming always for an even higher level of beauty.' She watched as he topped up her glass and then his own. 'Now tell me why you were in France.'

He was pleased with the effect that the champagne was having on her, because for the first time that deep-rooted hostility towards him was melting away from the violet depths of her very expressive eyes.

'You will remember that Grinling and I have both been involved in work for the actor, Thomas Betterton, in the building of his new London theatre?'

'Yes, of course.'

'Naturally Thomas Betterton wants his playhouse to be the best in London, although personally I doubt that it will ever rival Drury Lane Theatre. Nevertheless his playhouse is going to be the most advanced in its productions and the most innovative. For the first time in this country there is to be movable scenery instead of tapestry backcloths that are normally used. Some while ago the King heard about one of the theatres in Paris where this new kind of scenery

170

had been successfully installed. Always interested in anything to do with the stage, he discussed it with Thomas Betterton, who took me with him to look into the mechanics of this movable scenery.'

She regarded him in amazement. 'If the scenery can be changed constantly it will make any production more realistic.'

'That's right. A scene can switch from a forest to a palace or to any other setting required in a matter of minutes. Actors can enter or exit through side settings known as *slats*. I have enjoyed overcoming some minor matters in ensuring that everything can be moved swiftly and easily. Meanwhile Grinling has finished the decorative carvings for the proscenium arch as well as some other decoration and that is now all in place.'

'I remember him telling me about it,' she said quietly.

He topped up her glass again. 'You promised some time ago that you would let me take you to the opening night and I said you should have the next best seat to the King's.'

'Is that invitation still valid?' she asked with a boldness that she later blamed on the champagne.

'Indeed it is! I shall come for you next Saturday and you will get your chance to see the King as well as the play.'

'Then I shall postpone the opening of my stall until the next market day,' she said eagerly. 'I don't want to put off customers by closing early when they are still prepared to buy.'

'That is sensible.'

'What is the play called?'

'The Empress of Morocco.'

Robert left soon afterwards and she returned to her interrupted work, but she felt a little dizzy from the champagne and soon abandoned her task. Instead she went upstairs to decide which of her two silk gowns she should wear for such a grand occasion. Having made her choice, she decided she would also wear her mother's ruby pendant, which she kept for special occasions in its original place in the Spanish strongbox.

Then there came a knocking again on the door downstairs before it was opened.

'You here, Mistress Marchand?' a young man's voice called. It was Rufus with his pots.

'Yes!' she answered, tidying a strand of hair as she came downstairs. A tall, thin young man with shoulder-length straw-coloured hair greeted her with a grin.

'Good day, mistress. I'm here with the first lot of pots as promised.'

She looked in the box he had set down on the table. 'These are splendid!' she exclaimed, taking up one and then another.

'You like the colours?' he inquired anxiously.

'Yes! They could not be better. When shall you deliver again?'

'At the end of the week.'

'Good.' She fetched her purse and paid him.

After he had gone she washed every pot, not because they were not clean, but because she was always fastidious in preparing her products.

She went through the same procedure two days

later when a glass merchant delivered the little bottles she had ordered for her rose waters and perfumes. He had a well-stocked shop and was willing to let her have as many as she wanted at a discount.

When the day came for the visit to the Dorset Garden Theatre Saskia's feelings were mixed. She was looking forward immensely to the play and to seeing Grinling's work, but it was almost certain that he would be there with Elizabeth and she had not seen them since their wedding day.

Robert came for her in a coach. It was a recent purchase with a pair of fine horses and his coachman was in grey livery. It was indicative of his rising financial status as a result of the increasing demand for his work. Yet privately he was not satisfied. He wanted commissions from Wren, who could give him the kind of work that would allow him to give full vent to his imagination and his skills. But that pious gentleman still considered him too wild a fellow to be taken seriously. At a recent social gathering Wren had tapped him on the shoulder and given him some solemn advice. 'You need a good wife to steady your ways, Robert. Come and see me when you have achieved that goal.'

Now, as Saskia came out of her cottage, wearing a sea-green gown, a lace shawl about her shoulders and the glow of a ruby pendant at her cleavage, he knew very well whom he would marry if it were possible, but she was still lost in a girlish infatuation with Grinling.

They chatted easily all the way into the city, she wanting to know which of his scenery designs had pleased him best and how the actors and actresses had taken to such an innovation. In turn he asked her how she was progressing in building up her stock and she also told him of the advance orders she had already received and that she believed Mistress Henrietta had forgiven her for leaving to start work on her own.

'How do you know that?' he asked with interest.

'Because she sent her personal maid to ask me to continue making for her all the preparations that had suited her so well.'

Saskia did not add what an unpleasant interview that had been. Martha had been in a savage rage in her humiliation at the errand she had been given and had flounced in and out of the cottage, slamming the door after her with such force that Saskia had feared for its hinges. But she did not want to think of that this evening. Ahead of her lay some exciting hours and now she had fully prepared herself for seeing Grinling again, determined that Elizabeth should never suspect her feelings for him.

There was a large crowd streaming into the theatre when she and Robert arrived, but a footman had been instructed to watch out for them and they were escorted to their box, she glancing at the carved cornices and the abundance of ornamentation that was surely from Grinling's hand. As they entered their box Saskia saw at once that Robert had kept the promise he had made that day in the coffee house, for the garlands of fresh flowers decorating the neighbouring box showed that it was for the King. She turned to him excitedly.

'Thank you, Robert!' She did not realize that it was the first time she had ever used his Christian name, but he noted it while at the same time realizing that it was only a very small step forward in their relationship.

She sat down in the chair that the footman had placed for her and studied the carved, highly gilded proscenium arch that she knew to be Grinling's work. A pair of bare-breasted goddesses, representing comedy and tragedy, held back looped drapery to reveal a central armorial shield flanked by cherubs and all surrounded by flowers, foliage and fruit. She saw that it was not his best work, with none of his delicate carving, but it was perfect for a theatre and gave dramatic pleasure to the eye.

She looked down into the auditorium, the buzz of voices rising like a cloud. The seats were filling up very quickly and there was a brilliant sparkle from the jewels worn by both men and women. In the cheaper seats the noise was quite raucous and when the King suddenly appeared in the Royal box the cheer that came from that quarter drowned the applause from the rest of the audience rising to its feet to honour his presence.

He was not alone, having several people with him, including one of his beautiful mistresses with a fine white bosom rising from her low-cut gown. Saskia had a splendid view of him, for the wall between the boxes was low, and she stood applauding him enthusiastically. She had long

175

admired him for his mercy towards his treacherous enemies when he had returned home from exile. He had pardoned all of them, only signing a death certificate for each of those responsible for the beheading of his father.

She had seen the King's likeness portrayed often enough in drawings and on the coin of the realm and once in a painting, but now, seeing him in person, she thought him handsome, a thin black moustache adorning his upper lip. His strong features were set off by the black periwig flowing down over his shoulders while his height and broad shoulders matched Robert's fine stature. There he stood, smiling and at ease, clearly as one with his people, and he raised his hand in acknowledgement of the cheers and the applause. Then, as he took his seat in a large gilded chair, others in the royal party grouped around him, he happened to glance into the neighbouring box. Robert bowed immediately and Saskia curtsied deeply, rising up again to see the King staring hard at her. She blushed, taken aback by his intense gaze, which reminded her of the way Robert had so often looked at her. Then the royal stare melted into a smile before the King turned his attention to the stage where the play was about to begin.

It was then that Saskia noticed someone giving her a little wave from a box on the opposite side of the theatre. It was Elizabeth with Grinling. She felt an agonizing pang, but kept her smile and returned the wave. Then with a fanfare of trumpets the curtains of the stage parted and she became lost in the drama unfolding before her.

At last she saw for herself that Thomas Betterton was indeed the great actor he was reputed to be, his voice powerful and reaching every corner of the auditorium. Yet this evening often the applause was as much for the swift change of scenery and the transformation of a setting as for the actors themselves.

During the interval Elizabeth and Grinling came to Robert's box and greeted them both happily. Saskia was pleased and surprised when Elizabeth embraced her.

'I have missed you so much, Saskia!' she declared. 'We used to have such happy talks together and you were always there when I needed you. Lucy is helpful and does her best, but it is not the same as when you were my confidante. Do visit us at *La Belle Sauvage*. It's on Ludgate Hill. Grinling has carved some new works that I'm sure you would like to see.'

'Yes, do that, Saskia,' Grinling said encouragingly. Then he added with a grin, 'I've sold the Tintoretto carving.'

'That is good news,' Saskia said, well pleased for him.

Elizabeth gave him a loving look. The sum he had received for it had gone into the beautiful necklace of pearls and ear-drops that she was wearing. Surely no woman ever had such a loving and generous and passionate husband as he was to her. She suspected that she was already pregnant.

'Now promise you will come, Saskia!' she insisted.

'Perhaps when I have opened my beauty stall,'

Saskia answered evasively. 'I still have much to do.'

'Then it will be as soon as you can manage it.' Elizabeth turned to Robert. 'You shall bring her to dine.'

'I'll do that,' he answered.

A warning bell told that the interval was coming to an end. Elizabeth and Grinling hastily departed. Saskia gave Robert a very direct look as they took their seats again.

'Why did you accept?' she asked, thinking it strange that he was the only one who had guessed, probably from the start, her long-held love for Grinling.

'Because Elizabeth needs a friend and she has chosen you,' he replied succinctly.

Momentarily Saskia's voice broke. 'What of my feelings?'

'You've more stamina than you realize.' The glow from the stage was illuminating his face, his eyes holding hers. 'In the past ten minutes you overcame the first hurdle. It will get easier as time goes on.'

Later in the cottage as she prepared for bed she tried to hope that some ease would come one day from the pain of still loving in vain. She remembered Nanny Bobbins' warning given to her before she had ever seen Grinling and how lightly she had taken it at the time. Yet even with hindsight she knew that nothing could have been changed. Love dictated its own rules.

Eleven

By the time the stall was delivered Saskia had called on all the ladies, mostly acquaintances of Mistress Henrietta, who had previously purchased from her. With two exceptions, both women doubtful about her new circumstances, all the rest were agreeable to her calling to take orders for her preparations and then to deliver them. This was a great relief to her as she had feared losing their custom.

Always when she was visiting she took the chance to buy a news-sheet, for England had gone to war again with Holland and it distressed her deeply that this should be happening with no end in sight. Personally she could not see why men could not talk out their problems instead of taking up arms, which always meant suffering for the innocent as well as those involved.

On the morning when she set out her stall for the first time two sombrely dressed women, attracted by the rainbow colours of Rufus's containers, came to see what she was selling and both made a purchase.

She wanted male customers too and had made ready bottles of colouring used to match the fashionable arrow-pointed beards and thin moustaches to a favourite wig. It was something she had done for Grinling's father during her time in the Gibbons household. She had also made up several different fragrances with a tangy aroma for men too, for they indulged in perfumes as much as women, the dandies among them also using cosmetics that whitened their faces and rouged their lips, but as the whitener contained lead she did not make it. Instead she had concocted a white powder, which when properly applied, would have the same effect.

By the end of the first week she had done extremely well with her sales, but she realized that the appeal of her stall was in its unusually pretty colours and its unexpected appearance on its own at the wayside. She knew that regular passers-by would soon get used to her being there and interest would wane. Yet she hoped that those who had bought from her would return to purchase again simply because her wares suited them. As the days went by she noticed that although at first it was wives and sweethearts, who made purchases for their men, it was not long before a man came alone to make his own purchase.

She had finished work for the day and taken the remainder of her goods indoors when Robert rode up and dismounted. She opened the door to him.

'I've come on Elizabeth's and Grinling's behalf to invite you to dine with them tomorrow,' he announced as he entered. 'Just as we promised.'

Her immediate thought was that it was he who had done the promising, but as tomorrow was

Sunday she would not be opening her stall and had no reason not to accept the invitation. In any case if she did try to escape from the commitment Robert would see through it and goad her once again.

'That's very kind of them,' she answered, her voice subdued.

He had seen the flash of wariness in her eyes at the prospect of seeing Grinling yet again and he spoke out remorselessly.

'You faced the worst on the night of the play. Let's have no more dithering now.'

She turned pink with annoyance. 'You really know how to turn a knife in a wound!'

'It should have healed by now,' he said without pity. 'You've accepted that you can't have Grinling for a husband and so,' he added on a softer note, his eyes becoming amused, 'you can give me your time and attention. I'm young, strong and healthy with every chance of becoming rich one day. Am I not a good prospect?'

'Not for me,' she stated impatiently.

'But that is not all I could offer if all goes well for me. At the present time I'm involved in a lawsuit to regain the country house that has been in my family for many years and it is where I was born. You would love it there. It lies in the heart of the hills we call the Sussex Downs and it would be difficult to find a more peaceful place anywhere.'

In spite of herself her curiosity was aroused. 'If it is your birthplace why have you had to go to court to regain it? The King restored all properties to their rightful owners when he came home after his exile.'

'It is occupied by my stepmother, Caroline Harting. When my father fled with the King, taking me with him, she refused to go too, not wanting to give up her comfortable life at Harting Hall, and conveniently switched her loyalties to Cromwell and the Parliamentarian rule. Throughout his years of dominance she kept open house for him and his generals. There is even the suspicion that she betrayed two royalists.'

'Then why should there be any problem for your inherent right to your birthplace?'

'There is a complication. After Cromwell died and it became obvious that his son had none of his father's ability to rule, there was soon a movement to restore the King to the throne. It was then that my stepmother declared herself to have been a royalist all along and it was no fault of hers that the two royalists, whom she had hidden in the cellars, were captured and executed. It is that claim that has kept her in the house where she betrayed my father in more ways than one. The case has yet to come to court and my lawyers are gathering evidence against her. In the meantime I have to be patient, which is far from easy.'

'Indeed, yes. I understand how hard it must be for you. I wish you a successful outcome when the case does come to court,' she said sincerely.

'I thank you, Saskia.' He rose to his feet. 'Now I must go. Shall I tell Elizabeth that you accept her invitation?'

'Yes, please do that for me.'

'Then I shall call for you tomorrow.' He paused as he reached the door. 'How do you go about the delivery of your wares?'

'On foot after I have closed the stall.'

'But you should have a horse to take you around. I'll look out for one.'

She spoke firmly, 'Thank you, but no, Robert. I have never ridden in my life.'

'Then I'll teach you.' He turned away, the subject closed as far as he was concerned.

From the window she watched him ride away before she turned back thoughtfully into the room. She had known from the start that it would be useful to have her own mount to cover the distances when visiting the ladies who ordered regularly from her. But the old stable at the rear of the cottage needed repair, something the landlord had overlooked, and the cost of riding lessons as well as buying a horse and feeding it was an expense that she would have to postpone for the time being. Yet she would give the matter more thought one day soon.

The prospect of seeing Grinling and Elizabeth in their home did not stir jealousy in her, only regret that she still could not banish her love for him, no matter that she had fully accepted the situation. Since the wedding night it was as if a shield had gradually moulded itself around her heart, keeping in her love while protecting it against further anguish.

She was ready and waiting when Robert arrived to collect her in his coach the following day. They talked all the way and when the city began to close about them Robert pointed out

183

sights of interest. As the coach pulled up Ludgate Hill Saskia was surprised to find the area far busier than she had thought possible on a Sunday, but it had become clear to her that this was a city that never took rest. They arrived at *La Belle Sauvage* with a clatter of hooves, passing through the wide entrance into the cobbled courtyard. Two ostlers ran forward to take the horses' bridles.

When Saskia had alighted she looked up and around, amazed to find that this coaching inn was far larger than she had expected. It was several floors high and encompassed the whole of the expansive courtyard, each with a gallery along which people were passing, mostly travellers being shown by youths in fustian jackets to their accommodation or else making a departure.

Saskia wondered how Elizabeth endured the noise, for coaches and other vehicles seemed to be coming and going all the time. Apart from the stamping of horses' hooves and the rumble of wheels there were the shouts of the ostlers, drunken bellowing from those who had indulged too freely in the inn, the melodious cries of flower-sellers and the clamour of boys wanting to carry passengers' luggage or run errands for them. The wealthier travellers themselves were an interesting sight to see, the men all in large hats with nodding ostrich feathers, bunches of ribbons on their shoulders and swashbuckling cloaks, their women equally spectacular. These were in sharp contrast to some other passengers soberly dressed in black with white collars, who looked disapprovingly at everyone else in the old Puritan way. Saskia wondered if those sober-ly clad men noticed how the younger women with them could not resist glancing enviously over their shoulders at those of their sex finely adorned in silks and velvets.

There were steep flights of stairs to reach the top floor. Grinling, bewigged and beaming, came out on to the landing to meet them, his arms spread wide expansively. He had put on a little weight, which suited his broad-shouldered frame, and was well dressed, his coat of fine crimson velvet and his cravat a flow of truly exquisite lace.

'Welcome, my friends! Saskia! How good to see you! Elizabeth is eagerly awaiting you! Come in!'

As they entered the quite luxurious apartment Elizabeth came tripping forward, white lace dancing back from her sleeves as she reached out her arms to embrace Saskia. 'How well you look, my dear friend! I was so afraid you would be tired out after selling from your stall, but you are blooming like a rose. Have you had nice customers? I'm looking forward so much to seeing your stall for myself.'

As Saskia began to slip off her cloak Lucy came forward to take it from her. 'How nice to see you again, Mistress Saskia,' she said shyly.

'I'm pleased to see you too, Lucy. Are you still writing entries in your book?'

'Yes, mistress. I watch out for all the latest fashion trends and dress Mistress Gibbons' hair accordingly.'

Elizabeth stood smiling. 'Yes, have no fear,

185

Saskia. Lucy is doing very well.'

As Lucy went to hang away the cloak Elizabeth whispered to Saskia that the girl had a beau among the ostlers. His name was Ben, an agreeable young man, who aimed to have his own stables one day.

'It's good that he has ambition,' Saskia said, pleased for the girl.

Then Elizabeth, too excited to hold back her news any longer, told what she had been bursting to tell from the moment Saskia had crossed the threshold.

'I'm with child, my dear friend!' she exclaimed happily. 'Is it not wonderful?'

Saskia took Elizabeth's hands in both her own, thankful for the protective numbness centred around her heart, for she felt neither envy nor jealousy, her only thought being that Elizabeth and Grinling were deserving of all good things that came their way and she was thankful that she could rejoice for them.

'It is an early blessing on your marriage, Elizabeth.'

'Let me show you what I have made for the layette already.'

Proudly, Elizabeth led the way into what would be the nursery where she showed Saskia several small garments, most of them neatly embroidered. One little gown was trimmed with some very fine lace, which caused Saskia to comment on the beautiful lace of Grinling's cravat. Elizabeth, putting the garments back in a drawer again, looked up with her eyes twinkling with amusement as if she hugged some secret

186

joke to herself.

'It is very fine indeed,' she agreed, a laugh in her throat. 'In fact I doubt there is a finer lace to be found anywhere. You must tell him. He will be so pleased.'

Together they returned to the drawing room where the two men were talking and Elizabeth immediately announced to Grinling how much their guest admired his cravat.

'I think,' Elizabeth added merrily, 'Saskia believes that such exquisite lace should be used for our baby's garments instead.'

Saskia protested immediately. 'I said no such thing!'

Grinling laughed. 'If it could be put to such use you should take it from me now, but first of all you need to feel the quality of it. Only then can you decide if it is fine and soft enough for my son and heir. Come now!' He expanded his chest as if to display the cravat to better advantage.

'Yes, of course it would be,' Saskia said, smiling at his urging, but keeping her hands at her sides. 'Remember that I used to see Nurse Bobbins making lace as fine as yours.'

'You will never know if you do not test it for yourself.'

Robert stepped forward. 'I'll be the judge.' He touched the lace, met Grinling's eyes for a moment, and then stepped back again, a quiver of amusement at the corners of his lips. 'It really is up to you to decide, Saskia.'

She saw that Grinling's game was not going to end before she had fingered his cravat. To humour him she put up her hand to feel its fineness. Instantly her expression became one of total astonishment and then she dissolved helplessly into laughter, Robert and Elizabeth laughing too. Grinling was grinning widely in delight.

'It's not lace at all!' Saskia exclaimed, brushing a tear of mirth from her eye. 'It is wood! You have carved it, Grinling! What a delightful joke!'

'Congratulations on creating such a fashionable masterpiece!' Robert said, still laughing.

Grinling then demonstrated how the carved lace, which was perfect in every delicate detail, was fastened to a normal cravat around his neck. Saskia guessed it would be a joke played many times on friends and acquaintances in the future, but it was also proof of his marvellous skill in carving minutiae. The four of them were discussing it with amusement as they took their places at table.

Apart from a manservant, who waited at table and also acted as Grinling's valet, Elizabeth had a housemaid, a scullery maid and a kitchen boy, there being special accommodation for the servants of residents as well as passing travellers. She also had the services of an excellent cook, who in between duties worked downstairs in the inn's kitchen. On this Sunday Grinling and Elizabeth with their two guests dined handsomely on asparagus soup, fish cooked with cream followed by a dish of succulent guinea fowl before Grinling stood with a flash of a carving knife and fork to carve a large roast sirloin of beef into perfect slices. This was all accompanied by a selection of vegetables. Then came a delicious custard pudding that was light as air.

Saskia thought to herself that it was no wonder that Grinling was putting on weight, although Elizabeth assured her that they did not eat so grandly every day. Yet from the conversation it was clear that Grinling was being frequently wined and dined lavishly by important gentlemen at their clubs. Since becoming known to Thomas Betterton he was rising rapidly in the public eye through his growing reputation for beautiful carving. He had no shortage of work and the next day he was to interview several young woodcarvers with a view to taking on one of them as an apprentice to assist him in his workshop on the ground floor.

It was during the talk at table that Robert mentioned Saskia's need of a horse. Grinling immediately had the solution.

'The landlord has a couple of horses in his stable, which he took in lieu of payment from a husband and wife, who had imbibed so much during a week's sojourn that they could not meet their bills.'

Elizabeth nodded. 'We can ask Ben – that's Lucy's young beau – for his advice as to which would be best for Saskia.'

Grinling smiled benignly at her in gentle reproof. 'I think Robert and I are well able to judge which is the better of the two animals and if the one that the woman rode would be right for her.'

'Of course, my dear,' Elizabeth replied, suspiciously docile.

Saskia could see that she was making fun of

his moment of pomposity, but he did not see it. She hid a smile herself before making a statement to close the discussion. 'I'm afraid I'm not in a position to afford my own horse yet. Perhaps later—'

Elizabeth looked sternly at her. 'You need it now, Saskia. You can't walk everywhere.'

'If it is a question of cost,' Grinling said, 'you could rent one of those two horses by the month. Maybe until you are ready to buy?'

Saskia nodded. 'It would be a solution for the time being if I were able to ride.'

'You would soon learn.'

Robert intervened. 'I've already offered to teach Saskia.'

Grinling nodded. 'Then we'll talk to the innkeeper before you both leave.'

Then the conversation switched to other topics and the time passed quickly.

It was getting dusk when eventually the visit was at an end and the four of them went downstairs together to go first into Grinling's large workshop. He lit some candle-lamps which, combined with the lamplight illumining the courtyard, enabled the visitors to view some of his latest works. His interest no longer lay wholly in religious subjects, for festoons and foliage had presently captured his imagination and there were glorious outpourings as if his workshop were part of a forest blossoming with flowers and laden with fruit. These were surrounds for large portraits and doorways and some to create festoons around all or part of a grand room, much of it in his beloved lime

190

wood. Full daylight was needed to examine the work in detail and Saskia resolved to return one day to see these works at their best.

When Grinling had extinguished the lamps and locked the door again they went to view the two horses. Both Grinling and Robert looked at both of them carefully. Then, in spite of what Grinling had said earlier, he did question Ben, a tousle-haired, freckle-faced young man, as to whether either of two mounts was suitable for a beginner to ride. Elizabeth promptly nudged Saskia with her elbow.

'Men!' she whispered derisively, rolling up her eyes. They giggled together.

Ben indicated the darker of the two mounts with a white blaze, and he did not hesitate in his reply. 'This mare is old, but she is as gentle as a doe and would suit Queen Catherine herself, master.'

'What is her name?' Saskia asked. She had gone forward to pat the mare, already loving her for her beautiful eyes.

'Her previous owner called her *Acorn* after the oak tree that hid the King when he was in flight from old wart-on-the-nose Cromwell.'

Saskia smiled. 'In that case she was well named.'

'So is it agreed?' Robert asked her. 'You will let me teach you how to ride?'

Elizabeth answered for her. 'Indeed she will. It is very kind of you, Robert.'

Saskia felt as if everything had been taken out of her hands, but Acorn had won her over more than the persuasion of her friends. It only remained for an agreement with the innkeeper. Saskia went with Grinling back into the inn and the procedure was soon settled. Acorn was to be collected as soon as Saskia had had the stable on her land repaired.

Although it was dark when she and Robert arrived back at her cottage she went indoors to light a lantern and then he went with her to see what repairs were needed in the stable. There he took the lantern from her and held it high as he looked around, the glow highlighting the planes of his face as he gave his judgement.

'There's nothing seriously wrong here. A few new planks, some hinges and a serious sweeping out is all that's required. I'll do it for you myself.'

'No, that's too much,' she said sternly. 'You've already offered to give up time to teach me to ride.'

He lowered the lantern and set it on a ledge as he looked fiercely down into her face. 'When are you going to realize that anything I do for you is a pleasure to me?'

She drew back a step, causing some old straw to rustle underfoot. 'It should not be. I don't want to be under an obligation to you or any other man.'

He groaned in exasperation and seized her by the shoulders, pulling her to him. 'Wake up, Saskia!' he exclaimed angrily. 'I can't wait for you for ever!'

Then he clamped his mouth down on hers in a kiss that set up such a whirlwind in her mind that she trembled violently in every limb. She believed afterwards she would have fallen to the ground if he had not been holding her within the circle of his arm while his other hand caressed her. When the kiss ended his lips continued to hover caressingly over hers as if he would kiss her again, but he put her abruptly from him and went striding out of the stable, taking the lantern with him. She followed quickly to avoid being left in the dark. He deposited the lantern on her doorstep and went to his waiting coach. She thought that he was going to leave without saying anything more, but as he entered the equipage he spoke over his shoulder to her.

'You shall have your first riding lesson at six o'clock after you have closed the stall. These May evenings are light enough for at least two hours in the saddle.'

The coach door was shut after him and he was driven away.

She did not go indoors at once, the violent trembling having failed to leave her and her heart was still beating a race of its own. Robert had shown that he wanted her with a passionate ferocity that she had first glimpsed in his eyes without understanding when she had been standing on a staircase far away in Rotterdam. Now she forced herself to accept the fact that completely against her will and by its own volition her traitor body would have welcomed his passion, her breasts left aching for further caresses from his demanding hands. Yet he was a man she did not want and could never love. She stood quietly, breathing in the soft night air until calmed by it, all the while looking up at the star-filled sky.

Then a shiver passed through her and she rubbed her arms before picking up the lantern and going into the cottage. She bolted the door firmly as if she feared he might return and could not keep her thoughts from his kissing as she went upstairs to bed.

Twelve

In the early morning Saskia was awakened by a hammering. She left her bed to see from the window overlooking the road that a horse and cart was parked on the grass verge. Then, turning, she hurried across to the rear window, and saw a workman on a ladder repairing the stable roof. Opening the window, she called to him.

'Good day! Who sent you here?'

'Master Harting.'

'I thought from the way he spoke to me yesterday that he was coming himself.'

'I know nothing of that, mistress. I received my instructions late last night. Do you have a drop of beer? This is thirsty work.'

She had no beer, but took him a cup of tea instead. He had never tasted tea before and put it to his lips suspiciously. He had no idea what a treat it was, for tea was extremely expensive and Saskia rationed herself.

During the day there was a delivery of straw

and a sack of feed, which was properly stowed away with the amount she had already ordered. It seemed as if Robert had thought of everything. Later, when the carpenter had finished his task, he showed Saskia what he had done and she was pleased with the result, for now the mare would have a roomy stall under a watertight roof. The repaired stable-door would enable Acorn to look out at the world.

When Saskia would have paid the carpenter he waved the money aside.

'No, mistress. I'm getting paid from Master Harting's office.'

'But I want to pay you myself.'

'Begging your pardon, mistress, but I have my orders.'

She bit her lip, prepared to remonstrate with Robert that evening, but he was not the rider who came cantering up, bringing Acorn with him. Instead it was a well-spoken young man with dark curls to his shoulders, not handsome, but with a pleasant face. He dismounted to introduce himself as Allan Willowby.

'Was Master Harting not able to come?' she inquired on what she hoped was a casual note.

'I was unaware that he had any intention of coming,' he replied. 'Today I was engaged by him to make you a competent horsewoman and I'm sure that can be achieved without any problems.'

She was stroking Acorn's white blaze. 'I shall do my best.'

He helped her up into the side saddle and as soon as he saw that she was comfortable and he had given her some basic instruction he remounted himself and together they set off. It was from those first few minutes that she was to enjoy riding for the rest of her life and as her instructor had anticipated she was to prove quick to learn.

That night when she went to bed she pondered over Robert's failure to appear on two separate occasions in the same day and finally decided with a feeling of relief that he had accepted at last that he had no place in her life. There remained the problem of levelling out in some way his generous gift of the repairs and now of these riding lessons. She decided that she would present him with a selection of the very best products that she made for men, including a new fragrance for the male chin after shaving, which was superior to anything offered by a barber.

Elizabeth came to visit as had been arranged when Saskia was at her stall. She admired the layout of the pots and flasks.

'It all looks so pretty!' she declared, clasping her hands together in her enthusiasm.

There were no customers and they sat in the chairs by the stall to exchange news. Elizabeth was eager to tell that Grinling had plenty of work coming in all the time and that his first apprentice was skilful, quick and eager to learn.

'But Grinling still has not received any orders for his carving from Master Wren,' she said, a puzzled frown drawing her fine brows together, 'and the prestige of that gentleman's patronage almost outshines that of the King himself. It is so maddening when Grinling is being recognized by everybody else as a true artist in wood. It is not as though Master Wren was barring him for the same reason that he will not have Robert involved in his rebuilding.'

'Robert barred?' Saskia asked in surprise. 'Whatever is the reason for that?'

Elizabeth lowered her voice even though there was nobody in sight. 'When Robert was first in London after coming from Rotterdam with Grinling he soon gained a reputation as a rake and a ravisher. Being of an aristocratic background he had an entrée to St Luke's club and other such elite gentlemen's clubs where he drank heavily and played intensely, often risking everything on the turn of a card. Then whenever he was at a ball or any other grand social occasion women would not leave him alone and people gossiped about that too. He had a very beautiful mistress for a while, although his good manners prevented him from bringing her into my company at any time. That's why Master Wren has told him to gain a more respectable reputation before allowing him to work on hallowed ground.'

'Has Robert shown any sign of mending his ways?'

'Grinling says he has, but then they are virtually lifelong friends. Grinling would always defend him.' Elizabeth sat back in her chair and regarded Saskia with intense interest. 'Now you have Robert's attentions. He could scarcely take his eyes from you the day you both came to dine.' Then she tilted her head enquiringly at Saskia. 'Have you not been stirred by his male magnetism that seems to arouse so many women?'

'Only enough to make sure I keep my distance. Fortunately I think there must be somebody new on Robert's horizon, because quite abruptly he has cancelled two arrangements he had made with me.'

'Are you disappointed?'

Saskia smiled reassuringly, for Elizabeth looked so concerned. 'Not in the least! I'm grateful for the kindnesses he has shown me, but that is all. But what I do need from you is his London address.'

She explained about the gift she was preparing for him and Elizabeth wrote the address down. Just as she handed it over a coach stopped to allow a middle-aged woman and her two young daughters to alight and come across the grass to the stall. Elizabeth made a quick departure, not wanting her presence to interfere with business.

Saskia kept the stall closed every Monday afternoon, for that enabled her to visit the ladies that still wanted her products. She had not expected to continue to supply her former employer, but Mistress Henrietta's early alliance with Martha's own beauty preparations soon came to an end, resulting in Saskia receiving an order to deliver all the products previously used. She never saw Mistress Henrietta, but Martha was usually there to receive the items, a sneer on her face as if accepting poisonous substances. Once when Martha was out the housekeeper confided that the woman savagely resented Mistress Henrietta's conviction that nobody could make beauty preparations like Saskia.

'Martha is a vicious woman as I know to my cost,' the housekeeper continued, 'and she really hates you, so always be on your guard.'

'Thank you for the warning,' Saskia replied, although she could not think of any way that Martha could harm her.

By now Saskia rode well, her lessons having come to an end for a while, and when she delivered to her ladies she had two saddlebags containing her wares. It was rarely that she returned with any of the extra products she took with her and always with a list of what was wanted next time. She had employed Ted Robinson's younger son, Joe, to groom Acorn and keep her fed and watered as well as exercised when she herself did not have time to ride while in attendance at her stall.

It was Joe whom she sent to deliver her gift to Robert. The pots, which had been made by Rufus, all had striped blue and white lids and were neatly labelled as were the flasks containing a choice of fragrances, and she had covered the box in fine white paper. She hoped that the care she had taken with the presentation would show him how much his generosity had been appreciated.

Joe returned to say that he had handed the box in to a servant. 'The fellow said that Master Harting is out of London on a building project in York at the present time, but the box will be kept for his return.'

'Thank you, Joe,' she said.

Her days at her stall were not without problems. Until now the weather had been kind to her, the occasional light shower not deterring customers in any way, but then with the arrival of June the weather became unseasonably wet. Downpours were so heavy that it was pointless to open her stall, for coaches did not stop and people hurried by with their heads down.

Then when the sunshine did return other hazards awaited her. One morning a herd of goats started to eat the stall's canvas apron, making a hole on one side and leaving it ragged before she and the goatherd managed to drive them away. At this time gypsies were on the move, passing from one country fair to another, and their children came running up to swarm about the stall, their hands shooting out to grab whatever they could before bolting off again. She overcame this by getting a tightly webbed fishing-net and throwing it over her goods to secure them as soon as she saw caravans approaching. Although the majority of her customers were honest there were some people, respectably dressed and well able to afford her modest prices, who were not above slipping a pot into the pocket of an apron or a coat.

She began considering how much better it would be if she could turn the cottage into a shop. Then she would have most of her wares securely on shelves behind her and a counter would block unlawful access. It meant waiting until the end of summer as by then she hoped to have made enough money not to have to draw on her savings.

Unexpectedly one day Martha arrived at the

stall and showed immense satisfaction when she conveyed the message that Mistress Henrietta wanted Saskia to call on her without delay. It was a command.

'Don't expect to be treated like a visitor,' Martha said acidly. 'Rushmere House has not become as lax towards the social rank of its guests as a certain apartment in *La Belle Sauvage*. I happen to know that there is trouble in the air for you. You must realize that being as busy as you are with your stall also means that you are rushing through the preparation of your beauty products. They have been very poor recently. Mistress Henrietta has only to make her displeasure known and all the ladies in her circle will stop buying from you.'

Saskia looked the woman directly in the eyes. 'What have you been mixing in my products?'

It was a guess, but she was certain that it had hit home, even though Martha appeared unfazed by the question. 'What an absurd accusation!' she replied scornfully, tossing her head as she left again.

Saskia knew that Mistress Henrietta had never forgiven her for leaving Elizabeth's employ, but she had no qualms when she presented herself at Rushmere Hall when she was on her next Monday afternoon circuit. There was no sign of Martha and it was a young housemaid who took her up to the boudoir, even though she knew the way so well.

She entered the room with a curtsy and Mistress Henrietta flicked her closed fan in the direction of a chair. To her amazement, no sooner was she seated when the woman spoke in a whisper.

'I know that Martha listens at keyholes, so make sure that she is not in the corridor.'

Saskia rose to her feet again and looked out of the door, but the corridor was empty. She returned to her seat. 'There's nobody there.'

'Good. Now I believe you know why I have sent for you.'

'Yes, I understand that my products have not been pleasing you recently.'

'But I'm sure you can guess as well as I what has been happening to them after they leave you.'

Saskia had not expected the woman to be so perceptive. 'I'm making no accusations, madam.'

'But I am! You are the first to know that I am going to get rid of Martha. I should never have transferred you to Elizabeth, but I did it out of the goodness of my heart. Now I want you to come back to me. I'll treble your previous salary and give you better accommodation with a special room where you can make your lovely products, and I'll put no restrictions on your selling to other ladies that like to buy from you.'

Saskia was shaking her head. 'No, madam. You are making a most generous offer, but I never want to return to service. I enjoy having my own home and my own business. In fact I intend turning my cottage into a shop. I have already spoken to my landlord and he is agreeable.'

Mistress Rushmere stared at her in outraged

disbelief, unable to comprehend how this young woman could refuse such an offer. 'You have not given yourself time to think over my proposal. I shall withhold my dismissal of Martha to give you time to reconsider the hasty decision you have made.' She held up a hand as Saskia began to repeat her refusal. 'Not another word! Go now! I shall expect a different attitude when next you call on me.'

All the way home Saskia seethed inwardly at the woman's arrogance, even though she had been in England long enough now to know how class distinctions set people far apart through birth, fortune, trade or service. Her wide open Dutch attitude was that the good in people mattered, not their station in life. It made her exasperated with her new countrymen and -women on many occasions. Naturally there were social differences in her own country, but she had never been so much aware of the gaps between them as in England. She was thankful that Elizabeth saw no barriers between them in the friendship that they shared. It was probably Elizabeth's clear mind that had been one of many reasons why Grinling, a true Dutchman despite his English parentage, had fallen in love with her.

After several weeks Saskia received a formal letter of thanks from Robert for her gift. He apologized for the delay in his reply, explaining that he had just returned briefly to London and that was only for a matter of days before he left again. Although she knew from what was said by Elizabeth and Grinling that during the short time he had called on them, his visits and hers had never coincided. Then as Elizabeth's time for being brought to bed drew near she wanted Saskia to call in and see her as often as possible.

As for Mistress Henrietta, she had finally accepted that Saskia would never return to her. The result was that Martha had been ignominiously replaced by a smiling Swiss woman, named Dorli. According to Elizabeth the newcomer also had to face being constantly compared to Saskia, but fortunately the woman had supreme confidence in her own skills and so Mistress Henrietta's often cruel comments bounced off her, leaving no resentment. She even welcomed having Saskia's products supplied for her as it saved her a great deal of time-consuming work. There was no news of Martha, although Mistress Henrietta had been gracious enough to give her a character reference to help her get other employment, for as she said to her god-daughter it was no fault of Martha's that she had been unable to compete with Saskia's exceptional skills.

By now summer had waned and Saskia went ahead with her plans to make the cottage into a shop. The same carpenter that had repaired the stable did the work for her cheaply and efficiently, reusing some of the timber of the stall. She made a special trip into the city to order a swinging sign to set up above the shop door. The result was a double-sided sign displaying a flask of perfume and one of her decorated French pots.

On the eve of the shop's opening she took a

last look around before going upstairs. The counter was waxed and well polished and the rows of shelves on the wall behind her held displays of her wares, interspersed with some of the lovely French pots, which would not be for sale. Somehow she had at the back of her mind the vision of a truly elegant shop where she could preside and all her beauty products would be in pots and flasks as lovely as those in the chest that was stored upstairs. Was it a dream that her mother had had for her? She often wondered about it. But until then she would not part with any of those in the collection.

On the shop's opening day Saskia wondered at first if Robert happened to be in London would he call on her as he had done on the first day she had had the stall, but he did not appear. She was busy all day, for the cottage with its new sign, standing alone as it did in the countryside, caught the attention of all who passed by. Previous customers came to see what else she had to sell and to congratulate her on her venture. Other grander folk, who had not halted their fine coaches for a wayside stall, now alighted out of curiosity to see what was for sale.

As Saskia locked up for the night she did not see Robert come riding up in the darkness outside. He had been at his London residence for a few days before he had to return to York on the morrow where he was still engaged in the building of a fine mansion of his own design. He had been determined to stay away from Saskia, still angered by her rejection of him, and yet he had felt compelled to come and see what she had done to the cottage. At least, that was what he had told himself, but in his heart he knew that he hoped for a glimpse of her.

Now he reined in and watched the cottage where her lamp showed that she was on her way upstairs to bed. When he had seen her draw the curtains across her window he rode on into the city, his rage increased as he thought of her discarding her clothes and how eagerly he would have bedded her if such a chance had come his way. As soon as he found another woman with enough beauty, charm and sexual appeal to banish Saskia from his mind he would wed her.

In the bedchamber Saskia had undressed and had slipped a robe over her night shift to sit down and brush her hair. Afterwards she crossed the room to adjust the arrangement of some of her favourite little French pots on the chest of drawers as she did sometimes for her own amusement, for it always gave her pleasure to handle them. Now she brought forward one with a painted scene of two lovers meeting on a bridge and then she set back two others that were equally delightful. Over past weeks she had recounted every piece in the chest and had carefully listed each one in a sequence of pages at the back of her book of receipts. She thought with a smile that she was like an old miser relishing his money, although with her it was the beauty of the pots that gave her delight.

Suddenly hearing a sound that puzzled her, she went to the front window and looked out. The landscape was illumined by a full moon and she could see nothing that was untoward. She supposed it was a fox on the prowl or some other creature of the night that she had heard, but she was still not wholly satisfied and took up her candle-lamp to go downstairs to check that both the front and back doors were securely fastened. Only then, finding all was well, she was reassured and went back upstairs to bed. She was soon asleep.

Yet concealed in the deeper darkness of some trees, a rough-clad man, unshaven and sharp-eyed, had seen her come to the window and had held his breath for a few moments as he silently cursed the emptied gin bottle that he had thrown aside. He had not expected it to smash against some obstacle in the darkness. Then as the minutes passed he relaxed again. The candle in the upper room had been extinguished. Yet he was still tense as he fingered the coins in his pocket, which would be doubled when his assignment was done. The donor was an upper-class maid-servant that had sought him out in one of the taverns that he frequented, although on whose recommendation he did not know. He would wait another hour and then he would carry out his task.

Thirteen

Saskia awoke coughing and choking from the smoke billowing about the room. Tired from her busy day she had been in a deep sleep, but now, realizing in horror what was happening, she sprang from her bed. Grabbing her robe from its peg, she thrust her arms into it before darting to the head of the stairs. There she stopped, terror-stricken and drew back. There was no escape that way, for the flight was already a furnace, the flames greedily leaping up each wooden tread. She thought in despair of Grinling's looking-glass. There was no way that she could get to it. All she could save was the strongbox in her room. As she seized it and hurled it through the open rear window she heard Acorn whinnying in the stable, frightened by the proximity of fire and smoke, and to her horror she saw that the stable roof was already alight.

Swinging round to the wash bowl on its stand in the corner, she snatched up a towel and dipped it deep into the ewer of water to soak it as a cover for her head and to shield her face. Then darting once more to the rear window she looked down to judge her chances of escape that way. Cascading sparks and the crackling of straw overhead told her that the thatch was burning fiercely. There was the flat porch roof over the back door. If she could lower herself to get a foothold on to it she should be able to lessen a fall.

Then as she put her foot over the window sill somebody was shouting to her. She recognized Ted Robinson's voice.

'We're here! George and me will catch you!'

'Get Acorn out of the stable!' she shrieked, clutching the window- sill with both hands.

'Joe is seeing to her!' Ted Robinson shouted back in his deep voice. 'You get yourself ready now to jump.'

Not daring to look down, she found a foothold on the porch roof below, but almost in the same instant she slipped. She crashed against the porch roof and screamed as she fell, but Ted and George staved off the worst of her landing. Then Ted snatched her up in his arms and ran with her away from the burning straws being thrown wide like a wild fireworks display from the flaming thatch.

George shouted to her. 'Anybody else in the cottage?'

'No,' she cried, still clutching at Ted as he lowered her to the grass well out of range of the sparks.

'Do you think you've broken any bones?' Ted asked, his big red face hovering anxiously over hers.

She shook her head, aware of pain, but it seemed to be all through her and she could not locate the source. 'Has Acorn suffered burns?' she asked fearfully, drawing breath between coughing.

George answered, adding his face to his father's over hers. 'No. Joe was quick to lead her out of danger. Folk are coming from everywhere, bringing buckets with them, to see what they can do to help.'

'Take some deep breaths, girl,' Ted said, propping her up a little with his arms, almost causing her to pass out with pain.

As she tried to obey him she saw that people were moving around everywhere, the flames illumining their concerned faces as they trampled unknowingly over her herb garden. Some had formed a chain filling buckets from the nearby stream and she could hear the pump handle being worked hard. Yet she feared their task was hopeless, for the fire had gained such a hold. Amid the shouting and the crackle of flames she heard Kate's voice calling.

'Ted! George! Where are you?'

'Over here!' Ted answered, getting up from his knees at Saskia's side. Kate came panting up with a blanket in her arms, clearly having run most of the way from the farm.

'Wrap the girl up in this blanket,' she instructed her husband, 'and bring her home! Now!'

Effortlessly, he carried Saskia in his arms all the way, telling her jovially that she weighed much less than his prize pig in a vain attempt to take her mind off the scene they had left. Kate kept a few paces ahead, clicking her tongue at what she thought of as his nonsense. She carried the foreign-looking strongbox and wondered what it held.

At the farmhouse Ted left Saskia in his wife's

care and then returned to the site of the fire. Although there was nothing to be done to save the cottage, which now resembled a giant bonfire, there was the need to be sure that sparks did not ignite anywhere else. All knew that the Great Fire of London had been started by a fire in a baker's shop and the speed by which it had spread was still fresh in everyone's minds. When dawn came nothing remained of the cottage except smouldering ashes and blackened timber. Ted and George and the last of the watchers finally dispersed.

Joe had gone to find Acorn, whom he had left tethered to a distant tree, but the mare was still nervous and wild-eyed. Joe spoke to her soothingly all the way to the farm and then put her in the stables with a feed to quieten her.

Kate made Saskia rest in bed for two days. She was badly bruised and Kate, able to tell that the girl had cracked a rib and perhaps two, would have bound her up if the local wise woman had not always said it was better for nature to be left to heal ribs. At Saskia's request Ted had searched in the debris for the chest that had held the containers she had treasured, but it had been completely destroyed and only a few blackened bits of broken china were all that remained of the collection. There was also no trace of the looking-glass that she had cherished.

She wept desolately when he told her. Although she tried to tell herself that since Grinling's marriage had put an end to all her secret hopes it would be as well that she had nothing to remind her of her lost love. Yet the looking-glass

211

had been a work of art in itself and she had treasured it so much.

Ted, not knowing the importance of the looking-glass attempted to console her in a clumsy, good-hearted way. 'Don't distress yourself over some old china and a looking-glass,' he said, not knowing the significance of her loss. 'Be thankful that you're young and strong and can begin all over again.'

Going back downstairs he found his wife in the kitchen and told her how desperately upset the girl was over what he thought had probably been an old china tea-set lost in the flames.

'As for the looking-glass that has been destroyed too,' he said. 'I told her that I believed you had one that she could have instead. Joe won it for you at that fair we went to last year.'

'Yes, she can have it,' Kate replied willingly. 'Maybe if she came down here with me for an hour or two it would stop her dwelling on the loss of her nice little home.'

She took with her Saskia's newly washed robe, for it had been mud-stained and grass-flecked from her fall. As she went bustling into the bedchamber, she held it out in front of her.

'Put this on, Saskia, and come downstairs for a while. It will do you good to get out of this bedchamber.'

Saskia obeyed her listlessly, wincing at the pain in her rib. 'You're being so kind to me.'

'Nonsense! We're here on this earth to help each other.'

Kate assisted Saskia down the narrow stairs and settled her in a comfortable chair by the hearth. Immediately the house cat jumped up on to her lap and she smiled as she stroked it, rewarded by a deep purr. Kate, smiling at them both, dived into her apron pocket and brought out one of the little French pots that Saskia recognized immediately. 'I found this in the pocket of your robe,' Kate said, holding it up. 'It's lucky I didn't break it when I plunged the garment into the suds.'

Saskia had uttered a low cry of joy and held out her cupped hands to receive it. She remembered now that she had been adjusting its position on the top of the chest of drawers just before she had caught the unusual sound outside. Without being aware of it she must have put the pot into her pocket as she turned to the window. There was not the least doubt in her mind or anybody else's that the fire had been started deliberately. The only clue was the empty gin bottle that lay smashed against a large stone at which it had been thrown.

She gazed at the pot in her hands. How pretty this little survivor was in every way! How delicately painted with a pair of lovers meeting on a bridge in a rose garden! She turned her radiant face towards Kate. She had known in that instant of seeing the pot again that she would start to replace her heritage by building up a collection just as her mother had done. It was like a lifeline being held out to her and mentally she gripped it with all her strength. She would fill the gap that the fire had left in her life.

'Now I can begin again!' she exclaimed fervently.

Word of any fire spread quickly in these sensitive times and news of the destroyed cottage soon reached *La Belle Sauvage*. As a result Elizabeth arrived at the Robinsons' farm, followed by Wilkins, her coachman, carrying a large wicker basket, to find Saskia seated by the hearth in the farmhouse kitchen. Elizabeth was not far from her time and was awkward in her movements as she embraced Saskia in sympathetic understanding before settling herself in a chair on the opposite side of the hearth.

'Tell Wilkins where to find your room upstairs,' she said. 'I've packed a few useful things to tide you over for the time being.'

Saskia, still pale from pain, was lost for words at her friend's thoughtfulness, for she was clad in one of Kate's dresses that was too big for her and too short. When she attempted to express her thanks Elizabeth waved her words away.

'You must let me know if there is anything else that either Grinling or I can do for you. He doesn't know about the fire yet as he is out of town for a few days, having gone to measure up for carvings to surmount a number of doors in a house near Horsham. He will be devastated when he hears what has happened. I had a look at the remains of the cottage as I came by.' She shook her head sympathetically. 'Was nothing salvaged?'

'Only my strongbox with my precious book of receipts in it, my mother's ruby pendant and some money as well as – wonderfully – one of the little pots from my mother's collection, which was in my dressing-robe pocket. All the

214

rest were lost.' She paused and then her voice caught in her throat. 'The fire also destroyed a little circular looking-glass in a carved frame that Grinling gave me in Holland after he had come home from his travels abroad.'

'My poor dear friend,' Elizabeth said sympathetically, reaching out to take hold of Saskia's hand. 'You have lost so much, but I'm sure Grinling would carve a frame for another little looking-glass for you.'

Saskia shook her head determinedly. 'No. You must not ask him. He is too busy to be troubled with any extra task. That gift always reminded me of a happy time in Holland, which was the reason why it was particularly precious to me, and a replacement would never be the same.'

'I suppose not,' Elizabeth answered. 'I know if I ever lost that first beautiful necklace that Grinling gave me there could never be another to take its place. That is what happens when love or friendship is part of the gift, whether given or received,' she added dreamily. Then she became practical, sitting upright in her chair as if about to take charge. 'Is it too soon to ask if you have made any plans yet for the future?'

Saskia was thankful for a change of subject. 'I have given the matter considerable thought. I shall have to return to service as a personal maid until such time that I can launch out on my own again. Kate Robinson has told me that her husband had no insurance on the old cottage and I doubt if he has it on anything else he owns. All I do know for certain is that he will not be rebuilding on the site and intends to grow crops

215

there in future.'

'You've spoken of your ultimate plan,' Elizabeth pointed out, 'but what are you going to do in the next week or two? You could have come to stay with us if we had another bedchamber, but we could take a room in the inn for you.'

'There is no need,' Saskia assured her. 'I'm not exactly homeless. Kate and Ted are willing for me to stay on here for a while at a very modest charge. It will give me the chance to apply for employment and to start putting my life together again.'

'I think I have a better solution,' Elizabeth said, looking extremely pleased with herself. 'It is entirely my own idea. Would you consider becoming the caretaker of a London house during the owner's absence? You would have your keep and a small salary. It should give you the time you need to take stock and not rush too quickly through necessity into any position offered to you.'

Saskia's face had lit up hopefully. 'Oh, Elizabeth!' she exclaimed in a choked voice, clasping her hands together. 'Do you know of such a house? It is just the employment that I would welcome to see me through for a while.'

Elizabeth smiled, delighted that she was able to help in a practical way. 'Then it can be arranged. How soon do you think you will be fit to travel into the city?'

Saskia gave a little laugh. 'I would go this minute for such a chance, even dressed as I am!'

Elizabeth giggled, glancing over her friend's attire. 'I have seen you clad more elegantly.

Should we say in two days' time?'

'Yes! Who is it that owns this house?'

'Robert. Did I not say?' She did not notice that Saskia drew back warily in her chair. 'He dined with us three days ago before setting off north again. He is overseeing the final stages of a great mansion in Yorkshire that he designed. At the start he moved his London staff to a house he is renting in the city of York. His housekeeper's sister, who has acted as caretaker, left at a moment's notice when her daughter sent for her, needing help in nursing a sick child. At present I am sending Lucy into the house every day to make sure that all is in order, but that is only a temporary measure as I promised Robert that I would find a reliable and honest replacement.'

'Why doesn't Robert close the house up?' Saskia asked, still wary.

'With winter coming? No, it would get cold and damp without habitation.'

'Then he will be away for some time?'

'Probably for weeks yet.'

'Why is the position not for another house-keeper instead of a caretaker?'

'Because there will be nobody for whom to housekeep. Does the thought of being on your own in the house concern you?'

'No, not at all.' Saskia was welcoming the thought of it.

Then, after Elizabeth had arranged to send her coach to convey Robert's new caretaker to his house in two days' time, Saskia asked what Grinling had carved recently. Elizabeth answered with enthusiasm.

'He has just finished some carved doors with a theme of fruit and game for the dining room of a fine mansion owned by a young lord. They are extraordinarily beautiful.'

Saskia thought to herself that the timbers of England had met their master and were surging forth miraculously under his hands in a way never seen before. It was no wonder that Elizabeth's voice throbbed with pride in her husband's achievements.

'Unfortunately,' Elizabeth continued, 'no money has yet come forward to pay for these grand doors. Such carving takes so much time and Grinling, who never owes a penny himself, believes in his practical Dutch way that agreed interim payments for such work should be paid promptly. Now when he sees he will have a struggle to be paid, he leaves the pea pods open in his carving of them and his clients or, if they live far away, their representatives come to see how the work is progressing – as they frequently do – it is his own special reminder that they have yet to settle an account with him.'

'Does he often have to do that?'

'It happens, because it seems that the richer the client the slower he or she is to pay. Grinling, in his blunt Dutch way, allows them sufficient time with the pea pods and then, if nothing has been forthcoming, he arrives grandly attired on the doorstep with his bill. That usually has the right result, because almost always more of his work is wanted.'

It was at that moment that Kate Robinson returned to the farmhouse with a chicken under

218

her arm to pluck. She shook her head firmly when Saskia said she would be leaving in two days' time.

'You may have a fine coach, madam,' she said with a bob of her knees to Elizabeth, 'but it will still jolt up and down over the ruts and bumps of the roads, giving Saskia's poor ribs a lot of extra pain. Another week's rest here and then perhaps she will be ready to go off to London. And, if you'll forgive me for saying so, it hasn't done your condition any good to travel here today.'

'But I had to come and see for myself that Saskia is recovering from the calamity that has befallen her,' Elizabeth protested smilingly, although she accepted that Saskia's departure should be postponed. She rose from her chair to depart and gave Saskia a light kiss on the cheek. Then, at the door, she paused to look back at her. 'Get well soon, dear friend.'

Later that day when Saskia opened the wicker basket in her room she found two of Elizabeth's gowns, one silk and the other woollen, folded neatly on top of the rest of the contents. She knew that both would fit her, for until Elizabeth became pregnant they were as slim and narrow-waisted as each other. There were also two petticoats and other underwear as well as a thick shawl. Elizabeth had also thoughtfully included bindings for certain times in a month, a brush and comb, a toothbrush that was of Saskia's own design made up for Elizabeth to have in stock, and even a new pot of dentifrice that was another of her own products. She had never thought that she could be so pleased to receive the simple necessities of everyday living.

On the day Saskia left the farm Kate gave her a dozen new-laid eggs, a cooked chicken, two loaves freshly baked that morning, and a chunk of the farm's own cheese.

'Now I know you will have some nourishment to keep body and soul together until you can get to a market,' Kate said, embracing her. Yet that was not the end of the Robinsons' generosity, because when the coach arrived for her Ted came with a basket of good eating apples for her, some potatoes, a bunch of carrots and a cabbage. She was entrusting Acorn to Joe's care for the time being, but went to pat and say farewell to her mare before leaving.

When the Gibbons' coach came for her she waved to Kate and Ted from the window as she was borne away. Then she waved again to Joe as she passed him working in a field. When she went by the blackened ruins of her cottage she gave it one last look before turning her gaze away.

Soon the noise of the city was sweeping around her and she realized how much she would miss the peace of the countryside. With all the rebuilding that was going on everywhere London was a hive of activity with wagons delivering timber, bricks and much else with scaffolding encasing half-finished houses and municipal edifices. Now and again there was an explosion when gunpowder was being used to clear a site of burned-out ruins.

Harting House was grander than she had expected in a busy commercial area that had been well away from the reaches of the Great Fire. It was a large red-brick house with an elegant portico that faced directly on to the street. As the coach drew up at the entrance Saskia took from her purse the house-keys that had been delivered to her and went up the three steps to insert one into the dark red door with its brass knocker that was the face of a lion. She turned it and entered a spacious hall. A letter addressed to her lay on a side table and she recognized Elizabeth's writing. It was brief, wishing her well in her new abode and telling her which bedchamber had been prepared for her.

The coachman had unloaded Saskia's wicker basket and, as he had done at the farmhouse, followed the directions she gave him as to where to deposit it. Then, after bringing in the box of supplies, he left it on a bench in the kitchen before leaving the house and driving away.

On her own Saskia began an exploratory tour, guessing that it had been Lucy that had delivered the letter and was responsible for opening the shutters and preparing her room, which she had yet to see.

On the ground floor the rooms were large and well proportioned, which she thought would have attracted Robert into buying the house, and the decor of each was so pristine that Saskia was certain that total redecoration had taken place quite recently. Dust sheets covered all the furniture and linen bags enclosed the chandeliers, making them look like puddings ready for the pot, and even the paintings had protective cloths draped over them. There was the customary drawing room, a dining room with a long table that would seat twenty people, and a music room with a clavichord, a harp, some lutes and a fiddle in a case.

Robert's study had tall cabinets with shallow drawers to hold plans and designs while a specially constructed drawing board on a stand with a racket to adjust to the right sloping angle showed where he did much of his work, a high stool set in front of it. Interested to see what painting he had chosen for his office, she lifted a corner of its covering and saw that it was a Dutch landscape with a windmill and a grove of trees by a canal, the sky full of that special light that seemed to rise from the water that veined her rich green homeland. He must have brought it home to remind him of the land that had given so many of his countrymen sanctuary during the days of the King's exile.

The neighbouring room was Robert's library, the walls covered by shelves of books, and although there was a large section devoted entirely to architectural subjects there were others on a variety of subjects as well as some works of fiction that she was already eager to read.

In the kitchen she found the list of instructions on the table left by the caretaker, whose place she had filled, and she read it through. Her duties included forwarding mail by special messenger to Robert's Yorkshire address, keeping good fires stacked, supervising the two cleaning women, who would come once every two weeks, and, most important of all, making sure that the house was safely locked against intruders during absence.

Upstairs Saskia continued her inspection of the house. Entering the master bedroom, which would be Robert's, she was astounded by the enormous width of the bed. Its dark oak canopy was supported by bulbous-shaped posts, all as heavily carved as the great bedhead. A long time ago in Holland Grinling had spoken of oak being the wood most used in English carving and here was an example of almost overpowering magnificence. As well as trees and birds and flowers being depicted there were lightly-clad dancing maidens, all with flowing hair that coiled out towards the virile young men in the carving. With its crimson and gilt brocade curtains that would shut out the world it was a bed for seduction and for passion and for birth.

As she closed the door of the room behind her she smiled, thinking also that with so much room in such a bed long-married lovers could expand their girths as the years went by and never lack for space.

She soon found the bedchamber that had been made ready for her and her wicker basket had been placed on a side table in the adjoining dressing room where there was a hip bath painted with posies of flowers. She guessed that she had been given the most important guest room, which would have been at Elizabeth's instigation, and was sure that the previous caretaker would have occupied less grand accommodation.

She glanced about admiringly at the aqua-hued walls, the fine oak furniture and the four-poster hung with brocade drapery. She was going to enjoy being the sole occupant of this fine house.

Best of all there was a Dutch painting in this room too. It had been uncovered during the preparation of this accommodation for her. It showed a courtyard that could have been found anywhere in Holland and a housewife was sweeping up some fallen leaves. A passageway behind her led to the street with the glimpse of passers-by. It was such a simple subject, but Saskia felt a wave of homesickness engulf her as never before. Immediately she crossed the room to put up her hand and touch the painting with her fingertips.

'I haven't forgotten you, my homeland,' she whispered.

That night she had a dream that she was back in Holland, but it faded as soon as she awoke and could not be recalled.

Fourteen

Forty-eight hours after Saskia had taken up her caretaker's duties Elizabeth gave birth to a fine son. She had endured a hard labour, but the joy in her baby melted all memory of it away. Grinling was as proud as the proverbial peacock, picking him up out of his cradle at any opportunity, and showing him off to every visitor. He had even taken the baby downstairs to the tavern, wanting all there to see his handsome son.

'How is he to be named?' Saskia asked on her first visit to see the baby. She felt sympathy for the little one, for at her arrival Grinling had snatched him up from sleep to put him protesting noisily into her arms while declaring that his son had smiled at her. Now the baby was sleeping in his cradle again and Grinling had gone back to his workshop, leaving Saskia seated by his wife's bedside as they talked peacefully together.

'He is to be baptized James after Grinling's father,' Elizabeth replied, resting luxuriously against an abundance of lace-edged pillows, 'which should meet with my mother-in-law's approval and will most certainly delight my dear father-in-law.'

'Have they seen their new grandson yet?'

'No, they're coming up from Deptford tomorrow and bringing Godmother Henrietta with them.' Elizabeth glanced blissfully across at the crib. Then her eyes twinkled mischievously as she turned back to Saskia. 'Nothing ever really pleases my mother-in-law, but even she will not be able to find any fault with him!'

'That's true!' Saskia replied as they laughed together.

'Now tell me how you like living in Robert's house?' Elizabeth asked, enjoying her friend's company.

'I have every comfort there,' Saskia answered,

'and from my bedchamber window I have a splendid view of the knot garden with all its formal squares and twirls. There is also a splendid herb garden, but it is of almost no advantage to me in this wintertime, but I should have loved to gather from it in the spring.'

'If Robert is still out of town perhaps you will still be there.'

'That would suit me very well, but I think it most unlikely.'

'Who knows? At least I'm glad you are comfortable in your new abode,' Elizabeth said. 'I told Lucy to be sure to choose a pleasant room for you. It's a very grand residence for a bachelor living alone, but Grinling says that an architect has to look prosperous if he wants the big commissions. How do you pass your time?'

'My duties are so light that I have started to make my own beauty products again. I want to build up a good stock in readiness for selling again. It will have to be a hired market stall in the city this time.'

'But you will still have the ladies you have served before?'

'But they will think I have deserted them as I'm not fit yet to ride any distance.'

'Where is Acorn now? Is she back here in the tavern stables?'

'No, I couldn't bear to part with her and I'll go on renting her until such time that I can purchase her. She is being stabled at the Robinsons' farm and Joe is looking after her.'

By this time Saskia felt she had stayed talking long enough, not wanting to tire Elizabeth, but she had to stay a little longer as there was some especially good news for her to hear.

'Grinling has been made a member of the Drapers' Company!' Elizabeth exclaimed joyfully. 'It is a great honour. There are no guilds for woodcarvers, but as his father is a draper he is eligible to join.'

'That is splendid news,' Saskia endorsed. She knew that all these great trade companies were particular about who joins their esteemed ranks and it would take Grinling further up the social scale.

Before leaving the inn Saskia went to congratulate Grinling in his workshop. He looked extremely pleased and thanked her in Dutch, for they always spoke their own language when alone. 'I've had three commissions already from members,' he said. 'So I think it will be good for business apart from the honour bestowed upon me.'

Then he noticed that she had glanced in the direction of a new project he was working on and watched as she went across to it, wonder on her face.

'This is lovely, Grinling,' she breathed. It was a garland carved out of his beloved lime wood, abundant in flowers and fruit, strings of beans, flowers, pods of peas, oranges and grapes all nestling in thick foliage. She realized that the carved decoration on the little mirror lost in the fire had been the simple forerunner of this marvellous tribute to nature that had come from his hands.

'What do you think?' he asked.

227

She turned to him, her eyes shining. 'It's superb!'

He laughed with pleasure at her praise. 'I have it in mind to use such garlands when the right commission comes along. In the meantime I have plenty of other work in hand.'

Baby James was baptized on a cold and windy day at Aldgate Church, but was cocooned in shawls and suffered no ill effects. For the first important occasion in his life he wore the same long, lace-trimmed robe that his father had once worn for his baptism. There were many guests present, including Saskia, whom Mistress Gibbons only acknowledged with a nod. It was obvious that she disapproved of her former maid associating socially with her son and his wife. Yet since everyone present was linked to trade in some way Saskia did not see how, as a maker of beauty products, she should be treated differently from anyone else. Even Henrietta's fortune had come through trade and she had already chatted to Saskia. James Gibbons was also equally amiable and crossed the room specially to speak to her.

'I trust I find you well, Saskia?' he inquired. 'It was truly unfortunate that you should lose so much in that fire. I hope that from now on all will go well with you.'

'I believe that I shall soon be on my way up again,' she declared confidently.

'I'm very glad to hear it,' he replied, 'and you are being caretaker to Robert's property in the meantime?'

'Yes. The chance was most opportune.'

She had known that Robert would not be at the baptism, for she had been told at the start of becoming his caretaker that she would always be notified should he have to return to London on business at any time. He had sent his gift to the baby, which was a dozen bottles of good French wine to be put down until young James came of age. Her own gift was a garment she had made and embroidered herself since coming to Robert's house and which should fit the Gibbons heir when he was six months old.

Next morning Saskia was up early as usual, a robe over her night shift as she went downstairs with a candle-lamp. Outside it was still winter dark, but it was always cosy and warm in the kitchen. She stirred the glowing embers on the hearth into flames and added logs to heat the water in the cauldron suspended there. Then she went to drag a circular wooden tub from the storeroom as she did every morning for her daily bathing, for she was not going to haul cans of hot water upstairs to her dressing room, no matter that the hip bath there was the handsomest she had ever seen.

When the water was hot enough she poured it into the tub and then stepped into it and stood soaping herself with some new soap she had made. Then, using a jug, she doused herself several times.

She had just reached for a towel before stepping out of the tub when a chill draught from the door leading from the hall made her spin round in alarm. Robert, wearing a crimson dressing-robe, stood in the doorway, his surprise equal to hers, but without the hot rise of angry embarrassment that seared her through. He spoke at once.

'A thousand pardons, Saskia! Believe me, I truly thought that you were still abed!'

'Go away!' she hissed.

'Yes, of course. I came down for some shaving water. Is there any left in the cauldron?'

'No!' She did not want him walking around her to reach it. 'I'll bring some up to you.'

'Thank you. Please accept my sincere apologies again for my intrusion.'

He closed the door as he went and she was faced with having him in the house, which was not what she wanted at all. She hoped he would not be staying long.

When she was dressed and ready for the day more hot water was ready and she filled a brass water-can and took it upstairs where she knocked on Robert's dressing room door. He opened it and was dressed, but still in his shirtsleeves. Taking the can from her with a word of thanks he set it down by the wash stand.

'What time did you get here last night?' she asked coldly.

'About one o'clock in the morning. I knew you would be sleeping and I kept as quiet as possible in order not to wake you.'

'I was told when I had agreed to come here that I should always be notified when to expect you.'

'In normal circumstances you would have been informed. It was my original intention to come for the baptism and to stay a few days afterwards in order to settle a business matter. Then unexpectedly in Yorkshire I had a crisis on my hands, which needed my presence. It was only yesterday that the problem was finally resolved and that was when I made the decision to try to get to the christening of my godson.' He spread his hands expressively. 'But after all the heavy rain recently there were floods everywhere and diversions were lengthy. The final straw was when my coach slid off the muddy road into a ditch, smashing a wheel. That is when I hired a horse from the nearest tavern and rode the rest of the way.'

'So now you will be staying for those few days originally planned?'

'It depends on the outcome of the business matter.'

She nodded. 'Breakfast will be ready when you come downstairs.'

He caught her wrist as she passed him, bringing her to a halt. 'You'll take your breakfast and all meals with me. You shall not play the servant.'

She gave him a long cool look. 'Very well.'

As she went back downstairs she thought what a strange relationship she shared with him. He had a flair for sparking wariness in her and then, just like the turn of a card, she found herself feeling quite agreeable towards him. Yet always she sensed his determination to slice away all she would always feel for Grinling, not knowing that she had come to terms with that impossible love by tucking it away in her heart. Every instinct told her that it was and always would be an

231

insurmountable barrier between them.

Over breakfast they talked quite companionably, he wanting to know what plans she had made for the future. She replied that she would rent a market stall just as soon as she had enough products to sell and would take a room she could afford. Then she asked him about his work in Yorkshire.

He described the house he had designed and it sounded as if it were a very grand mansion that was taking shape under his supervision. Then he talked descriptively of York that had not changed in some parts since its days as a Viking settlement as well as its importance in Tudor times. She listened avidly as he described the great Minster with its glorious stained-glass windows, its arches and carved stonework.

'Do you think the new St Paul's Cathedral will compare with the Minster?' she asked.

'Having seen some of Wren's work elsewhere I'm sure it will be a Holy jewel in the crown of London for ever more. It is a great pity that some of Master Wren's other plans for wide streets and squares throughout the burned down areas were rejected. He would have made the city beautiful beyond compare.'

'You feel very strongly about it,' she commented.

'Indeed I do. I fear that a great many badly built habitations are going up in areas beyond his jurisdiction, but the need for housing is desperate.'

They sat talking over the breakfast table long after both of them had finished eating. Now and again she had the feeling that he was eyeing her speculatively, even while talking on some mundane plane, and it puzzled her as to the reason. The trouble with this man was that she could never tell what he was thinking and it was as if all his soul were hidden behind those penetrating and calculating black-lashed eyes.

When he left the house later that morning it was to visit Grinling and Elizabeth. He had said that he would be out all day and not to prepare any meals for him, but she went to market to buy bread and some vegetables as well as a few other items she might need for herself. It was late in the evening when he returned to find her reading a book by the fire in the library.

'What have you found to read?' he asked, sitting down in the leather wing chair on the opposite side of the fireplace. She handed the book to him, unaware how the firelight was illumining her face and creating red-gold lights in her hair. His gaze lingered on her for a few moments before he glanced at the title and read it aloud. *'Ancient Greek Architecture and Statuary'*.

'I'm finding it very interesting,' she said. 'You have quite a number of books about Greece on these shelves.'

'I visited Greece with my father when I was still a boy, and all I saw made a great impression on me. I believe it was then that I made the decision to be an architect one day.'

'Was that your father's profession?'

He shook his head. 'No, my late father was what is known as a country gentleman, and he became one of the King's cavaliers immediately when the call came. After defeat at the Battle of Worcester he escaped to the Continent, taking me out of school to go with him. But he had suffered wounds during the battle and never quite recovered his health again. He died shortly after I had completed my apprenticeship in Amsterdam. It was then that I went to Italy with Grinling.'

'What of your mother?'

'She died at my birth.'

'That was a sad loss for you,' she said sympathetically. 'I never knew my father and when I was young I envied my friends who had fathers to take them skating and to fairs and all else.' She did not want to bore him with her reminiscences and gestured towards the library shelves. 'I should like to publish a book one day. But before that can come about – and how one gets a book published I do not know – I aim to have a little shop in which to sell my wares.'

His interest had sharpened. 'What would your book be about?'

'How my products can improve and even restore women's beauty. I have a record book where I have written down countless receipts that I learned from my mother, including many that were handed down to her from her mother, and others that are of my own invention. Most of them are herbal and none contain anything at all harmful. I've looked at books on the subject that appear sometimes in a tattered state on stalls or pristine in bookshops. Not only is it alarming to read some of the ingredients that are included in lotions and other products for the face, but without exception all of the books I have looked at combine the subject of beauty with household hints and medical advice of a frightening nature. I believe that such a book as mine would be welcomed by women if ever it could come into print, even though my mother always told me to keep the secrets of my products to myself.'

'Maybe she meant until the time was right,' he suggested, but then paused briefly on a frown as he glanced around the room. 'Is there any wine here?'

'No. Only in the cellar.'

'I'll fetch a bottle.' He returned quite quickly with a dusty bottle and two glasses. After pouring the ruby-red wine he handed a glass to her and then sat down again in the wing chair. As he sat back comfortably against the padded leather, he raised his glass ceremoniously to her before putting it to his lips. 'Now,' he began, 'getting a book published privately can be a costly business unless it is done by the subscription method.'

'How do you mean?'

'You would call on all your clients and ask them for a subscription towards the publishing of your work. In return their names would be printed in a list of donors and it is usual to give a complimentary copy to each person. People like to see their names in print. If I wished it I could publish a book on architecture by the same means.'

She smiled, shaking her head to dismiss his suggestion. 'I'm able to see how it would work with architecture or with any other such subject, but – being a man – you're not able to see the barrier that would make my book impossible to publish by that method.'

He looked puzzled. 'I don't understand.'

'None of the ladies that I deal with in my work would want the world to know that they rely on cosmetic artifices to remain beautiful.'

'But paint and powder on women's faces are so obvious!' he exclaimed on a laugh.

'Only when cosmetics are used crudely. My products are made to enhance.'

He narrowed his eyes at her. 'Do you really believe a book such as yours would be sought after?'

'I'm sure of it, but it is just a dream of mine. At the present time I have far more practical matters on my mind. As soon as I leave here I have first of all to make a living with a market stall. Then with time I should be able to rent a small shop.' Her eyes began to twinkle. 'Who knows? I might gain royal patronage from the Queen herself one day.'

'A commendable aim,' he said with a grin. 'But now I want to discuss the business matter with you that would have brought me to London with or without my godson's christening. I want you to hear me out before you voice any opinion.'

Smiling, she raised her eyebrows questioningly. 'How on earth do you expect me to advise you on any business matter?'

'You will be able to do very well in this case. I believe you have heard from Elizabeth – and perhaps from others – that Master Wren does not consider me a sufficiently pious man to work at his right hand on the cathedral and the many churches that are to be rebuilt, even though I know he approves my talents.'

Saskia nodded. 'I have heard your situation mentioned.'

'What's more, he would have no hesitation in taking me on if I could present myself as a reformed character.'

'Are you leading such a wild life?' she asked teasingly on a smile.

He threw back his head and laughed. 'In the dales of Yorkshire? There it is all fresh air and long walks!' Then he paused briefly. 'I'm not ashamed to admit that I have sown plenty of wild oats in my earlier years and some would say until comparatively recently, but those times are past. If I can present myself as a responsible man settled into marriage Master Wren will accept me into his fold.' He tightened his hand into a fist on his knee, unconsciously displaying the intensity of his feelings on the matter. 'To have the chance to design beautiful houses for graceful streets where once there were only slums and wretched pest-ridden alleys is every architect's dream.'

'Then you must find yourself someone to love and marry,' she advised sensibly.

He had turned his head to gaze unseeingly into the fire, his thoughts far distant as he paused for a few moments before he spoke again.

'I have found her,' he said quietly, his frown heavy and his tone deeply serious. 'Her name is

Jane Montgomery and she would marry me tomorrow if the chance were ours. Unfortunately she is the daughter of the baronet for whom I'm building the York mansion and she is already betrothed. Her parents had arranged the marriage some months before I first went to view the site for the house and to have preliminary discussions about what was required in style and embellishments.' He got up from his chair and moved restlessly across to the bottle he had left on the library table. There he poured himself a refill, she having shaken her head when he had glanced enquiringly at her half-emptied glass. 'I wish you could meet her, Saskia. I believe you would have liked each other. She is beautiful and intelligent and everything any man could wish for in a wife.'

'Is there no chance at all of her breaking that betrothal?'

He shook his head. 'No, it's signed and sealed.' Then he returned to stand with his back to the fire as he looked down at her. 'So now you and I are in the same boat. You can never have Grinling as a husband or lover and Jane is beyond my reach. Neither of us can have the one person that matters most to us.'

'I'm learning to live with the situation and so must you.'

'I'm taking the first step by being here to talk over with you the business proposition that I have in mind.'

'What is it?' she asked, her curiosity roused.

He sat down again, leaning towards her with an elbow on his knee. 'As I said to you earlier, I must have a wife if I'm to get the work I want from Master Wren. Marry me, Saskia. It will be a business arrangement, a marriage of convenience as most are these days, but without demands. Separate bedchambers and, in a way, separate lives beyond necessary appearances together. In exchange for marrying me you'll have a comfortable home and, if you should wish it, a shop in an elegant street where you could sell your beauty preparations and become financially independent. Then I'm sure you would find among your clientele some ladies willing to subscribe to your book. In return I can promise you without any false pride that my architecture will enhance Wren's own beautiful works for centuries to come. You have nothing to lose, not even your virginity.'

She had sat still and speechless, but now her eyes widened even more. 'You are very blunt in your speech!'

'I'm putting all my cards on the table,' he said in the same controlled and yet curiously angry way. 'We should be equal partners, but – using discretion – we would go our own ways, although I suppose in your devotion to Grinling you are hardly likely to fancy anyone else. But it is not in my nature to live like a monk. I'm not asking for a reply now, but I want you to think about it.'

She had risen slowly to her feet. 'I can tell you now that even a marriage in name only would be too high a price to pay for the loss of my freedom.'

'Would it be freedom to end up managing a
239

stall in a dirty London square in all weathers? All your grander customers would desert you. None would ever buy from a market woman.'

'It did not put them off when I had my stall at the cottage!' she retaliated fiercely.

'Then you were a novelty. A pretty young woman with charmingly presented wares outside her own cottage. It was fast becoming a vogue to buy from you.' He saw that he had surprised her. 'Did you not know that?'

Subdued, she shook her head. 'No, but I'm well aware how women can be swayed by fashionable notions that come and go.'

'If it had not been for the fire you might eventually have made enough profit at your stall to rent a property, but it would have taken a long time again – if ever – before you could get a shop in an area where the right kind of affluent customer would have come to you. Now I'm giving you the chance to get business premises of your own a deal quicker than the decades that it would take otherwise.'

'Aren't you forgetting something most important of all?'

'That we each may meet someone to love again?' He gave a careless shrug of his broad shoulders. 'Divorce is not impossible, although it's a lengthy process.'

'I'm not listening to anything more,' she replied emphatically, rising to her feet. 'You have put a most extraordinary proposition to me and I'm quite stunned and bewildered by it.' She made a wavy movement with her hands. 'I'm going to bed. Good night.'

He made no attempt to detain her. 'Sleep well, Saskia. If you have any doubts about me I can assure you that as a royalist and as a gentleman I always keep my word.'

She did not doubt that he meant what he said. Englishmen of breeding were renowned for their word being their bond. In the hall she took up a candle-lamp from a side table to light the way upstairs. One phrase he had used danced in her mind. He had said she could make herself financially independent. It was like a beacon in the darkness. Therein lay the only true independence for a woman, but few could obtain it when by law upon marriage everything the bride owned became her husband's property. Yet Robert had made it clear he would want nothing from her in any way. Had she become so mercenary that independence meant more to her than any relationship?

She shook her head fiercely against the thought. Since the love she had yearned for could never be hers she had to be practical about her future, fulfilling her life in another way. She would give his proposal very careful thought. If she should decide to accept him on the terms he had put to her she would in return do her utmost not to let Robert regret his generosity. She was determined that to the world she would appear to be the perfect wife for him.

In the library Robert refilled his glass again and sat down to finish off the rest of the bottle. He could not understand now why he had ever thought that if Jane had been free that she could even begin to take the place of the only woman he wanted above all others. Saskia was always a challenge and created depths of feeling in him as no other woman had ever done.

His thoughts drifted back to when he had seen her earlier that day and lingered on the memory of when he had opened the kitchen door. Botticelli's Venus, rising from the waves, was not more alluring than Saskia in her wooden tub, reaching for her bath-towel.

Fifteen

Saskia gave her answer to Robert three days later on the morning he was to journey back to Yorkshire. His coach had been repaired with a replacement wheel and the restoration of the damaged paintwork before being returned to him. The horses, although they had been frightened at the time of the accident, had been unharmed. She had seen little of him. He had been out most of the time, keeping appointments by day and involved in social occasions by night, but now there was half an hour remaining before his departure and they had left the breakfast table to go into the library where a cheerful fire was blazing.

She held out her hands to the flames. Right up until this last minute she had been undecided whether to accept the offer he had put to her or to turn it down. She could tell with every nerve in her body that he was watching her, knowing that she was about to announce her decision.

In a curious way she felt that because of her mother's hours of self-sacrifice in making up the collections of pots and flasks she was equally committed to such a task. It made no difference that the conflagration that had destroyed the collection had been no fault of hers. The guilt of losing what had been bequeathed to her would remain a torment until somehow her heritage was fully restored. Only then could she pick up the threads of her life again. Robert's offer was a swift route to achieving her goal among other advantages.

'I will enter this marriage of convenience with you,' she stated decisively as she turned to face him, 'but it will be exactly on the terms that you stated and we shall remain totally independent of each other.'

'Agreed,' he replied without hesitation. 'In the meantime go ahead with the marriage arrangements. Get the banns read and order a whole new wardrobe of clothes for every occasion. I confided in Elizabeth that I hoped we would soon be wed. She will help and advise you. We'll be married at Aldgate Church and have a banquet after the ceremony.'

She frowned. 'Why were you so sure I would not refuse?'

He smiled slowly at her. 'Because I know you better than you realize. You have the same ruthlessly ambitious streak in your nature as I have in mine and when you have set your mind on a goal nothing will deter you. Admittedly you

243

failed to win Grinling, but that matter was entirely out of your province. So, since my terms suit you, I think we shall do very well together.'

'You can be very cruel at times,' she said, wincing at what she saw as a taunt.

'It is not my intention,' he said, holding out his hand for hers, not to put it to his lips as she would have expected, but to clasp it firmly as if she were a man with whom he had reached a satisfactory business arrangement. 'I want us to share an agreeable partnership.'

'I have one stipulation,' she said. 'We shall not be married in Aldgate Church.'

'You have another that you prefer? It is of no consequence to me.'

'No. It is just that I could not in all conscience stand before a holy altar in any church and make false promises to love, honour and obey you till the end of my days. I want a Fleet wedding.'

He stared at her in astonishment. The notorious Fleet prison had become a place where those in haste to be married could be wed at short notice without a licence or banns being read as well as no awkward questions asked. The reasons for such marriages might be an unexpected pregnancy, men departing overseas with the armed services sooner than expected, elopements when couples needed to escape parental wrath, and sometimes simply to avoid the cost involved through the festivities that accompanied a church marriage. The reason why it had become quick and easy to arrange a wedding ceremony within the prison's dank walls was that among the many prisoners there was always a small

244

number of clergymen incarcerated for various crimes, some of them defrocked, and all thankful to earn a little money to help towards their debts that had put them behind bars or to purchase ale and other comforts to ease their grim circumstances.

'Do you really want to be married in that notorious, fever-ridden place?' Robert questioned on a note of total disbelief.

'Yes, I do. Find a defrocked clergyman in there. One who is no longer ordained and without authority to perform marriages or anything else. He will be only too eager to carry out the charade for good payment and any words spoken by us will have no more meaning than if we were actors in a play.'

He regarded her steadily. 'Did you keep awake all night thinking this out?'

She nodded. 'Yes, and the other nights too. In fact, I have not stopped considering every aspect very seriously ever since you put your proposition to me. I know as you do that the alternative would be very bleak for me. You said yourself that my previous success with well-to-do clients was only because I was a novelty, and I know that none would ever buy from me again if I sold at a common market stall.'

'You can be sure of it,' he agreed. He could see that although she wanted no part of his life, she was also too level-headed to take the grim alternative. It pleased him that she lacked foolish sentiment and had so much common sense.

'If you delay your departure just by a few hours,' she continued, 'we could get the whole

245

business of a sham marriage over and done with completely today. People will think that we were swept away by love and wished to marry before you had to return to Yorkshire.' Then she smiled wryly. 'I believe that should convince Master Wren that you have finally mended your ways and settled down.'

He gave a quiet laugh on a triumphant note. 'It should indeed.' Then he reached into his pocket and drew out a small box. Opening it, he presented a very fine emerald and pearl betrothal ring set in gold for her inspection and with it was a gold wedding ring.

'Allow me to put this ring on your finger now that we are betrothed,' he said courteously, but with no more emotion than if he was wanting her to pour him a cup of tea.

She held out her hand once again and this time, after slipping on the ring, he did raise her fingers to his lips with a formal bow.

'It's a beautiful ring,' she said quietly.

'I chose it to match your eyes,' he replied, his fierce dark gaze holding hers as he pocketed the wedding ring. 'Now is there anything more we have to discuss?'

'No. I think we have settled everything.'

'Then I'll delay my departure until this afternoon and go to the Fleet prison now to make the necessary arrangements.'

It was just before noon when Saskia arrived with Robert at the great grey stone building that was the Fleet prison. There was to be a hanging of a highwayman that day and people were already gathering around the scaffold outside the

246

prison walls.

Inside the prison the stench from the cells wafted around the wedding couple as they were led along a wide hall into a side room. They had been offered the use of the chapel for their marriage, but Saskia had been swift to refuse. The clergyman, who awaited them, had creases at the corner of his eyes as if he had once enjoyed laughter and jovial company in the past, but judging by his oversized cassock and desperate expression he must have lost a deal of weight as well as his *joie de vivre* since coming into prison through gambling debts. He introduced himself as the Reverend William Walburton. Two of the wardens, who had followed Saskia and Robert into the room, were to be witnesses.

It was all over very quickly. The marriage certificate was signed and handed to Saskia. Robert gave a purse of money to each of the witnesses and a heavier one to the clergyman, who clutched it to his chest, closing his eyes in thankfulness for the jingle of gold.

They returned to the house where Robert discussed the financial arrangements he had made for her with his banker before he had made the wedding appointment, putting no limit on whatever she wished to spend.

'There is no equipage for you to use in my absence,' he said, 'except a little carriage for two in the coach-house, which was here when I bought this property. Get some advice from Grinling and buy a pony for it. Then you can use it to go visiting.'

Now it was time for him to leave and his coach

stood waiting. As he and Saskia stood facing each other in the hall by the open front door she spoke very seriously.

'You said you wanted me to let our marriage be known.'

'Yes, of course. The sooner the better.'

'Yet I shall wait until I receive word from you, because if you and Jane should decide to elope I would never breathe a word to anyone of what has taken place here today. You would be free to make a marriage of love.'

He eyed her cynically, taking her chin between his finger and thumb to tilt her face upwards. 'An elopement would cost me all my ambitions for this life. I know of nothing that could cause me to jeopardize my ultimate aim, least of all the scandal that such an action would create.'

Then he lowered his lips on to hers into what became a deeply passionate kiss, holding her locked in his arms as they swayed together. Then gently he released her, aware that she was flushed and breathless.

'That was to seal our bargain,' he said drily. 'Nothing more than that. It will not happen again.'

She stood at the door to watch him depart, but when seated in the coach he did not glance back or raise his hand in a wave as he was borne away. As she shut the door again she was left wondering just how deep his feelings were for Jane Montgomery since he would not risk endangering his future through an elopement to win her.

Upstairs she gazed into her looking-glass,

expecting to see her lips swollen by such a kiss. It had been an experience she would not easily forget. In fact it seemed to have inflamed her whole being in a way she had never known before. Remembering what Elizabeth had said about his male magnetism she supposed that briefly she had fallen victim to it.

In the coach Robert congratulated himself on his restraint. It had not been easy, but he would keep his word. At least Saskia could never marry anyone else now, which had removed his fear of losing her. If she had already gained a husband during his absence from London he would have probably made Jane his wife. She was beautiful, well educated, intelligent and also passionate, which he knew from the occasions when he had been alone with her. If he had given her the slightest encouragement she would have told her father that she had changed her mind and no longer wished to marry her betrothed. She would not have been denied, for she was the apple of her father's doting eye. Yet Robert knew that her chief attraction for him had been in a faint resemblance to Saskia, who was as firmly entrenched in his heart as Grinling was in hers.

Later that same day Saskia went to see Elizabeth, who immediately started chattering away about wedding gowns and dishes for banquets before Saskia could break her news.

'Robert and I were married today at noon.'

Elizabeth looked at her incredulously. 'You can't be! You have not had any banns read in church!'

'There was no need. We had a Fleet marriage.'

249

Elizabeth looked aghast, throwing up her hands in dismay. 'That dreadful place! Why?'

'Robert and I decided between us that we should be wed before he left for the city of York today.'

Immediately Elizabeth's expression changed and she became quite dewy-eyed. 'He could wait no longer to make you his wife! I wish you both all the joys of marriage, but,' she added mischievously, 'I'm sure that Robert initiated you into some of its pleasures before he went away.'

Saskia ignored the comment. 'He is sending his staff back to London from Yorkshire to take care of the house, and so I shall have plenty of time on my hands. I have a project that I have planned. I'm going to try to replace all the little pots and flasks that were lost in the fire. If my mother was able to put a collection together of such lovely old ones in Paris I'm sure I could do the same in London.'

'But you could buy new ones.'

Saskia nodded. 'Maybe if I find any worthy to be added to the only one I have from the original collection. My mother had added two or three little Delft jars to it that were new, but I'm hoping that each one I buy will be antique enough to have its own little history, even though I shall never know the origins of any of them.'

'What a fascinating task you have given yourself! May I be allowed to start off your new collection?' Elizabeth sprang up from her chair and went into her bedchamber to return with a tiny glass pot, its colour a rich blue.

'It's lovely!' Saskia exclaimed as it was handed to her.

'It's from Venice. It is one of the souvenirs that Grinling brought home from his trip, but I know he will be pleased for you to have it.'

'Together with the one sole surviving pot from the cottage fire it makes a wonderful commencement of my task. I thank you so much.'

'Have you selected a room in the house where you can make your products?' Elizabeth asked.

'Yes, there's one above the kitchen with a view over the herb garden. As soon as I leave here I'm calling in a carpenter to equip the room for me with a work bench, shelves and all else that I'll need. It will be the kind of working area that I have always wanted. Somewhere in the house I shall have a glass-fronted cupboard from floor to ceiling where I can place all the little treasures that I'm hoping to find. It will probably be in the music room.'

'That is an excellent idea! But at the present time you should also be thinking about clothes. Robert is very sociable and when he returns to London you'll be invited with him to all kinds of events.'

'I'm engaging the same dressmaker as you had. I have contacted her and she is coming tomorrow afternoon.'

'Excellent! May I come and help you choose as you did with me?'

Saskia laughed. 'Yes, indeed.'

After drinking tea with Elizabeth and before leaving the inn Saskia went to see the landlord. After paying him up to date for renting Acorn she then made an offer to buy her, knowing from Joe what the mare was worth. The offer was accepted and the following day Saskia sent a message to Joe, asking him to bring Acorn to her, for there was stabling for eight horses beside the coach-house.

When Joe arrived with his charge Saskia met him with a gold coin and gave Acorn a juicy apple. She could see from Acorn's condition how well the lad had cared for the mare.

'Mistress,' Joe began tentatively after Saskia had given him food and drink in the kitchen and it was time for him to leave again, 'do you think you might have a place for another stable lad when the staff come back from Yorkshire? Acorn has become used to me and she won't like anyone else grooming her.'

She realized how strong the bond had become between him and the mare. 'What of the farm, Joe?'

'My brother won't even notice I've gone and the farm will be his one day, never mine.'

'But your parents?'

'Ma thinks it would be good for me to get out in the world and she has already talked my Pa into agreeing.' Then he added eagerly, 'I looked at the accommodation in the stable loft. There would be plenty of room for me.'

She smiled. 'In that case you'd better go home and collect your belongings.'

He gave a yelp of jubilation and then coloured beneath his freckles. 'Your pardon, mistress. I'll be back here this evening!'

After he had gone she went upstairs to transfer

her clothes and other items into the closets and chests of the bedchamber and its adjoining dressing room that were next to Robert's. Since they would now appear to be husband and wife it was right that she should occupy the rooms of the mistress of the house. The communicating double doors had the key on her side and were securely locked.

Now she realized that she must have a personal maid. She would need help in dressing in more elaborate gowns, for so many bodices hooked or laced up at the back. She would visit an agency in the morning.

Joe returned with his few possessions and moved into the stable loft. It was divided into three rooms, which were furnished, and there was more accommodation above the coach-house. Finding a spare bed stacked against the wall, he set it up for himself and then made it up with the bedclothes that Saskia gave him. He was content as he fell asleep.

Saskia was late to bed, for she had sat studying a detailed map of London that Robert had left behind. It had been printed to show the vast area that had been devastated by the Great Fire and he had made crosses or else encircled parts that were of special interest to him. She in her turn was highlighting with a pencil the markets left in the city and the streets of shops where she might acquire items for her collection.

Next morning Saskia visited an agency to state her requirements and the following day she interviewed three women in turn, questioning them about their experience and getting each to dress her hair. One young woman in her mid-twenties, named Joan Pomfret, stood out from the other two, being neat and competent. Saskia had deliberately dressed her own hair in an unfashionable style and whereas two of the personal maids repeated the same style, Joan chose the very latest mode. She brushed Saskia's hair until it shone like bronze silk and then drew it back from the face in the very latest mode, securing it in a way that allowed the rich tresses to fall in long soft curls down her back. Saskia was reminded how she done something similar to establish herself with Mistress Gibbons one wet night far away in Holland.

Joan was plain-featured, but had a ready smile, the high curve of her brows giving her the look of being perpetually pleased and surprised by life. Yet it was clear from her references that her previous employers had all been elderly and difficult, much that was written suggested to Saskia that a spiteful pen had inscribed it.

'I'm so happy to come here, madam,' Joan said after Saskia told her she was appointed. 'I have never before had someone young to serve.'

Saskia felt well satisfied with the choice she had made. Joan was as delighted with the room she was given and also to learn that she would have new clothes for her duties. It gave Saskia special pleasure to have been instrumental in improving two people's lives. She was certain that both Joan and Joe would serve her well and loyally.

Yet she was to be rewarded in her turn, soon finding out that Joan had an interest in cosmetics that matched her own. Soon she was entrusting Joan with weighing and mixing and filling pots with various creams.

'Would you be prepared to become my full-time assistant?' she asked the girl one day.

Joan's brown eyes widened. 'Yes, mistress! It would be wonderful! But I was employed to wait on you personally and take care of your clothes and shoes and all else.'

'I shall take on a minor personal maid, who will be your assistant and do all that you'll no longer have time to do for me.'

'But I'll still dress your hair, mistress! I should not want anyone else taking over that responsibility.'

'It shall be as you wish.'

So a young girl named Matilda Durrant joined the household. She was short, dark-haired and eager to learn. Joan made a point of training her well to look after their mistress and everything continued to run smoothly.

Sixteen

The household staff arrived on a rain-soaked evening two days later. Saskia, reading in the library, raised her head with a start. Although she was expecting them to arrive at some unspecified time the sudden explosion of voices, hurrying footsteps, the thumping of baggage and a snatch of laughter made it sound as if the house had been invaded. She put aside her book, but before she reached the door it opened and a middle-aged woman in a rain-spattered cloak, her features quite fine and her dark hair neatly dressed beneath her hood, entered to bob a curtsy.

'Good evening, madam. I am Mistress Seymour, your housekeeper. The staff are here with me. Do you wish to see them now?'

Saskia shook her head. 'No. You have all had a long and tiring journey. There is a large game pie and a cold cooked chicken among other foodstuffs in the pantry. Let them eat their supper and then I will see them. Afterwards I shall discuss domestic arrangements with you. I dined early and so there is nothing to be done for me this evening, except to prepare my bed.'

Alice Seymour raised her eyebrows slightly in surprise. She had not expected such consideration. 'I thank you, madam.'

An hour later she returned, changed now into a dark-blue gown and a neat white cap. She stood back to allow Saskia to pass by her into the hall where the servants waited in a line, each bowing or bobbing according to their sex and all regarding her with intense curiosity. This was the Master's bride! She was younger than they had expected, but her beauty came as no surprise, for they knew their master's taste in pretty women. But she intrigued them, for there was an air about her that showed she was in full charge of herself and in spite of her smile there was sternness in her glance that showed she would expect the best from each of them.

She in her turn was studying them with interest. Four footmen, four housemaids, two scullery maids, the kitchen boy and the chef from France, whom she knew had been employed by Robert's father during his exile and who had recently come to England, wanting to serve his late master's son. She thought it extremely unselfish of Robert to have deprived himself of the chef's expertise in order that she should benefit. At the end of the line the coachman and grooms were easy to distinguish by their ruddy complexions, the result of hours in the open air. Last of all in the row was Joe, looking highly pleased with himself in new clothes that Saskia had bought him that same day. Joan and Matilda were also present, but as befitted their positions as lady's maid and assistant already established in the house they stood apart from the rest, although they had already introduced themselves.

Saskia spoke to each of the new arrivals in turn, asking their names and where they were from, most of them proving to be London-born. Then she beckoned the housekeeper into the library while the rest of the servants dispersed.

'Tell me how you have managed the household whenever Master Harting has been in residence,' Saskia said. When the woman had answered her fully Saskia gave a nod. 'That all sounds very sensible and practical to me. There is just one other matter. I have converted what was previously a bedchamber into a workroom where I shall be making my own cosmetics, salves and unguents, which is something that I have done for a long time. Joan will be assisting me. Although my wardrobe will have priority, with her there will be Matilda on hand for any mending of linen or other such tasks should that be needed.'

'Very good, madam,' the housekeeper replied, impressed again by this new mistress's practical attitude.

From then onwards the house settled into a regular routine. Saskia began happily to make her beautifying products again. She contacted Rufus to order finer wares from his kilns, for she had observed many times that items expensively presented were more highly esteemed by those who could afford to buy them, no matter that there was no difference in the contents. He brought her some samples.

'Do you like these, madam?' he asked. 'The china is thin as a fine teacup and the decoration on each one is different. I've a new artist and her work is very delicate.'

She did like them and placed her order. It was all part of her careful preparations for relaunching herself into business. She had not forgotten Robert's words that at her cottage stall she had been a novelty and a whim of fashion, which was why she had been successful during the short time she was there. Now she was going to become a novelty all over again, but on the London scene this time, for that was the way to get herself and subsequently her cosmetics back into the public's notice. All of it would pave the way to getting a shop of her own one day and then she would be completely independent and free from all obligations to Robert. The farce of their marriage could be allowed to fade away and then both of them would be at liberty to live their own separate lives.

There would be no more deliveries by horseback, although Acorn was hers to ride in her leisure time. Instead she had the elegant little carriage in the coach-house restored to its former splendour of pale green paintwork with discreet gilding. She intended that the colour green should predominate throughout her enterprise, for it was the colour of nature and would help to emphasize the healthy and natural ingredients that she always used in her products.

With Joe advising her she purchased a sturdy young pony to pull the little carriage. Joe in his turn was measured for a white livery with bunches of green ribbons at his shoulders and also a green band around the crown of his wide-brimmed hat, all from the many yards of ribbon that she had specially dyed to ornament her presentations. Having noticed early on how he reeked of the stable, in spite of cold water ablutions every morning at one of the pumps, she moved him into a bedchamber on the top floor of the house in the male servants' quarters. He was now ready to drive her about.

She had plenty of new clothes now and all were discreetly fashionable, for in no way did she intend to appear lacking in good taste. A milliner made her some hats to her own design. All were wide-brimmed in a fine straw and curved up away from her face, each trimmed with enormous clusters of ribbons, silk flowers or ostrich feathers. Joe, smart in his livery, drove her to the races, to exhibitions, to the theatres and to any event where she would attract attention.

It was not long before it was well known that the beauty in the green and gold carriage was the wife of Robert Harting, the architect. At the same time Elizabeth was helping to circulate information about her expertise in beauty aids, although Saskia's lovely face was its own advert, and many women became eager to consult her. Those who had purchased from her in the past began to boast of having tried her wonderful products. It was not long before carriages brought would-be purchasers to Saskia's door.

None was received. She did not intend that Robert's peace should be disturbed in his own home when he returned, but the footman gave each caller a pale green and gold card with the announcement that Mistress Harting would be holding consultations in the Grand Salon at the recently rebuilt assembly rooms for three hours on a forthcoming date.

Saskia was only too aware all the time how she was spending Robert's money in a way that he could never have foreseen at the time when he had put no limit on her expenses. She was keeping a ledger in which she entered every penny that she owed him. He should be paid just as soon as she began making a profit from all she had prepared.

On the afternoon of the consultation there was a traffic jam with carriages outside the assembly rooms. Women, who had never before alighted from their equipages until they had been brought right to an entrance, now sprang out of them and sped on foot not to be too far to the rear of those already entering.

When they came into the salon there were chairs in semicircular rows, which were soon filled, and then the doors were closed. On the arm of each chair was a sample of hand cream, which was examined with interest and popped into purses. Saskia sat by a table on which her products were displayed, backed by an arrangement of flowers, and with Joan in attendance. Saskia was well aware that there were plenty of charlatans that preyed on people's gullibility, and at all costs she was determined not to let herself be tainted in any way by such a false accusation.

She had seen Elizabeth arrive in the company of a sweet-faced, quietly composed woman, who was dressed in modest colours with none of the flamboyance of the more fashionably attired women present. They took two seats at the end of the seventh row. Saskia exchanged a smile with Elizabeth before standing to address her audience.

'I bid you welcome, ladies. As you will have noticed, the colour green is important to me as it is Nature's hue and I'm here today just to talk about my products, but not to sell.' There was a rustle of disappointment, which she ignored. 'I should not want anyone to think I have discovered some magic way in which to create a transformation from normal visages into startling beauty. That is impossible. There have been many false claims made over the years. All I have to offer are simple herbal products that are free of white lead, which I believe to be the most dangerous of all the ingredients used in many beauty aids.'

Again there was whispering among her listeners. Then a voice spoke up. 'How else is one to get a truly white complexion?'

'There are ways with balms and powders. Leave the white-painted faces to the dandies.'

There was a ripple of amusement. Many dandies not only used cosmetics to whiten their faces, but contrived with lip rouge to give themselves a rosebud mouth, their lashes blackened and high, pencilled eyebrows, which all combined to give them a mask-like look. Unfortunately, due to the poor quality of some cosmetics, many women present had the same unfortunate appearance without realizing it.

More questions followed. Saskia felt that she

262

was only giving sensible advice and was inwardly surprised by the ignorance of many of the women, for by their clothes and jewels it was apparent that all present enjoyed an affluent way of life. She would have expected better from every one of them.

Finally she closed the meeting by saying that she would receive by appointment any ladies who wished to consult her privately here in the assembly rooms one day a week. Her assistant would take their names.

There was a rush towards Joan, who had seated herself at the table with pen, ink and a book in which to record names and appointments.

Saskia managed to ease her way through to Elizabeth and her companion. With sparkling eyes Elizabeth said immediately, 'Allow me to present you two ladies to each other.' She gestured gracefully towards each of them. 'Mistress Wren and Mistress Harting.'

Saskia showed her pleasure and curtsied deeply. 'It is an honour to meet you, madam. I admire what I have already seen of your esteemed husband's fine work.'

Mistress Wren smiled. 'I've been told by Mistress Gibbons that you have a talented husband too.'

'I believe him to be.'

Elizabeth explained how this unexpected acquaintanceship had come about. 'We met by the side door that you had advised me to use. I had seen Mistress Wren most rudely pushed aside at the main entrance and immediately I beckoned her to enter with me.'

'I'm so glad you did,' Saskia said.

'I found all you said most interesting,' Mistress Wren commented. 'I could have listened to you for much, much longer. Now I'm like the rest of your audience in still having questions I'd like to put to you.'

'Then may I offer you some hospitality,' Saskia asked. 'My home is not far from here.'

Mistress Wren hesitated only briefly. 'That would be most kind.'

The three of them drove in their individual carriages and were soon settled in Saskia's drawing room with tea and small cakes being served to them. It had been Saskia's mention of her herb garden at the meeting that had particularly interested Mistress Wren and after they had finished tea Saskia took her out to see it, Elizabeth following. There were two medicinal herbs that Mistress Wren did not have at home and Saskia gave her clumps of each in a basket that she could plant in her own herb garden in the country.

'I come to our London home infrequently,' Mistress Wren said as they wandered back indoors again. 'My husband prefers the quiet of the countryside just as I do, and so we retreat to our country house as often as possible. Fortunately he is able to leave London tomorrow with me for a few days respite from the city. Although he will not be idle! He will be poring over his plans and drawings or making models of buildings that he will create. There are not enough hours in the day for him.' In the hall Mistress Wren paused, ready to depart, and smiled at

Saskia. 'I congratulate you. I'm like my husband in admiring those who work hard and overcome odds to make a success of life, whether man or woman. He will be most interested when I tell him about you.'

After she had gone Elizabeth stayed on for a while as she discussed excitedly the success of the afternoon. 'I recognized Mistress Wren immediately. I had seen her at a banquet with her husband, but never supposed our paths would ever cross. Unless,' she added wistfully, 'Grinling should ever get a commission from him.' Then she clasped her hands together joyfully. 'But the whole afternoon was a triumph for you! My congratulations once again!' Then she remembered that she had left her baby son with his nursemaid far longer than she had intended and departed in a hurry.

Joan was waiting to show Saskia the list of appointments that she had written down. One glance was enough for Saskia to see that it would take her at least six weeks to get through them.

'Every item you left on the table disappeared,' Joan said, shaking her head at such dishonesty. 'I was so busy taking names that I did not notice. I never expected ladies of quality to be light-fingered!'

'Never mind,' Saskia said. 'Let us hope that each of those items will result in orders for more of the same.'

She recalled how Elizabeth had declared the meeting a triumph, which could not be denied. There had been waves of goodwill wafting towards her all the time. Yet she felt that her true success was in being presented to Mistress Wren. Now the person whose approval mattered most to Robert would know that he was married to a wife of whom his wife approved.

The next day a letter came in which Mistress Wren thanked Saskia for her hospitality as well as the kind gift of the herbs. She also expressed the hope that they would soon meet again.

Seventeen

Saskia had returned with Joan from her seventh weekly gathering of ladies to find that Robert was home. It was not a surprise as he had notified her of his forthcoming return, his task at an end in Yorkshire and everything concluded satisfactorily. She had not been looking forward to his coming home again, but she had made sure that everything was prepared for him. The cold March wind swirled her skirts as she entered the house just ahead of Joan, who swiftly closed the door after them.

He was standing in his study doorway, his frown deep, and he had one hand behind his back. She guessed immediately that he was holding the file of her bills, which she had left on his desk.

'Welcome home, Robert,' she said, slipping off

her hooded cloak, which Joan immediately bore away.

'I trust you are well, Saskia,' he said grimly.

'Yes, indeed,' she replied, leading the way into the drawing room where she held her hands to the flames for a few moments before sitting down in the nearest chair. 'I know by your expression that you wish to discuss money matters with me.'

'Yes, I do.' He had remained standing and now he brought the file from behind his back, opening it to reveal the wad of its contents. 'These accounts have certainly surprised me,' he challenged. 'When I gave you *carte blanche* with your expenses I had not expected you to run up bills to this amount! You appear to be producing your cosmetics on a grand scale, judging by the apothecary bills, and the cost of the china pots seems astronomical to me.'

She thought what a typical husband-and-wife scene was being enacted between them, although it was not about an extravagance in clothes, hats and general fripperies as was most likely with other couples. 'You have no need to be concerned,' she replied. 'I shall repay every penny. As you will see I have kept careful account and have already paid some of the smaller bills out of the money I have earned so far.'

'So how do you propose to settle the rest?' He put the file on a side table and then sat down, his elbows resting on the chair arms, his fingertips propped together in an arch as he gave her his stern attention.

'By building up my business sufficiently to pay back all that I owe you. You know from what I have said in the past that my ultimate goal is to rent a shop in a prosperous street and conduct my sales from there.'

He saw through her words. The financial independence that he had once forecast for her would rebound against him, for she was planning an escape from their marriage. The bills themselves were of no importance to him, for he could settle them without a second glance, but he had seen them as a warning and that had seriously alarmed him.

'How long do you expect it to be before you can carry out this ambition of yours?' he asked bluntly.

'Not as long as I first thought. Already I have an enthusiastic body of women eager to purchase from me, although,' she added frankly, 'I find the richest women are the slowest to pay. At first they seemed to think I should present my account at the end of the year as tradesmen are expected to do, but I consider myself to be an artist. So I have been following Grinling's pea pod method, which has worked very well.'

'Whatever is that?' he exclaimed.

'If Grinling sees that he is to be kept waiting for his account to be settled he leaves pea pods open in his carving. In my case whenever a debt is mounting I switch to presenting my cosmetics in plain pots without the green ribbons that I always have specially dyed. Without my saying a word my clients soon understand just as Grinling's clients do at the first sight of an open pea pod when they visit his workshop to see how the piece they have commissioned is progressing. Now my bills are like his in being settled promptly.'

Robert was grinning widely. 'I remember admiring your business acumen some time ago and now you have proved it once again. Are your wares expensive?'

'Yes, they have to be or else they would not be valued. Nobody appreciates something for nothing.'

'I know that to be true.'

'Let us not fall out over this matter of my work, Robert,' she urged, holding out her hands in appeal. 'I'll not let anything interfere with the running of this household. We shall have people to dine and hold parties and card-playing evenings and all else. I shall be a perfect wife.'

'In all ways but one!' he gave back with sudden harshness.

She caught her breath. 'We have an agreement.'

'Yes,' he replied impatiently, flicking a dismissive hand. 'Forget what I said.'

She saw it was time to disclose what she was eager to tell him. 'We shall have our first dinner party next week with two important guests.'

'Grinling and Elizabeth?' he assumed casually.

'No, he's away. It is Master and Mistress Wren that have accepted our invitation.'

He stared at her in astonishment, leaning forward in his chair. 'How on earth did that come about?'

'Mistress Wren came to my first gathering at

the assembly rooms. She had heard of my use of herbs, which particularly interested her. I have met her several times socially since that day. It is my belief that her husband agreed to an acceptance of the invitation because he wishes to see for himself just how you have settled into married life.'

He gave a shout of laughter, throwing his head back and clapping his hands down on his knees. 'You're a genius, Saskia! Are you sure that you don't create magic spells with those herbs that you use?'

She laughed with him. 'Perhaps I do.'

He sprang to his feet and took her hands to draw her up out of the chair. 'How shall we celebrate your success?'

'Wait and see the result of the dinner party first,' she advised, smiling. He was holding her hands against his chest, but when she would have drawn them away his clasp tightened.

'Why not weave a spell for us?' he said softly, looking down into her eyes. 'One that would banish Grinling from your heart for ever.'

She turned her face away from him, unable to make any reply. She was aware how his gaze grew cold on her and she shivered. Then he let her hands drop as he took a step backwards. Pausing only to pick up the file of bills, he left the room and went to his study.

She remained standing in the firelight, accepting now what she had always been reluctant to admit to herself, ever thrusting the thought away. The reason why Robert had refused to consider eloping with Jane Montgomery was now very clear. It was not from a mercenary reason as he had said, but because he had been so long in love with her that she had eclipsed all other women for him. She saw now that it dated from their first meeting in the Rotterdam house when the stare he had fixed on her had been the beginning of it all.

She took a few paces up and down. Between them they had created an impossible situation. She must leave his house just as soon as he had gained Wren's patronage on a permanent footing. Robert had been kind to her in many ways. She would not desert him while her presence at his side was needed for their masquerade.

With Robert's return she saw again the portrait medallion that Grinling had carved for him all that time ago. She had gone into his study with a letter that had just been delivered, for she allowed nobody else to enter there when he was working. She came to an abrupt halt.

'You still have it!' she exclaimed. In her surprise she forgot the letter she was holding.

He was seated at his desk and looked up to follow the direction of her gaze. 'Did you suppose I had thrown it away?' he asked drily.

'Where has it been? Has it been kept in a box or a drawer?'

'No. I've always had it with me on my travels.'

She gave him a surprised glance and then went closer to it. 'How young I look!'

He gave a mirthless laugh. 'You look no older now. In fact you still have a virginal bloom.'

She flushed and remembered why she had come into his study. 'Here's a letter for you.'

He took it from her. 'I can see it is from my lawyers. Wait a moment, Saskia,' he added as she would have left the room. 'Let us see if it contains any good news about regaining my family home.'

She waited until he had read it through and then saw him shake his head ruefully. 'The case is still being heard. By the time the lawyers finish their game I'll have no money left to enable me to live in the house.'

She knew he was jesting, but his frown had shown a deep anxiety that he might yet lose the case and have to wait until his stepmother's demise before the family home came at last into his rightful possession.

They spent Christmas Day with Grinling and Elizabeth, who with Lucy's help had decked the rooms with evergreens just as Saskia had done at home. While doing it Saskia had remembered nostalgically the clog filled with sweetmeats that Vrouw van Beek had always given her for St Nicholaes Day.

Robert's gift to her was a gold bracelet, which she thought was beautiful, and hers to him was a book on old London. He was extremely pleased with his gift, for it was a volume for which he had been searching and he had not known that she was aware of it.

She wore the bracelet every day from that time on.

Eighteen

Saskia discussed the menu at length with Louis, the chef, for the evening when the Wrens would be present. When the day came she spent considerable time decorating the table as she had once longed to do when watching Mistress Gibbons give the final touches. As it was early December there were few flowers to be had anywhere, but she used what she could find and added rowan berries for colour while ivy trailed delicately along the table and encircled the bases of the silver candelabrum with the tall white candles. The effect was later admired by Mistress Wren herself.

Saskia was fascinated to meet that lady's famous husband with his strict principles and extraordinary talents, for not only was he a brilliant architect, but also a mathematician, a geologist, an astronomer and much else, and had once successfully transferred blood from a healthy animal to a sick one, which had never been done before and would probably never be done again. Yet he had given lectures on its possible benefits for human beings instead of the bloodletting that most physicians considered essential for most ailments.

Saskia curtsied deeply to him when he and

Mistress Wren arrived and Robert had welcomed them.

'I have been hearing about you from my wife, madam,' he said, smiling at her. 'Your success is much to be admired. We need beauty in all its forms in this world of ours and you are contributing in your own unique way.'

She had liked him on sight and his compliment meant much to her. He was not a commanding figure, being slight of build, but she thought him most remarkable for his keenly intelligent eyes that seemed to encompass everything at a glance. His nose was long and thin with finely curved nostrils, his cheeks clear cut and his mouth pleasingly indented at the corners. His periwig, which flowed over his shoulders, was a dark coppery shade that most surely echoed his own hair colour to judge by his brows and lashes. He was handsomely dressed in a sea-green coat of richest velvet, and the lace trimming his cravat and flowing from his cuffs was as fine in appearance as the lace that Grinling had once carved.

There were only eight guests and conversation flowed freely around the table. One gentleman, forgetting that his hostess was Dutch, brought up the subject of the current war with Holland. Immediately Wren intervened.

'Remember that we are both great maritime nations,' he said, 'both expanding our colonies and our trade routes. Friction has been inevitable, but all will settle down again before too long.' He turned to Saskia, for he was seated at her left hand. 'Believe me, madam, it was only a squabble between two seafaring friends. Our bonds with your nation are too strong to be severed. Even the King's niece is wife to the Prince of the House of Orange, and your country gave refuge to our Merry Monarch himself during his years of exile. Bonds have been formed over the years that will never be broken.'

'I thank you for your kind and reassuring words, Master Wren.'

He had averted what could have been an embarrassing interlude for her and after that the talk was mostly light-hearted and amusing. Once during dinner Saskia's glance was caught by Robert at the head of the table. He gave her a smile that told her the evening was already a success.

It was as the guests were leaving that Wren spoke quietly to Robert. 'I shall be in my office tomorrow morning. Come and see me about eleven o'clock if that is convenient.'

'Indeed it is, sir,' Robert replied swiftly.

'Good. Thank you again for a most enjoyable evening.'

When the last guest had departed Saskia and Robert faced each other in the drawing room. 'Tomorrow I've an appointment at eleven o'clock with Master Wren at his office,' he said triumphantly.

'That's wonderful!' she exclaimed, glad for him. 'I wish you well there.'

'It's all due to you,' he said appreciatively.

She shrugged. 'It was bound to happen for you sooner or later. I've heard praise for your work from different sources. I'm only sorry, as I am sure you are, that this chance had to be achieved through a deception.'

'But there was none,' he said.

She looked at him in cool surprise. 'How can you say that when we are only posing as a married couple?'

He had decided that the time had come to tell her the truth. 'But it is not a pose, Saskia.'

She looked puzzled. 'I don't understand.'

'The Reverend Walburton was still ordained when he married us at the Fleet prison. What I paid him settled his debts and afterwards his bishop was merciful and restored him to his parish in Berkshire.'

All colour drained from her face and in distress she pressed her fingers against her cheeks. Her voice came in a whisper. 'You tricked me.'

'Not in the way that you imagine. I have wanted you for my wife ever since I first saw you on that day of my return to Rotterdam with Grinling from abroad. He has known my feelings for you ever since that time.'

She sat motionless, her head bowed, and he could not see her face. Dropping down to one knee beside her, he would have taken her hands into his, but she snatched them away and her expression as she jerked her head towards him was one of total fury.

'You are the one who has always stood between Grinling and me!' she accused fiercely, her eyes flashing. 'Not Elizabeth! Not then! If you had never told him he might have looked at me in a different light. We both know that out of the binding loyalty of friendship he would never have vied with you over me.'

'I cannot deny that,' he said, rising to his feet again. 'He did think you were a lovely girl.'

She gasped, hearing no hint of remorse in his voice. 'This is beyond endurance! I cannot stay in this room with you for another second!'

She threw herself up out of her chair, her silken skirts swirling about her, but when she would have flown past him he caught her by the shoulders and jerked her to a halt.

'Not before we have settled how we are going to spend the rest of our lives together!' he declared firmly.

'That is easily answered!' she retorted. 'I'll stay long enough for you to establish yourself with Master Wren and then I'll go back to Holland! I'll find some way to be free! Then you and I need never meet again.'

'Do you really suppose that I'd allow that to happen?' he demanded on a note of angry disbelief that she should have thought it possible. 'You are legally my wife and therefore you have become a British subject. Dutch laws would no longer apply in your favour.'

She gave a sharp cry. 'You have taken away my freedom and my country!'

'Don't be so dramatic!' he replied impatiently on the brink of anger. 'I have no intention of restricting you in any way. You can continue to sell your products and if you need financial aid in getting a shop you shall have it.'

'No! I want it to be through my own enterprise! Not a means by which you can entrap me still further!'

277

His jaw tightened and a vein throbbed in his temple. 'Stop turning me into a jailer and listen to me, Saskia!' he demanded dangerously. 'As soon as there is peace again between our two countries you can visit Holland as often as you wish. All I ask is that you will always come back to me.'

All the fight seemed to drain from her and her whole frame sagged, causing her to clasp the back of a chair as if for support. She turned her anguished face to him. 'Is that all you will expect of me?'

He shook his head, his deep gaze fixed on her. 'No. I hope in time you will be a true wife to me.'

She straightened up and her eyes blazed. 'Not unless you are planning rape!'

He caught his breath in such a great surge of rage that his whole face flamed as if speech would have choked him. She backed away from him, fearful that she had goaded him beyond restraint. There was no sound in the room except the crackle of burning logs in the fireplace and her frightened breathing. Yet, after a few tense seconds during which they faced each other as if on the brink of an abyss, he turned away from her to fling the double doors wide and stride from the room, leaving them open behind him.

She stood trembling from the shock of all that had taken place. It was in such moments of high tension and savage words that violence could occur and an end put to love. She believed she had ruthlessly murdered whatever tender feelings he had had for her. Somehow all the anger she had felt initially at the revelation of his tricking her into a legal marriage seemed to fade before the much greater harm that she had done to whatever future they would have together. She had the feeling that she had ripped both their lives into shreds.

Slowly she went out into the hall and paused at the centre of the wide marble floor, her shadow thrown in all directions by the crystal chandelier suspended overhead. A streak of light under the study door showed her where he had gone, perhaps to put her from his mind in the absorption of work. Momentarily she wondered whether she should go to him and try to heal in some measure the searing rift between them for both their sakes, but the harm that had been done needed the solace of time before such a move could be made and even then might prove impossible to mend.

It was in the early hours of the morning that she heard him go to bed in the neighbouring room. She had found it impossible to sleep. Dawn came before she finally dozed.

Nineteen

Robert was gone from the house when Saskia came downstairs, his place at the table cleared away. Ever since his return they had had break-fast together. She made no comment, determined not to give the servants any cause for gossip, but she wondered where he had gone so early when his appointment with Master Wren was not until mid-morning.

She aimed to spend the morning going to two different markets. Although Joe drove her when the distance was too far to walk she always left the carriage to go on foot into markets and side streets and alleys in her search for unusual and beautiful items for her collection. She also dress-ed inconspicuously, not wanting her purse snatched in dubious areas.

In the first market, looking with interest at the goods on the stalls of what others would con-sider rubbish, she found a tiny glass bowl, covered with dirt, which in its better days would once have held finger-rings. It would be perfect for presenting one of her products that did not need a lid. After paying for it she put it into the basket she had brought with her and covered it with a patterned cloth.

She had no luck in the second market, but went

down a narrow alleyway where she had never been before and found a little curiosity shop. The proprietor's name was above the door. *William Jenkins.* Looking through the small grimy panes of the shop window, she was amazed at the variety of second-hand goods on display. Everything from painted masks to wooden toys, spades, gardening forks and tools of every kind, jugs and chamber pots and worn-out rugs. She entered to the smell of dust and dirt and a foul aroma of tobacco smoke that came from the long-stemmed clay pipe being smoked by the old man behind the counter, his spectacles tied on by a faded ribbon around his bedraggled grey wig. Yet he moved with an unexpected sprightliness at her entrance, getting quickly to his feet. She guessed that this was William Jenkins.

'What 'ave you brought me?' he asked without preamble. 'A pendant? A ring? Your 'usband's watch?'

She realized that he thought she had come to pawn something. 'Nothing,' she replied. 'I'm on a quest for anything small and antique and still beautiful.'

'What's it for?'

'I need containers for the cosmetics I make for the face.'

He gave a hoarse chuckle. 'You don't need paint on that visage of yours.'

'But I'm in business. I produce my powders and balms for other people too.'

He frowned at her warningly. 'I don't give no special prices for those in trade. It's the same prices for all.'

She doubted that was true, but shrugged her shoulders. 'I'm going to look around. You may not have anything suitable.'

'Oh, I will, madam! You take your time and 'ave a good look and I'll see what I can find for you.'

He dived behind a ragged curtain into the back of the shop. She heard him rattling around in there while she looked along the crowded shelves where festoons of cobwebs showed how long some of the items had been undisturbed. But she was rewarded in her search with a little pink-tinted flask, the stopper intact. She had put it on the counter ready to be paid for when the old man returned, holding a collection of items by an arm across his chest. He set them down one by one on the counter. Most of them were worthless rubbish, but there was one of silver with a screw lid, but black through lack of polish, There was another of Indian origin studded with semi-precious stones, which looked as if it were gold, and also a little china box, so charmingly painted with a primitive portrait of the King that she could not resist it. These three objects she set aside with the flask she had found.

'Well?' the old man prompted as she lingered over some of the other items on the counter, discarding in turn those that were cracked or otherwise damaged.

She stood back to gesture towards those she had chosen. 'What is your price for these?'

He made a great show of pursing his lips and shaking his head as if she had given him a difficult task in estimating what he should charge her. Then he asked her far too much, but after some bartering they reached a figure agreeable to them both.

He made some attempt to wrap her purchases individually, but the paper he found was filthy and so instead she laid each purchase carefully in her basket and covered them with the cloth...

'Call in again from time to time, madam,' he invited. 'I get pretty things brought into me now and again from folk in urgent need of money.'

'I will do that,' she said.

They bade each other good day and then she left. Outside it was snowing slightly. It was now late morning and she was eager to get home with her purchases. Joe was waiting for her, but as they were not far from *La Belle Sauvage* she decided to call first on Elizabeth, whose time was drawing near for the birth of a second child.

The warmth of the inn was welcome after the cold outside. Saskia found her friend in the early stages of labour, but not yet ready for bed.

'A message has been sent to Grinling,' Elizabeth said, her cheeks very flushed as she paced up and down, finding it impossible to sit comfortably. 'I do hope he can get home in time, but Robert said it is at least a five-hour ride away.'

'Robert was here?' Saskia questioned in surprise.

Elizabeth paused in her pacing with a little grimace as she experienced another wave of pain. 'Yes. About half an hour ago. He expected Grinling to have arrived and came to bring us the good news that Master Wren has given him a special assignment. Isn't it wonderful! Now we are hoping that Grinling will have the same good fortune one day.'

Saskia felt a curious pang that she had not been the first to be told the good news. Then she reminded herself that there was no longer any unity between Robert and her to make him want to bring word to her before anyone else.

Later at home when she had washed her purchases she placed them in the glass-fronted cupboard in the music room with those she had already collected. All the time she was listening for Robert's return, wanting to congratulate him and to hear what assignment had been given to him.

He did not come home and she dined alone. It was four o'clock next morning when she heard him kicking snow off his boots before entering the house. His unsteady tread on the stairs was a clear indication that he had been drinking and he crashed open the door of his bedchamber as he entered. Then his great bed creaked as he threw himself across it and afterwards there was no further sound.

Surprisingly he joined her for breakfast, although he came late when she had almost finished. She had heard the servants taking cans of hot water for his bath, but thought the effect of the drink he had consumed during the night hours would have kept him in bed much longer. He looked strained and pale, which indicated that he had a severe headache, but he nodded appreciatively when she congratulated him on winning an assignment from Master Wren.

'It's beyond anything I expected,' he answered almost in awe. 'I am to be one of his team in building the new cathedral!'

'Again I congratulate you, Robert!' she exclaimed with delight. 'What an honour!'

He sat back in his chair. 'There is only one snag. It is that nobody knows, not even Master Wren himself, when the building will commence. So far no date has been fixed, the reason being that the King has rejected two of Master Wren's designs. It seems that the clergy are clinging to old-fashioned ideas instead of accepting Master Wren's new and exciting plans. They want the cathedral to be rebuilt much as it was before. Unfortunately it appears that they are influencing the King towards their way of thinking.'

'But he also rejected Master Wren's plans for the vast area destroyed by the Great Fire. Why was that?'

'My guess is that the King lacked control of the necessary funds, because he is not a man without foresight. Instead of the wide avenues and fine open plazas that Wren visualized for London, the rebuilding is taking place mostly along the same old routes as before. Worst of all, rogue builders are taking greater advantage all the time and a deal of bad housing is going up. Only last week another new house collapsed through poor foundations and I fully expect that state of affairs to go on happening in the years ahead. Fortunately so far nobody has been killed, although there have been casualties.'

'I remember that was your concern a while

ago. So what shall your tasks be until the re-building of St Paul's commences?'

'Today I'm going with him to look over some sites where the burned-out churches are to be rebuilt. He wants to hear any suggestions I have to offer, but the final decision will always be his.'

'So you have an interesting time ahead of you.'

'Indeed I do.' He glanced at the clock and pushed back his chair. 'I must go. I'm meeting Master Wren at the ruins of St James' Church just off Piccadilly.'

As he made for the door she half rose from her chair. 'Robert! Please tell me about your day when you come home this evening.'

He paused, raising an eyebrow in surprise at her request. 'Yes, Saskia. I'll do that.'

She sank back in her chair and after a few minutes she heard the front door close after him. Since they had to live together she must at least share his life and his interests as much as possible.

Later that morning a messenger brought the news that Elizabeth had given birth to a daughter. Saskia was mixing a dye at the time, but she stopped work to let Joan continue with the mixing while she wrote a congratulatory note to send back to her friend by the messenger.

As she returned to her work her thoughts drifted. When she was growing up in Holland she had always supposed she would marry a fellow countryman and have lots of children. Being an only child had probably made her long for a family more than most girls of her age, for she had envied her friends with brothers and sisters. She had also deeply missed having a father, aware to this day of a gap in her life. Once, after her mother had inadvertently revealed the location of her father's house on the far side of the city, she had gone to look at it. She had stayed long enough to see three of her half-sisters come out to play with a ball along the street. One had the same colour hair as her own. Once the ball had bounced to her feet and she had picked it up to throw it back to them. Later she had seen two of her half-brothers come home from school. Both were tall and fair. Neither of them had looked in her direction. When they had entered the house she turned away, wishing that she could have spoken to them.

She had never lost hope for a family of her own one day until Robert had played that devastating trick on her. Now that dream had to be put aside with others that had faded away with time.

That evening Robert clearly took pleasure in relating to her all he had done and she was caught up in his enthusiasm and examined with interest some sketches and plans that he had brought home with him. Yet she could see that his mind was not really focused on her. It was clear that he would have gained the same satisfaction in relating everything to a perfect stranger. She felt a chill descend on her. Was it an early sign that his love for her was fading? She could scarcely blame him if it was, for she had done nothing to sustain it.

They settled to a routine whereby they each dealt individually with the events of their working days. She continued to hold her weekly consultancies and the clients that had placed regular orders did not always continue attending, for their cosmetics were delivered by Joe in the smart little carriage, but wearing a green livery. His white attire had served its purpose, but had not been practical wear. Yet the chairs on a Wednesday afternoon were never empty as new clients came out of curiosity or through recommendation. Her success continued to grow.

Twenty

Once again Saskia went to congratulate Elizabeth on the birth of a fine baby and was delighted that she was asked to be godmother. The choice of names had been left to her, but between them they had decided on Alice.

'She is like a beautiful rose,' Saskia declared, looking down into the face of her godchild, whom she held in her arms.

'I think I'm going to have a whole garden of roses before my childbearing days are over,' Elizabeth replied, laughing. 'In the days of my innocence I had never supposed that babies could be conceived so quickly. In fact, like most girls, I did not know how they were conceived at all! I thought it happened through kissing and that was why girls had to be chaperoned!'

'I was aware early on in my life as to what was entailed,' Saskia said, amused. 'My mother was very plain speaking and full of warnings as to what could happen to me if I did not keep young men at bay.'

Elizabeth had suddenly pressed her fingertips to her lips in self-reproach. 'I'm sorry, Saskia. I spoke thoughtlessly about my babies when you have yet to conceive. I'm sure you will find yourself with child before long.'

Saskia spoke lightly as she returned the sleeping baby to the crib. 'I have your two dear children to love in the meantime.'

It was the truth. She enjoyed playing with little James and now there was his sister to bring pleasure into her life, easing the craving in her for a child of her own. As agreed from the start she and Robert were leading their own lives, although they accepted all invitations that came to them jointly and were socially much in demand. They entertained lavishly, saw all the new plays and attended balls, card parties and soirées. She guessed that Robert had a mistress, but preferred not to think about it, uncertain as to why she should find it painful. She told herself it was from resentment that somewhere another woman thought her too dull to keep such a handsome man faithful to her.

Her relationship with him was not easy. There were times when they laughed together, but others when the strain between them was intense and they quarrelled heatedly. Then she was almost afraid of him, for he looked at her so passionately. Yet never once had he tried the handle of the communicating double doors between their two rooms. She decided that for his sake and her own she would have to return to Holland as soon as the war ended. She was certain he would give his consent now when their marriage was proving to be so difficult for them both.

He had kissed her on occasions. Usually it was when they were on exceptionally good terms. Then he would take her by the shoulders and kiss her on the brow, but never on the lips. She believed he did not trust himself to put his mouth to hers, for she was well aware that his desire for her had not waned.

Her collection of little treasures had now reached the figure of one hundred and twenty. On her natal day and at Christmas time Robert had given her something that she could add to it, each being new and of beautiful French porcelain. She had one cracked little pot in her collection that could never be used, but it was of blue Delft just like one she had had in the original collection and when she had seen it languishing on a market stall she had bought it immediately.

It was an evening in early summer when Saskia decided to broach the subject of a return to Holland. Robert had gone out into the garden to see what the gardener had done that day, for he was extremely interested in plants and new ones were being introduced into the country from far away places all the time. She found him strolling along a path and increased her pace to catch up with him. He turned to her with a smile.

'You've come to enjoy the evening air with me. Good.'

'Yes, but I also want to discuss a very serious matter with you.'

'What is it?'

'It is about our relationship. You have to admit that it is quite impossible at times. We would be much better apart and I'm sure after the difficult months we have shared you feel differently now about my original request to go home to Holland. This war will not last for ever. I'm looking ahead to when peace is restored and I could safely return without causing any gossip. Nobody would be surprised that I should wish to go home and see how friends have fared during the conflict. You are so firmly established with Master Wren now that when I fail to come back again you would not be blamed for my apparent desertion. You can also query the legality of our Fleet marriage, because I believe that can be done under certain circumstances and then you would be a free man again.'

He must have been expecting such an approach from her, for all the time she had been speaking he had shown no surprise.

'Yes,' he replied evenly. 'You can go back to Holland whenever it is safe for you to travel, but on one condition. In return I'll raise no objection to your departure. Previously when you asked me to let you go I was against it, because I wanted to give our marriage a chance to survive. Unfortunately it has proved to be a pathetic sham.'

291

'I regret that too, but I never deceived you. From the start you knew I loved somebody else, even though his love was directed elsewhere.'

He gave a nod. 'So how soon after we have news of a peaceful settlement would you expect to depart?'

'I have to wind up my business first. What is the condition that you mentioned?'

'That you share my bed before your departure.'

She gasped in angry astonishment at his demand, withdrawing a step from him. 'That would be breaking our agreement!'

'Just as you intend to break it by leaving me!' he gave back bitterly. 'So make up your mind. Meet my terms or stay as we are in this wretched relationship.'

She felt overwhelmed. 'Do you hate me for it, Robert?'

His gaze was incredulous. 'Hate you? No! I pity you for throwing away the good life we could have had together.'

She experienced a deep stab of sadness. 'I wish it had been possible.'

He shrugged and continued his way along the path while she walked slowly back into the house.

Several weeks went by with no more talk about a future departure. During this time, after a long legal tussle Robert's case to reclaim his family home and evict his stepmother had finally come to court. On the day the verdict was given in his favour he did not go home to convey the news to

Saskia, but went to celebrate with friends. The hour was late when eventually he arrived home.

Saskia was waiting up for him. 'How did the case go?' she asked anxiously, able to see that he had been either celebrating or drowning his misery.

He beamed at her. 'It is wonderful news. The verdict went in my favour and Harting Hall has been returned to me.'

'I'm so glad for you, Robert,' she said sincerely.

He ambled across to the staircase, but reeled slightly and caught at the newel post to steady himself. 'I think I must have done rather well this evening,' he commented with a grin, 'but I did tip the waiter to keep the wine flowing.'

She watched him go up the stairs. It hurt her deeply that he had shared his news first with friends just as he had done when Master Wren had appointed him. Surely, even though they were estranged, she held more importance in his life than his friends. Then on reflection she realized that over past months Robert had been slowly cutting her out of his life in preparation for her departure, which he must have always foreseen. All he had originally hoped for through capturing her in marriage had faded away. Now he would adjust easily enough to being on his own again when she finally left him.

Next morning Robert outlined all that had happened in court, but it gave her less pleasure than it would otherwise have done as his account was coming to her after being celebrated by others.

'After all this time everything is returned to

me,' he said. 'The house and the whole estate! At my father's untimely death my stepmother was left well provided for in his will and she can live in comfort at any other house of her choice for the rest of her days.'

'My felicitations to you,' Saskia said. 'You have waited so long for what is rightfully yours. I have often wondered why your stepmother has been so stubborn about surrendering the house to you, knowing that you were the rightful heir to your father's property?'

'Revenge perhaps?' he suggested. 'She was quite savage about my father's loyalty to the King. What seems worst of all to my father's memory is that she entertained Cromwell, his greatest enemy, twice under his roof and all her acquaintances were Parliamentarians. Now she has to vacate the house immediately and the present staff will remain other than her personal maid. But I thought I should send two of our senior servants to make sure all is in order and then I'll go down to Sussex for a few days. I have plenty of work to take with me.'

She experienced a sense of shock that he intended to go alone, but she remained silent. In the past he had often talked to her about the house and all that he would show her in the surrounding countryside whenever he should win the family estate back again. Now she was no longer included in his plans for the future.

A week later, after word had been received that all had been made ready at Harting Hall, Robert bade her farewell and set off for Sussex, his valet travelling with him. She stood on the steps to watch him leave and she felt strangely bereft. It was becoming all too clear that his love for her had faded and she should be glad of it instead of feeling increasing sadness as the gulf between them widened. He had been patient for so long and had accepted at last that her love for Grinling would always stand between them.

As she turned back indoors a thought struck her and she hastened to his study. Opening the door, she looked in and with a curious pang of her heart she saw that the portrait miniature of her was still hanging on the wall there. For the first time he had not taken it with him. During the next few days she wondered whether he would send a messenger to collect it, having simply forgotten it in his excited anticipation of seeing his home again after so many years, but nobody came.

Although he no longer cared about her she knew that he would continue to be adamant that she could not leave England without his ever having possessed her. She feared his angry lust, but it was the doorway to her freedom. She might be left pregnant and that thought alone gave her comfort, for she was financially secure from her business to keep herself and a child in moderate comfort until she had re-established herself and her cosmetics in Holland. She thought she would settle in Amsterdam, for it was the heart of Holland where merchants of the East India Company thrived on the rich comings and goings of their vessels and their wives and daughters would be attracted to her beauty products.

She began looking for a letter from Robert, but she received no word. Neither did he send a messenger with news of how he was dealing with everything at Harting Hall. The two senior servants returned and assured her that everything was running smoothly there after – on their recommendation – some of the staff had been replaced.

Three more weeks went by and then a month. She heard by chance that Robert had made a swift visit to London in order to discuss some matter with Master Wren, but he had not come to see her. From being irritated by his neglect her feelings turned to anger and then to outrage when she considered the possibility that he might have installed his paramour at the Hall to keep him company in her absence. It never occurred to her that her fury sprang as much from a shaft of jealousy as from his neglect.

Finally she summoned Joe. 'I want you to drive me down to Sussex. I intend to visit Harting Hall.'

She gave other instructions to Joan. 'You must be early to the assembly rooms this week and apologize while making a deep curtsy for my having to postpone my consultations for that day.'

'Am I not to accompany you, madam?' Joan said in disappointment. 'How will you manage without having me to unhook your clothes and brush your hair and see that the servants bring you anything you want? Do you intend to take Matilda with you?'

'No, because it will be a very short visit and I

need to rely on you to deal with my ladies. Probably I shall only be gone for no more than two days. I am not taking any grand clothes. Just pack my sprigged cotton gowns and the essentials that I shall need.'

It was a warm sunny day when Saskia and Joe set off on their journey. When they had left the stench of the London streets behind them Saskia inhaled the sweet country air with quiet pleasure. The fields were full of ripening corn and every meadow was sprinkled thickly with wild flowers. The road was hard and dry, there having been no rain for some weeks, and the wheels of the carriage bowled along.

Saskia was always to remember her first sight of Harting Hall at early evening and thought it beautiful, although the great size of it surprised her. They had passed through some woodland and suddenly there it was, lying in a curve of the softly rounded hills that in her opinion were curiously called the Downs. It was a Tudor building with grand chimneys and the panes of the many casement windows were blinking back gold and orange and pink at the exceptionally beautiful sunset. A long gravelled drive led between an avenue of trees to the steps of the entrance, which was protected by a large stone porch under which equipages could come to a standstill and give arriving passengers protection from any inclement weather.

There was no sign of human habitation anywhere, but as she alighted the great door in front of her was opened and a manservant bowed to her. She entered the house with a flourish.

'Tell your master that Mistress Harting is here.'

Momentarily he showed surprise at hearing who she was, but bowed again as he stood aside for her to enter. 'The Master is not at home, madam. He went riding this morning with company and has not yet returned.'

She was gazing around at the wide hall with its dark linenfold panelling, the ancient but still colourful murals that followed the wide sweeping staircase to a gallery, and the heavy chandeliers from another age suspended from the ornamentation of the plastered ceiling.

'Notify my husband when he returns that I am here,' she said authoritatively, intending that the servants should know from the start that she was in charge, no matter if Robert was keeping his mistress under this roof. 'I want the best bedchamber in the house prepared for me immediately. I have not brought my personal maid, so send me one of the maidservants able enough to attend me.'

'The room you require is already prepared, madam. So are a number of the other bedchambers, because after a card party or any other social gathering here guests sometimes stay overnight.'

'Do they?' she commented drily.

The bedchamber was spacious and very fine with rich brocade hangings draping the four-poster bed and a Turkish carpet on the floor. She went to look out of the window and saw that she had a wonderful view of the parkland where a herd of deer was grazing in the distance.

She dined alone at a long oaken table where thirty or more could have sat down together. Afterwards she took a little tour of some of the ground floor rooms, but not upstairs in case she should see signs of a woman's occupation in one of the bedchambers, for she had not come to spy, only to assert herself as mistress of the Hall whether it pleased Robert or not.

When she was getting ready for bed, attended by a young maidservant, she thought she heard the clop of a horse's hooves in the drive, which surely meant that Robert had returned home. She was seized by an intense desire to go and meet him, but she crushed it down, for it was likely that his mistress was with him and he would be hostile at what he would see as her intrusion. Then, as the maidservant was nervous and clumsy, although doing her best, Saskia sent her away downstairs again, preferring to brush her own hair.

She was in her night shift, wielding her brush in long swift strokes as she stood in front of a Florentine looking-glass, when the door of her room was suddenly opened wide. Startled, she glimpsed Robert's reflection, and turned swiftly to face him where he stood framed in the doorway, a red silk dressing-robe covering his nakedness. Never before had he come to a room that was hers.

'I did not hear you arrive home,' she said almost in a whisper, unaware that the candle-lamp illumined her silhouette through the diaphanous silk and lace of her night shift. Her eyes were held by his concentrated gaze just as once on a staircase in Holland all that time ago. She stood as though rooted to the floor.

He did not move from the threshold of the room, but held out his hand towards her. 'Come to bed, my love,' he said very softly. 'It is time now and the hour is late.'

She put down the hairbrush and went slowly and unquestioningly towards him, her feet as bare as his. It was as if this moment had been predestined and only she had not known it. When she reached him he put an arm about her and guided her along the wide corridor to the door of his own room, the wall sconces throwing their shadows fore and aft as they went by. When he opened the door of his bedchamber she saw in the glow of many candles that his Tudor bed here was even larger than in his room at their London house and was as heavily carved, but here cherubs were pouring fruit symbolically from a cornucopia.

With the door closed behind them he led her by the hand to the bedside. As she stood there he kissed her lips softly as he released the silken ribbons of her night shift and it slipped from her to the floor. Then he tossed aside his own robe and lifted her up in his arms on to the great bed, her head coming to rest against the pillows. There he took his place beside her, his long limbs and handsome body warm against hers.

'I knew,' he said softly, putting his arms lovingly around her, 'that if one day you came looking for me it would mean that you had discovered at last where your heart belongs.'

Her eyes were wide and frightened. 'I'm not

sure if that is true.'

'You will be by morning, my darling,' he whispered before he buried her mouth in his, gathering her to him in a loving embrace.

It was as he had long anticipated. After he had tenderly caressed her whole body and when his lips had awakened her lovely breasts, she was totally ignited to sexual pleasure, responding joyously to greater intimacies as under his lips and tongue and hands she became afire with passion. When eventually he took her she cried his name aloud at the moment of ecstasy and he knew that at last he had truly won her.

The night they shared was one she was never to forget. In the soft glow of dawn she lay awake for a while, still a little dazed by all that had taken place between them in this great bed and yet glorying in being so loved and desired. His arm was encircling her as he slept, his head beside hers on the pillow.

She knew now that her love for Grinling had been a girlish infatuation, deep and true in its own way, but built on a dream without substance or reason. Lying beside her was a powerful man who had given her his whole heart long since and she had failed to accept that he was the other half of herself until this night that had passed in such passion. She would never cause him pain and disappointment again, but love him as he deserved to be loved until the end of her days.

His eyes opened as if he had heard her thoughts and she cupped the side of his face with her hand. 'I love you,' she whispered tenderly for the first time, repeating what he had said many times over to her during the night hours.

He drew her closer to him. 'My darling wife,' he murmured in reply. Then again he took her, causing her to arch under him with the force of her ecstatic fulfilment.

They stayed two more weeks at the Hall during which they walked hand-in-hand or rode in the parkland, he showing her where he had played as a boy, and they took a boat on to the lake in which once – as a three-year-old – he had almost drowned. One morning they came across an old swing hanging from the stout branch of an oak tree and after he had tested the rope he swung her to and fro, her petticoats fluttering, as she rose high into the air. Now and again they made love in sheltered groves with only birdsong to accompany her softly joyous cries.

One morning as they went riding she told him how mixed her feelings had been when she found he had not taken the portrait medallion of her with him.

He gave her a sideways glance. 'I was so furious with you at the time that I was afraid that I might hurl it away somewhere, which was why I left it hanging where it was.'

'What a torment I must have been to you,' she said regretfully.

'In more ways than one,' he replied wryly. 'But when we get back to London I want you to have your portrait painted. Grinling's portrait medallion will always hold your likeness as a young girl, but it is time now for your beauty as a woman to be captured for ever.'

'Then let it be done according to the Dutch way.'

'How do you mean?'

'Surely you remember from your days in Holland that it is the custom for dual marriage portraits to be painted? There will be one of the bridegroom looking towards his bride while she in her portrait gazes towards him, and they hang side by side from then onwards. It means that we shall be looking into each other's eyes for all eternity.'

He smiled. 'What could be better than that? It shall be as you wish.'

Neighbours soon heard that Robert Harting's wife had joined him at the Hall. It was then that their peaceful isolation was shattered as invites came and people called, all so full of goodwill that it was impossible not to welcome them. But the disruption lasted only a matter of days as word came that it was imperative that Robert should return to London.

He looked up from the letter, his face alight. 'It's splendid news, although it means we must leave here sooner than we had intended. Wren's third post-Great Fire plan for the cathedral has finally been accepted by the King and the clergy! Now work can begin!'

The letter had come from Wren himself, for he was summoning his assistant architects to a final consultation, for at last the great work was to commence immediately.

Twenty-One

It had been a strange little scene that took place in the Palace of Whitehall when Wren arrived to discuss some minor details about his accepted plan, for His Majesty wished to be enlightened about some aspects of the new building, even though all was settled. There were several courtiers in attendance when Wren entered the royal presence and six of the King's pet spaniels, which came scampering to greet him, tails wagging.

Charles was seated at a table with the plan spread out before him and after initial greetings he motioned for Wren to take the chair set ready for him.

'No doubt you are able to sleep again at nights,' Charles began jovially, 'now that the way is open for your great work to begin and all with the full approval of the archbishop and the clergy. Were you told that there was not a single dissent?'

'Yes, sire. I was mightily relieved. It must be the resemblance to the old Norman cathedral that pleased them,' Wren replied evenly, no hint of his own opinion of them in his voice. 'Ever since you first entrusted me with the task ahead I have never stopped receiving letters from the clergy, all pointing out all that was beautiful about it and emphasizing that there was no need to look beyond it to anything new or different.'

Charles smiled. 'Some people always cling to the familiar and are ill at ease with anything new.'

Wren nodded. 'Frankly, sire, I should not have been surprised if they had wanted the building to resemble the early Saxon church that was the first Christian place of worship on the site!'

The King laughed. 'At least it would have stopped there. They would not have wanted the original Roman temple to Diana to be re-erected on that same location!'

'Indeed not, sire!'

The King leaned over the plan on the table. 'Now I'm particularly interested in these arches by the nave. Tell me how they are to be constructed.'

After all the royal questions had been answered Wren expected to leave, but Charles had one more query to put to him and there was a conspiratorial flicker in the dark depths of the royal gaze.

'I suppose you will be using a great deal of scaffolding during the construction of this mighty masterpiece,' Charles remarked casually. Then he glanced down to scoop up one of his spaniels and fondle it.

'Indeed, sire. The world will see very little of the new cathedral until it is almost finished.'

Now the King's gaze met Wren's eyes again with that same meaningful flicker. 'I'm extremely pleased to hear it. My goodwill will be follow-

305

ing every mounting stone of it.'

Around them there was applause from the courtiers in honour of the great project that was to be started at last and the spaniel in the king's arms yapped as if in assent.

Originally the replacing of the old Norman cathedral had been planned in the early days of the Restoration, for the Parliamentarian troops had stabled their horses in it and defiled it further by using it for dubious entertainments at night. Nobody knew then that the Great Fire would consume it before Wren's first great plan for it could be carried out. The burned-out ruins were still being brought down by gunpowder explosions.

Now as Wren made his way out of the great palace a smile was twitching the corners of his normally serious mouth. Without a single word or gesture the King had let him know that he had a free hand to go ahead with his advanced ideas for the cathedral, all of which had met with His Majesty's enthusiastic approval right from the start. Then, by the time most of the scaffolding was removed, it would be too late for any reversal to the plan approved by the clergy. It was exactly what Wren had intended to do as long ago as when he had seen his first plan turned down by the clergy, but he had not expected to carry it through with unspoken royal approval. It should not be a steeple that would rise above London rooftops as before, but a beautiful dome such as had never before been seen against an English sky.

* * *

When Saskia and Robert were on their way back to London news-sheet sellers ran to the coach in every town. Robert had bought from the first one, for the great news was that the war with the Dutch Republic was over and peace between the two countries was restored.

'What splendid news to greet our homecoming,' Saskia said thankfully.

When they entered the London house she thought how different everything was for her now from that time of leaving. The first thing she did when she went upstairs was to unlock the dividing doors between Robert's room and her own. He had told her that many times he had come close to forcing the lock, but her taunt of rape had always stopped him.

'If only I had known how it was to be with us,' she had sighed in his arms.

'You needed time, my love,' he replied, kissing away her frown.

Elizabeth came visiting the day after their return, looking beautiful in a splendid straw hat, its wide brim half covered with silk flowers. Immediately she saw a change in Saskia.

'You look radiant, my friend,' she exclaimed, sitting down in a chair with a sweep of her blue-striped skirt and using her fan, for the August day was extremely hot. 'What has happened? Are you with child?'

'Not to my knowledge,' Saskia replied on a soft laugh.

'You look so – so – happy!' Elizabeth declared, being at a loss to find any other words to describe the difference she saw in Saskia.

'Yes, I am. Robert and I had a delightful time at the Hall.'

'I'm so glad the property is his again at last. I gave Grinling the good news when he came home from measuring up for his carving at yet another great mansion that is being built – the country home of a duke this time. He has been called publicly an artist in wood, a compliment that pleased him mightily. He is constantly in demand these days and his workshop is full of wonderful pieces that he is working on.' Then she added on an unconscious note of pride, 'Yet he has agreed that now he has established himself as a craftsman of high repute and a personage of some importance that it is time we had our portraits painted.'

Saskia raised her eyebrows in pleased surprise. 'What a coincidence! Robert has decided that we should have our portraits painted too!'

'How exciting! What are you going to wear?'

'I have not given it any thought yet.'

'Oh, but you must! It is very important. Grinling wanted our likenesses to be portrayed in the Dutch manner of two wedding portraits, but I said we had been married too long to be depicted as a bride and groom.'

Saskia smiled to herself. The length of her marriage to Robert was immaterial since it had been consummated so recently.

She resumed her afternoon consultations, but some while since had reduced them to one Wednesday afternoon a month, which made women all the more eager to be there. These afternoons had become important events in themselves with tea being served and ratatouille biscuits handed around by two pretty young girls in green gowns. To be present at one of Mistress Harting's consultations was to be seen as knowing the high points of London's social scene.

Saskia was wryly aware that once again she had become a vogue, a whim of fashion having taken her up, but one that could just as easily drop her again. She also knew that she must continue to keep these gatherings exclusive by limiting admission, or else they could become commonplace.

Some time after her return with Robert to London a long-delayed letter from Holland, held up by the conflict, came for her. As she broke the seal, recognizing Cornelia van Beek's handwriting, she hoped that those to whom she had written during the past four years would be receiving her letters too. The date of this one showed it had been written over a year ago and it brought sad news. Nanny Bobbins had died, a peaceful end in her sleep.

She treasured the letters you sent her and she has left you some of her beautiful lace – Cornelia had written – *either for your wedding gown or, if you are married already, for your first baby's christening robe.* *

Saskia, folding the letter again after reading it through a second time, sat for a while with a handkerchief to her eyes as she wept in her grief that she would never see the old nurse again. Always at the back of her mind had been the hope that one day she would be able to visit her old home and see again the friends she had made there.

Rising to her feet, she wiped her eyes and went upstairs to take from a drawer the Nordland cap that Nanny Bobbins had made her all that time ago. She often wore it, for fashion decreed the wearing of a cap under a wide-brimmed hat on wild and windy days to keep curls in place. Yet today she wore it as a sign of respect for someone who had brought a special kindness and affection into her life and whom she would never forget.

Over the next few months some other long-delayed letters arrived. Her friend, Anna, with whom she had been skating the day that Grinling had joined her on the frozen lake, wrote that she was married to a successful artist and presently living in Amsterdam. She also included news of mutual friends, which Saskia appreciated. Amalia Visser's letter also told of Nurse Bobbins' passing, not knowing when she wrote that Cornelia's letter would be first with the news. She was very distressed, having been fond of the old nurse and they had shared living accommodation at the Gibbons' house. Although Dinely Gibbons was willing for her to stay on there, according to the arrangements that his mother had made, she was going to move to Delft and live with her widowed sister there.

The bequeathed lace arrived not long afterwards and consisted of exquisite lace collars that would flow over the shoulders and many lengths in various depths to trim gowns and petticoats.

Among them was included a tiny Nordland cap, exactly like the one Nurse Bobbins had made for Saskia, which would fit a little baby's head.

'Perhaps one day,' Saskia whispered, placing it in a drawer with her own cap.

Saskia felt that it was fast becoming time to find a shop and she had seen one near Piccadilly that she thought would suit her perfectly. Her beauty products were now sufficiently in demand for her to risk such an enterprise.

Robert went with her to view the premises as she wanted his opinion on its location, for the shop was sandwiched between a hatter's high-priced establishment and an expensive boot-maker's. There was also a gentlemen's exclusive club in the street and she wondered if it was too masculine an area for her wares, for although she wanted male customers her primary concern was in maintaining a feminine demand for her products.

'There is a milliner's shop only two doors away,' she pointed out to Robert. 'So I should not be quite alone in the street in dealing with women customers.'

He shook his head. 'This is not the right place for you. I happen to know that the milliner – like many that follow her trade – has rooms above her shop available for liaisons, which means that your shop would be near enough to get the wrong kind of customer calling in and expecting to be offered the same upstairs facilities. I know you're disappointed, but something else will come along.'

So the purchase of a shop was postponed until

a better location could be found. Saskia was disappointed, but she had seen the wisdom of Robert's advice. In the meantime she continued to search out small treasures for her collection, which brought her into contact with people in all walks of life. Some, such as old Will in the curiosity shop, had become very friendly, always on the watch for something that would please her. Sensibly he always saved any spare glass or porcelain stoppers for her as often the little bottles she collected were missing them and she was able to match them up or at least top them suitably.

As her collection had grown so had her respect for her mother increased beyond all bounds, for by the very nature of Diane's employment she would have had little leisure time in which to search for what she wanted, and yet she had achieved it so magnificently. For that reason alone Saskia never let heavy rain, snow or fierce winds deter her from going out on her search, always remembering that her mother must have done the same.

Twenty-Two

Grinling and Elizabeth held a party for friends to celebrate the completion of their joint portraits by a prominent English artist. At an arranged moment a draped cloth, which was covering it, was removed and there was a burst of spontaneous applause from all present. The painting was quite large and showed them sitting side by side. Elizabeth was sumptuously gowned, her lips curved in her attractive, impish smile, and she was holding up for view the necklace of pearls that Grinling had given her from the proceeds of his first important sale. He, grandly wigged, was clad in a rich blue silk coat with diamond buttons, a well-fitted waistcoat and fashionably full cut breeches, his triumphant smile revealing his happiness in his marriage and in his success.

Recently he had installed for the first time his beautiful lime wood foliage carvings at Holme Lacy House, which was a grand house in Herefordshire, and also at another fine mansion in Hertfordshire. Already he was receiving enquiries from those who had seen the carvings in situ.

His likeness on canvas also showed something that Saskia had not really noticed over the passing of time. He had become quite portly from

313

good living and fine wine. He looked every inch of what he was, a prosperous craftsman moving in gentlemen's circles, who was able to command whatever price he wanted for his wonderful work.

She and Robert had almost decided to commission the same artist to paint their portraits, but then one day he came home with the news that he had seen the work of a Dutch artist living in London and thought he was the one they should choose.

'He came to England as a young man and over the years has established himself as a fine portrait painter.'

Saskia was delighted with this news. 'He will know exactly what I want in our marriage portraits,' she said enthusiastically. 'When can I see some of his work?'

'I'll take you to his studio tomorrow.'

It was a successful visit. Saskia liked the artist's work. Johan Rykers, originally from Amsterdam, was in his early sixties, a tall, gaunt-faced man with remarkably alert blue eyes. He bowed low to Saskia when she announced her decision.

'I look forward to sitting for you, Master Rykers,' she said, 'and I hope you will be patient when my husband is only able to spare a short time now and again.'

'It will be an honour to portray you and your husband, *mejuffrouw*,' he answered courteously, 'and I have had to paint busy men before now, so do not concern yourself. It will be a particular pleasure to paint a pair of marriage portraits

314

again. The last time was for a young couple of your nationality and mine, who had eloped here to England in order to be married.'

'I hope there was a happy ending for them,' Saskia said sincerely.

He nodded. 'I'm glad to say that her father relented and they returned to Holland with their portraits.'

Before leaving his studio, appointments were made for the first sittings. Now Saskia gave thought to what she would wear and, equally important, what Robert should wear too. Eventually she had a new gown of cream silk made for her, which was embroidered with roses. It was an appropriate choice, for the artist painted her looking over her shoulder, her hand lifted gracefully as if to accept the red rose that Robert, handsome in ruby velvet, was handing to her in his portrait. They were looking into each other's eyes just as she had wished.

They went down to Sussex with the paintings, wanting them to be at Harting Hall. There the portraits in gilded frames were hung side by side in the grand drawing room. As the servant, who had secured the paintings, left the room they stepped back a pace, hand in hand, to regard their likenesses in these new surroundings.

'I'm glad we did not have the kind of conventional portraits normal to this country,' she said. 'All your ancestors in the portrait gallery gaze out into the distance, whereas you and I will be looking at each other for ever and ever.' Then she added softly, 'I hope our descendants will always refer to us as the lovers.'

He smiled at her fanciful notion. 'I'm sure they will,' he endorsed, putting his arms around her and lowering his head to kiss her. Then, as they looked back at the portraits again, he said thoughtfully, 'Something is missing that would truly compliment Ryker's work and would also ensure that these portraits were never moved from their present position.'

She raised her eyebrows in surprise. 'Whatever could that be?'

He gestured towards the portraits. 'A while ago when I visited Petworth House in Sussex to discuss some building work with the Duke of Somerset, who owns it, I was shown into a large room where Grinling had recently completed what was most surely some of his greatest work. His foliage carvings were more abundant and intricate than anything he has ever done before, even surpassing what he has already done for those great houses in Herefordshire and elsewhere. He had garlanded the doors and the wainscoting and also surrounded important ancestral portraits with his decorative carving like second enhancing frames, every small detail perfectly executed. In fact,' he added, glancing up and around the spacious room, 'we could make this our Grinling Gibbons salon with festoons around our portraits and all else in a similar way.' He looked back at her. 'What do you say?'

'Oh, yes!' she declared, her eyes shining. 'Let's ask him as soon as we return to London, because it is a commission that will take a great deal of time and we cannot expect him to give us priority when he has so many orders to fill.'

He smiled at her. 'What does time matter? When the carvings are installed we'll still have the rest of our lives in which to enjoy them.'

If Robert had needed further proof that he had replaced Grinling in her heart he saw it in her obvious joy at the forthcoming beautification of an already finely proportioned room. There was no lingering sign in her eyes or her voice that a constant reminder of a man she had once loved would be painful to her. Yet he knew her well enough to guess that not even he could entirely banish the nostalgic affection that she most surely still felt for her fellow countryman. But, most important of all in his view, it was no longer a threat to their marriage.

He was right in his supposition, for at his mention of garlands surrounding their portraits she had remembered vividly the garland that had encircled the little looking-glass that had reflected her face daily before it had been destroyed in the fire.

They stayed a few days at the Hall, even though the November weather was cold and damp, for crackling log fires welcomed them back after they had been walking or riding. Then they returned to the noise and hubbub of London.

Good news awaited them. Grinling's work had been recognized at last by Wren, who as the royal architect embarking on a great task had just been knighted by the King. So it was Sir Christopher Wren who had commissioned Grinling to carve the choir stalls for the new cathedral. It was to be a colossal amount of work and

317

Grinling was overjoyed at being entrusted with this tremendous commission. Yet he promised Robert and Saskia that he would do the carving for their country home since it would be a very long time before the cathedral reached the stage when his choir stalls could be set in place.

Elizabeth, blooming as she always did in pregnancy, began to talk about moving to a house of their own, thinking how much she would like a room garlanded with her husband's work such had been ordered by Robert and Saskia. He had recently made her an exquisite carving for her natal day. It was a bowl of flowers, all carved out of one piece of lime wood and so delicately and realistically executed that the blossoms and their foliage quivered on their stems at the slightest vibration.

'There are so many fine new properties going up,' she said to Saskia, 'but Grinling is too busy to view anything. It is time we had a flower garden for the children to play in and I'm tired of all the stairs I have to climb at *La Belle Sauvage,* especially when I have little Alice in my arms and James by the hand.'

'Should you like me to go viewing with you?' Saskia asked.

Elizabeth looked grateful. 'Yes, indeed. Then if we find a property which I really like, I can persuade Grinling to spare an hour or two to view it.'

The viewing period did not last long. Elizabeth was too near her time to have much energy for going up steps and stairs and in and out of rooms and basements. She soon gave up and a month later gave birth to a second son, named Charles. Then she was too occupied to think of moving, which was a relief to Grinling, who found living and working at the inn highly convenient. There was a small room at the inn that he used for private meetings with clients, and it was very agreeable after a commission had been settled to seal it on the spot by having the best of wine served, usually by the innkeeper himself.

Saskia continued to keep a lookout for any house that she thought would please Elizabeth, but mostly when on foot she was in busy commercial areas in her search for more items to add to her collection. At the same time Saskia always considered the size and location of any empty shop she happened to see, but as yet there had been none of any consequence in the right fashionable area.

She was in a market near Piccadilly one morning when she found a pretty little pot in a rose colour, which she thought was extremely old. She had developed an awareness of value and rarity, always making sure that she paid a fair price, often adding a coin or two if she felt the seller was ignorant of the true value of his wares. She would not cheat anyone with whom she dealt.

It was as she was turning away from the stall that a woman at her side gave her a hefty thrust with an elbow, causing the little pot to leap out of her hands and smash on the cobbles. She turned swiftly to face the woman, expecting some apology, but it was her old enemy, Martha, smirking at her, triumph in her eyes.

'What a pity, Mistress!' she exclaimed mockingly. 'You've broken your dainty purchase.'

Saskia had seen immediately that the woman was shabbily dressed, something that would not have been allowed by a respectable employer. 'I'll find another to take its place,' Saskia replied quietly. 'How are you, Martha?'

'What do you care?' the woman hissed in reply. 'But I tell you that nothing has gone well for me since you connived to get me tossed out of work.'

For a moment Saskia stared at her in astonishment. 'Indeed I did not! However can you imagine anything so foolish?' She was outraged by the accusation. 'I heard when you lost your employment with Mistress Henrietta, but I can assure you that it was nothing to do with me!'

'Liar! It was your wagging tongue that brought me misfortune by passing on false information about me to young Mistress Gibbons, who in turn fed her godmother with your lies.'

Saskia gasped. 'You are totally mistaken! I have never spoken ill of you to anyone!'

'I choose to think differently!'

'I deeply regret that you are not prepared to listen to me,' Saskia replied with quiet fury, 'but I have told you the truth. Now I bid you good day.'

She walked quickly away, making for the place where Joe was waiting for her with the carriage. The encounter had upset her deeply. She knew well enough that Martha had been jealous of her when they were both in Mistress Henrietta's employ, but she had never suspected that

320

the woman's bitterness would fester into such terrible hatred.

The following day she discussed the encounter with Elizabeth, who nodded her head sagely. 'I've never discussed her with Godmother Henrietta, but I was always able to see that the spiteful creature was envious of you. After all, there you were! Young, pretty and talented! Poor Martha knew she could not match you in any way. I fear some people have no generosity of spirit in their natures and sadly she was eaten up by jealousy.'

'But why should she think I was in any way responsible for her downfall?'

'I blame my godmother for always singing your praises to the unfortunate woman and making comparisons between you both, Martha always the failure. It was no wonder that Martha sought comfort by helping herself too liberally to anything alcoholic that she could swig secretly from a cupboard. It was that offence that made my godmother get rid of her, not anything said by me.'

'I do remember the smell of wine on her breath sometimes before I left the household, but I never suspected I was the cause.'

'She probably had a weakness in that direction already.'

'What employment did Martha get next?'

'I've no idea, although I know Godmother Henrietta did not give her a good reference, because she judged the secret drinking of the household wines to be akin to thieving, which it was of course.' Elizabeth shrugged. 'So perhaps

Martha never found work as a personal maid again.'

'I'm truly sorry to hear that!' Saskia exclaimed, full of compassion. 'Then I can understand how she must be blaming me for her ill fortune. I could see from her clothing that she has been reduced to hard times. Why have you never told me this before?'

'Because I know how soft-hearted you are where other people's troubles are concerned, and I did not want to upset you.'

But the thought of Martha's misfortune stayed with Saskia and she felt responsible for the woman's plight, no matter that she had been the innocent cause. Yet even if they should ever meet again she knew any offer of help would be thrown back at her, for Martha had her pride as well as her hatred.

Twenty-Three

It was springtime again before Grinling found time to measure up at Harting Hall. He brought Elizabeth and the children with him at Robert and Saskia's invitation, for they thought that Elizabeth would enjoy a change of scene. It did delight her and also three-year-old James and two-year-old Alice, who were noisy, happy and exuberant with so much space, indoors and out, in which to play. Baby Charles enjoyed himself too, crawling about on the lawn and then taking his first tottering steps. Saskia yearned anew for children of her own to fill the house with young life and laughter. Twice she had believed herself to be pregnant only to find that it was yet another false hope.

Neither Robert nor Grinling could stay long at the Hall, business compelling them back to London, but their wives remained with the children for another two weeks. Then Saskia also had to return for her consultation afternoon and Elizabeth, who had become secretly homesick for London, having long since taken to city life as the proverbial duck to water, was eager to be with Grinling again. Then Saskia inadvertently delayed the planned early morning departure by a violent attack of sickness. Pale-faced and exhausted, she nevertheless embraced her friend with joy.

'I really think I might be pregnant this time!' she declared, her eyes shining.

Elizabeth, who was equally certain of being in the same condition again herself, rejoiced with her. 'I'm so happy for you, Saskia!'

As the days went by there was no mistaking the fact that Saskia was pregnant. Robert would have fussed over her if she had allowed it, but she declared she was too busy to make an invalid of herself and that Elizabeth was a perfect example of how pregnancy could be taken in one's stride.

'Babies pop out of her like peas from a pod,' Saskia declared, 'and it will be the same for me.'

She lost all interest in having a shop, her thoughts filled with the joyous prospect of starting a family at last, and yet she wanted to continue supplying her products that had benefited so many women in keeping them away from harmful substances. Then something Robert had once said came back to her. A book! Why not publish all she had written down in her red book over the years? She remembered saying that no woman would wish to support a subscription book that gave away the fact that she used beauty aids, but now she believed differently. Her products were in such demand that she was sure that her ladies would pore over every receipt, hassling their personal maids into making this or that cream or fragrance.

Saskia made her announcement at her next consultation afternoon, explaining exactly what the book would contain. 'All my beauty receipts will be in this subscription book. Nothing will be omitted. Some of the very best were given to me by my late mother, who once told me never to reveal my secrets, but I know that now I am drawing my consultations to a close she would agree that the time has come for them to be shared. If any of you here wish to become a subscriber your name will be listed in the book and a copy delivered to you on the day of publication. There is pen and paper on the side table for anyone who wishes to subscribe.'

As she had expected there was an immediate hubbub of voices, but also several women were already out of their chairs to hurry across to the table and see what they would be expected to pay in advance and in every case they set their names down. Others hesitated, for a book on beauty treatments was very different from sub-scribing to a book on flowers or wild birds or embroidery. Some of the women present had to wait and get permission from their husbands, but all wanted the book, for as far as anyone knew there had never before been a volume devoted entirely to such a fascinating subject as beauty. There were plenty of medical aid books, which usually included ways to soften chapped hands, cure rashes and the care of toenails, but nothing to enhance eyes or lips or cast lights into a pretty arrangement of curls.

There were fifteen names on the list when everyone had gone, but at the following consul-tation afternoon twenty extra names were added and finally fifteen more, which was well over the amount needed and would ensure a good quality leather binding. The subscription money flowed in and everything was arranged. Eliza-beth, Mistress Henrietta and even Mistress Gib-bons had sent in their names too.

Saskia had already arranged everything with a publisher, who was pleased enough to go ahead with a subscription book, which was to be bound in green leather. She had written an introduction, which he approved, and he edited her entries, grouping fragrances together, face creams in another section and so forth.

She also had a special section of the table decorations for all occasions from banquets to buffets, ideas of her own which she had set down ever since Vrouw Gibbons had inspired her interest in artistic presentation. The chapter was to be on the theme of the beautiful hostess with a table to match her perfection. She knew her ladies would love it.

The day came when Saskia held her last consultation afternoon, for she was now into her fifth month of pregnancy and wanted to be free of outside obligations. Orders had still come in, but she knew she could entrust Joan to carry them out efficiently. Champagne was served instead of tea and while some departed in a merry mood at the end of the afternoon there were others who deeply regretted the end of these occasions, having enjoyed chatting together as much as listening to whatever Saskia had to say to them.

The publisher had promised prompt delivery and kept his word. On publication day some of the copies were delivered by Joe in his best livery with bunches of green ribbons on his shoulders and several times a presented book was snatched from his hands before he had time to bow. The rest were delivered by well-dressed young men specially hired, all with bunches of green ribbons on their shoulders. The publisher filled his window with copies and as the word spread he sold out and the book immediately went into reprint. It was the first of many reprints.

In spite of her optimism Saskia had a lengthy labour before giving birth to a son, but her happiness in starting her family at last had already wiped out all memory of the pain.

'Next time a daughter,' she declared blissfully

to Robert as he sat on the edge of the bed, unable to take his eyes from his son as he stroked with a careful fingertip the baby's wispy black hair.

The baptism of young Richard Harting took place three weeks later at All Hallows Church by the Tower with Grinling and Elizabeth as two of the godparents. The baby wore a long robe trimmed with some of Nurse Bobbins' exquisite lace and also he wore the little Nordland lace cap that had been made by her skilful old hands far away in Holland. He blinked when Elizabeth as his godmother removed it, for one of the tie-ribbons had stroked his face, and he gazed up wonderingly when she handed him to the vicar at the font. Then he bawled lustily at the chill of the holy water until a soft cloth dried his head again.

As the weeks went by Saskia radiated happiness as she watched her son thrive and grow. With the certainty of most mothers she knew that no child had ever been so alert and advanced in every way. When he was sleeping she often went into the workroom to assist Joan in mixing or stirring or weighing up ingredients, for orders had increased again as personal maids had failed to produce exactly the same effect from the beauty aids as when they had been made by Saskia. She always experienced a sense of peace as she worked and sometimes used it as an escape from tension in the house. Her relationship with Robert was highly passionate and deeply loving, but they both held strong views and their arguments often developed into quarrels that invariably ended in fierce love-making. Recently he had begun to object to the fragrances that wafted from the workroom. Everything came to a climax one evening when he arrived home after a difficult day that had been full of unexpected problems, his nerves on edge, and the perfumes drifting through the house gave him an outlet for his anger.

'Our home has the stench of a bawdy house!' he exclaimed furiously, throwing off his hat and cloak. 'One could expect to find whores draping themselves on the stairs!'

Saskia, who had come into the hall to meet him, frowned sharply in annoyance at his words. 'Today we have been dealing with a lot of orders that have come in for fragrances, but Joan has opened the windows in the workroom and they should soon blow away.'

'It has to stop!' he declared as if she had not spoken and strode ahead of her into the dining room where he seized a decanter and poured himself a large glass of wine. 'We must find a workroom somewhere else. I thought when the book was published that it would mean an end to interference in our lives, but it seems as if it has increased instead of diminishing.'

'Yes, I admit it has done in recent weeks. Well, I have a choice. It is either to stop taking any more orders or open a shop with a workroom on the premises.'

His mood eased and he turned to look at her through narrowed lashes. 'I thought you had given up all idea of a shop.'

'So I had, but I can reconsider.'

He shook his head. 'It would take you away from the house and Richard. He's more important than anything else.'

'I would put Joan in charge and employ some women to do the work. She could manage very well without my constant supervision.'

He studied her again as he handed her his untouched glass of wine and then poured another for himself. 'How long have you been thinking this over?'

'Ever since it became apparent that my book was not the answer to everything as I thought it would be.'

He raised his glass to her. 'You are a victim of your own success, my love. I suggest that for the time being a workroom should be found and deliveries take place from there.'

She nodded. 'Agreed,' she said.

Later in the great Tudor bed he made love to her so passionately that she was sure that she would conceive again from such a night. Her supposition proved to be right. Nine months later she gave birth to twin daughters, Mary and Sarah.

By that time the workshop, which had started at the back of an office, had taken over the whole property. With a shop window installed and a new pale-green decor there was a swinging sign over the door that was a replica of the one that had once hung above the door of the cottage that had burned down. Saskia had put Joan in charge of all the ordering and dispensing, and after a period of guidance let her take over and manage everything in her quick and efficient manner. Joan had also found time to marry a childless widower of similar age to herself, who had become the porter and proved to be invaluable in keeping the property in good repair and was always on hand in any emergency.

It left Saskia with all the time she wanted for her family. Her dream was coming true at last. When the great day came for viewing the carvings that Grinling had finally installed at Harting Hall Saskia and Robert took the three children with them. Grinling met them at the door, a little more portly than when his portrait had been painted, but handsomely bewigged and dressed in perfect taste as always and beaming with pride at what he had to show them.

'I regret that you have had to wait so long,' he said, 'but such a commission as you gave me requires countless man-hours as you know.'

He went ahead to the grand drawing room and threw the double doors wide. Saskia caught her breath at the sheer beauty of his decorative carving that met her gaze. His garlands, far more luxuriant than any she had ever seen before, were looped along the wainscoting, the paleness of the lime wood that he had used making a striking contrast to the dark oak. All his love of nature and music had been poured into the flowers and foliage, the fruit and the berries, the tightly closed pea pods and the musical instruments that peeped out here and there. There were also scrolls of music, every note authentically carved, and any musician could have taken up an instrument and played from any one of them. Perhaps most impressive of all was the great overmantel surround that encompassed the twin portraits of her and Robert in the gilded frames, enhancing them dramatically. Then she spotted something else in the carvings.

'Dutch tulips!' she exclaimed. 'You have given us some tulips from home!'

Robert glanced swiftly at her, thinking that she should have remarked on the roses, for her home was in England now, but he said nothing. He knew that she would always cherish memories of her homeland and he had no wish to deprive her of them.

'What could be better,' Grinling said jovially, 'than to carve tulips for these two lovers who first met under Dutch skies!'

Now Saskia turned her gaze on Robert, meeting his eyes as they both remembered her wish that their likenesses should always been known as *The Lovers*. She thought again that the artist had captured their feelings exactly and their love for each other would for ever show in their eyes.

Grinling left after taking some refreshment with them and they saw him off in the fine new coach that he rode about in now. Elizabeth had her own carriage housed at *La Belle Sauvage* and that was almost as splendid. They were enjoying their prosperity, their marriage and their increasing number of children, for Elizabeth had given birth to a fourth son, named Harry, not long before Saskia had given birth to Baby Richard.

Saskia rejoiced for her two friends, for Grinling worked hard for long hours and deserved all the good fortune that came his way. He had taken on a second assistant and could have had more, but he was so meticulous in his work that he would only consider employing carvers of exceptional talent and they were hard to find. His only extra employee was a lad that put together various pieces of wood for when a three-dimensional effect was required in a finished carving. As this included much of the work that Grinling and his assistants did the lad was kept busy most of the time.

Now as Saskia went back into the grand drawing room, which she already thought of as the Grinling Gibbons room, she stood alone to gaze around again at its new magnificence. She understood from what Grinling had explained to her that time would darken the lime wood as the years went by until it was likely to become almost as dark as the oak itself in centuries to come, but she was certain that would only give another dimension to Grinling's work and further enhance the beauty of it.

Twenty-Four

Elizabeth, knowing for certain that she was not pregnant at the present time, had decided the day had finally dawned for Grinling to face the upheaval of moving into a home more suitable for family life. She knew he was busier than ever, which had caused him to employ another young carver for the basic work. He also had in hand carvings for Windsor Castle where the King was having some rebuilding done. It was his most prestigious commission to date. As he took a sip of wine while dining at home with Elizabeth, the children all tucked up in bed, he had no idea that his wife was about to startle him out of his comfortable mood and tasty dinner.

'Grinling,' she began, gathering herself for what she had to say. 'There are plenty of fine new houses built now on many desirable sites here in London and I think we should purchase one.'

'All in good time, my dear,' he answered mildly. It was not a subject he cared to discuss, being still perfectly content with their present abode.

'A craftsman of your standing in society should have a better address,' Elizabeth said firmly, having privately rehearsed all the angles from which to attack him.

'There is nothing wrong with the one that we have,' he replied, tucking into his plate of roast beef and vegetables. 'This is a highly respected inn and everyone knows to find me here.'

'But as I have said before, we need a garden where the children can safely play.'

'There's the park only a short walk away.' It was an argument that had taken place any number of times before.

'No, Grinling! That is not good enough!'

The unusually sharp tone of her voice caused him to look at her in surprise, halting his fork halfway to his mouth. 'Is it not?'

'Remember how we have had to rush out into the courtyard to save one child or another from getting under the horses' hooves in the stables or running too near rolling coach wheels.'

'That has not happened very often and every time we were near enough to avoid any danger,' he commented, although the force of her words had struck home. His children were very precious to him.

'The day could come when we are all too late to prevent a tragedy and we cannot risk that happening!' she continued heatedly. 'I want a house that I can make a home and where our children are safe! I have been patient long enough!'

She had brought the subject up at regular intervals ever since she had first suggested a move, but now he could tell by her whole attitude that they had reached the point of no return. He was too busy and had too much on his mind to be harassed day after day, which he could foresee happening with Elizabeth rebelling at last. She had an iron will beneath her gentle exterior, although it rarely showed, for she loved best to keep all happy and peaceful around her. Now she would keep a vice-like grip on the subject and there would be no letting go until she had her own way. He had known for a long time that he would have to make the decision to change residences sooner or later and now clearly the time had come.

'Very well. I agree,' he said calmly. 'We can consider a move from here.' Then he saw the whole of her dearly loved face lighting up for him and he smiled indulgently. 'You have waited a long time for us to have a home of our own, my dear, and, as you say, most important of all, we

334

cannot risk our little ones getting into danger.'

'Yes, indeed!' she replied ecstatically.

He frowned warningly. 'But I shall retain my workshop here,' he stated in case she expected him to uproot himself too.

'Yes, of course,' she agreed willingly. 'In any case I would not want wood shavings following you into a new home as they do here.'

His frown did not lift. 'You realize that I have no time to go looking for a house with you?'

'No matter. Saskia will accompany me as she did once before.'

He gave a nod. 'Remember that there are still some poorly built structures on the market that have been thrown together in the still high need for housing. So when you have found the house of your dreams I want you to ask Robert to survey it for any structural faults. Too many rogue builders are using defective materials with disastrous results. So if he approves the property I'll sign the contract.'

'You darling man!' Elizabeth sprang up from her seat and flew round the table to kiss him heartily on the cheek, hugging him about the neck until he eased her arms away.

'Don't choke me, my dear. I have not finished my good dinner yet.'

She returned to her chair, too excited to eat any more, already thinking about the decor she had long dreamed of having in a real home.

Saskia always enjoyed Elizabeth's company and was as willing as before to help her find a new residence, for she was interested in viewing the various properties, although she had no wish to move from her and Robert's home.

Naturally Elizabeth knew exactly what she wanted in the house for which she had waited so long, but it meant that it was not an easy task to find one that fulfilled all her requirements. It had to be a house where her four children could have sunny rooms with adjoining accommodation for the nursemaid. The kitchen had to be large and the servants' quarters in the attic of reasonable size, for Elizabeth believed in giving consideration to those who worked for her. Lucy had left to be married, but Elizabeth's new personal maid was Isabelle, a widowed Frenchwoman in her forties with a charming manner and an enthusiastic regard for Saskia's products. Elizabeth did not want to lose her and so a pleasant room for her was also on the agenda as well as quarters of equal standard for the housekeeper. Elizabeth was particularly looking forward to having her first housekeeper, for previously she had managed everything herself and often matters had become quite chaotic.

There was one asset in which she was not interested and which Saskia would have considered first of all. Elizabeth did not want a quiet street or square on which to live for the rest of her days, because she still loved being at the hub of London life as much as when Grinling first took her to live at the inn. The stench of the streets did not trouble her, for she always carried a pomander or a posy of scented flowers to keep unpleasant odours at bay.

She liked to hear the songs of the women selling lavender, ripe cherries or whatever else was in season, backed by the shouts of the pedlars and the water-sellers, the muffin men with trays on their heads and the whistling of tradesmen's lads delivering goods. Some of the milkmaids kept up a musical chant as they ladled out milk into people's jugs. Then there were the stirring sounds of pipes and drums whenever a troop of soldiers marched to or from Whitehall Palace as well as the music of wandering minstrels. Almost always there was the colourful bellowing of coachmen when their way was blocked, which combined with everything else to bring all life pulsating outside her windows.

'Oh, no,' she said determinedly to Saskia. 'A quiet tree-lined avenue amid grand mansions is not for me.'

After three months and just when Elizabeth realized that she was pregnant again the house she wanted was finally located in Bow Street, Covent Garden. Here on both sides of the bow-shaped street there were plenty of grand mansions as well as other houses not so fine and some that had seen better days a hundred years before. In days gone by it had been notorious as the haunt of criminals, but that had changed long since. These days a prestigious number of intellectuals, including some members of the nobility, resided now in Bow Street side by side with clergy, three doctors, a lawyer, two actresses and a flamboyant actor, who always dressed in purple, these three performing regularly at nearby Drury Lane Theatre. There was a magistrates' court, several workshops, a library and the popular Wills coffee house on the corner with Russell Street where Saskia had once drunk coffee with Grinling and Robert. Altogether Bow Street housed a colourful cross-section of society, which made it all the more interesting to Elizabeth.

The house that had captured her heart was newly built on a site where previously an ancient coach-house had stood in ruins. It had a fine facade and three steps up from the street to the imposing entrance, which had a pillared porch. To the rear was what would become an enclosed garden with trees, but which presently had the appearance of a ploughed field. Yet when laid out with lawns and flower beds it would be a beautiful place in which to watch the children at play. Then Elizabeth was exasperated to hear from Saskia that Robert was out of London on a project and was not expected back for another month.

'I cannot wait that long for him to survey the house!' she exclaimed to Saskia, throwing up her hands in dismay ... 'Other people will be after such a gem!'

'Robert is a full day's journey away,' Saskia answered, 'but I'll write and ask him if he can spare a day to come home and check on the property for you.'

'Would you? I should be so grateful!'

Robert replied at once, willing to come, but it could not be until the following week. That night Elizabeth was unable to sleep, tormented by the fear of losing the house that she had fallen in love with on sight. She could not and would not risk losing it to anyone else! It had been such a long and tedious search to find it.

In the morning, without saying a word to anyone, she went to see the builder, a sly-eyed fellow with an enormous girth, named Alfred Smith. He had received her in his office, and his expressionless face did not change as she offered the sum he wanted for the property without quibbling over the price, which any other would-be purchaser would have done.

'I must have your husband's signature on the contract, mistress,' he said, for he knew that even if this woman had money of her own she was under her husband's jurisdiction. No woman had a legal right to sign anything after she had written her name on a marriage certificate. He also knew an eager buyer when he saw one and added a much-used lie to spur her desperation to purchase. 'I feel obliged to tell you that I have two more prospective buyers coming to view the property later today.'

'But Master Gibbons is too busy to come here to your office!' she exclaimed frantically. 'Take the contract to him now at his workshop at *La Belle Sauvage*. I'm going back there now and will alert him to expect you.'

He stood to bow her out of his office. 'I will be there at noon,' he promised.

Grinling was instructing his youngest apprentice in the use of a finely bladed tool and gave a smiling, but somewhat abstracted nod, when she told him that the builder was coming with the contract for his signature.

'I'll be here,' he said.

She kept watch and saw the builder arrive.

When he had departed she went down to the workshop full of trepidation. There was the possibility that a casual comment by the builder would have given away that there had been no inspection by Robert or anyone else, which would have resulted in Grinling's refusal to sign the contract. But she need not have been fearful, for to her intense relief Grinling greeted her with a smile.

'I managed to get a better price for the house than was originally quoted to you, my dear. Now the house of your choice is ours.'

She burst into tears, overcome by emotion, a sense of guilt mingling with intense relief. He put down his chisel to leave his work and put his arms around her. 'This is no time for tears,' he said with a little laugh to cheer her. 'You can go upstairs now and start planning everything for the move to Bow Street.'

'Yes, I can.' She began drying her eyes, comforting herself in the knowledge that when Robert eventually saw the house he would congratulate her on the purchase. Then she could confess to Grinling and he would forgive her little deception.

It was usual for a newly built house to stand empty for three to six months in order to allow the plaster and all else to dry out completely, which to Elizabeth seemed the longest time that she had ever known. Fortunately she was having no trouble with her pregnancy and was looking forward to bearing her seventh child in her new home.

She had confided her little sin of deceiving

Grinling to Saskia and asked her to beg Robert not to give her away. Fortunately Grinling never questioned him on the matter and when he inspected the property he kept his opinion to himself. He and Saskia had called in not just for him to view the house that day, but also for Saskia to take a new toy for one of the Gibbons children, who was still in bed with a chesty cough. As she disappeared upstairs, calling to the child as she went, Elizabeth, rotund in her pregnancy, took Robert into the grand drawing room.

'Look at my flowers,' she said, indicating the carved bowl of lime wood blossoms that she had placed on the sill of a window facing the street. 'Here they sway and dip with the vibration from every passing wagon and loaded stagecoach just as if they were newly picked from the garden. That did not happen where we lived before, because we were too high up in our apartment at the inn. It makes the blooms more realistic than ever. What a genius I have for a husband!'

'Yes, his skills are beyond comparison,' Robert agreed, but he did not care for the amount of vibration that the house was experiencing. He glanced up at the ornately plastered ceiling. 'You must get the builder back to see to that crack, Elizabeth.'

She followed his gaze. 'I did send for him, but somebody else had taken over his office and nobody knew where he had gone. But Grinling has a plasterer coming tomorrow to put it right.'

'Who surveyed this property for you?' he asked-ed.

'Nobody.' She blushed scarlet at having to make a confession. 'But Grinling thinks you did. It was a little – er – misunderstanding, but I was desperate to get this house.'

He raised an eyebrow at her in mock reproof. 'Should you like me to look around now?'

'Oh, yes, because I'm sure you'll find no fault in it.'

He spent about an hour checking on various things. He thought the finishing off was extremely bad in some places, there being every indication of work having been rushed, and up in the attic the rafters were not what he would have selected, but were secure enough. He also found some slight evidence of subsidence on the ground floor, but the property seemed to have settled.

'Well?' Elizabeth asked, putting aside some sewing as he returned to her.

'I'll be blunt, Elizabeth. The house has its faults, although I have no quarrel with its design, the rooms being well proportioned with high ceilings, but I would not have advised the purchase.'

'Don't ever tell Grinling that!' she implored. 'Choosing this house was the only decision of importance that I have ever made in my life – apart from accepting Grinling's marriage proposal – and I do not want him to think me foolish and deceitful.'

Tears welled up in her eyes and she fumbled in her pocket for a handkerchief. Robert smiled and patted her arm.

'He would never think that. Just make sure that

any repairs needed are carried out promptly.'

She nodded, cheering up, and before he left she showed him a marble bust of Grinling, which had just been finished by a talented sculptor and had been given pride of place in the library. It was a striking likeness, the fashionable size of the large, intricately carved wig was matched in abundance by the billowing of lace at the throat. Robert thought that any stranger to whom Grinling was unknown would see at once that this was indeed a man who knew his own importance to the world and was well pleased with it.

Elizabeth gave birth to another daughter in her new bedchamber and, as was usual, she suffered no ill effects. Her godmother had died earlier in the year and so it seemed right that the new baby should be baptized Henrietta in her memory. Once again the little family procession entered Aldgate Church for the ceremony, although Grinling's parents were now missing, he having lost them both through a fever. Saskia carried the new member of the family and Robert was godfather for the second time.

He and Saskia were also expecting another child, but a few weeks after the christening she miscarried and, according to the doctor, she was unlikely to conceive again. She was deeply distressed, having hoped so much to increase her little family, but Robert consoled her by reminding her how fortunate they were to have three healthy children, all of whom had already battled through measles and whooping cough, which so often proved fatal to the young.

Elizabeth had been through similar crises with her young ones and blamed her premature streaks of grey hair on countless sleepless nights at nursery bedsides, for she was like Saskia in never relying on a nursemaid at anxious times. Saskia concocted a special dye that exactly matched Elizabeth's golden tresses. It could be combed through to disguise the loss of colour completely and had the effect of restoring lost highlights.

'Everything you produce always makes me feel beautiful,' Elizabeth declared, looking at her reflection and touching a curl into place, 'and it is the same for all your ladies. I believe,' she added knowingly, lowering her handglass to gaze in amusement at her friend, 'that is the real secret of your success.'

Saskia gave a delighted little laugh. 'It's true that beauty comes from within, so I think you have found me out at last, my dear friend. For a woman to believe she is beautiful, whether she thinks the source to be from a pot of facial cream or a special lotion, it gives her self-confidence and a glow to her eyes. Therefore she is beautiful.'

Elizabeth nodded in admiration. 'I'm sure that is true. I've seen it happen in my own looking-glass.'

Saskia thought as she had done many times before that Elizabeth had a loveliness that had nothing to do with the symmetry of features.

Twenty-Five

It was to be an evening without any social engagements and after Saskia had seen the children tucked up in bed she went downstairs again to have a quiet hour or two alone with Robert after what had been a busy day.

In the drawing room he was rereading a letter that he had received that morning. Then, when Saskia had taken up some embroidery and was settled opposite him by the fire, he flicked the letter in his hand, his expression serious.

'My lawyer has written about the arrest of a much wanted arsonist, named Walter Thornberry.'

She raised her eyebrows enquiringly. 'That name means nothing to me.'

'Nor did it to me until I read the name of the woman whom Thornberry declares paid him to burn down a cottage out in the country, which is only one of many charges against him. She has been arrested as the instigator of this particular crime with intent to murder. They are both incarcerated at Newgate prison awaiting their trial.'

Saskia stiffened in her chair. 'Not Martha!'

He nodded. 'She has denied the charge, but there is little chance of her being believed,

345

because there is strong evidence against her.'

Saskia bowed her head, covering her face with her hands. 'I never thought she had anything to do with the fire,' she said in a distressed whisper.

'It was no fault of yours.'

She lowered her hands again and looked at him as she shook her head. 'How can I ever be sure of that?'

'You must never think otherwise.'

She looked at him fearfully. 'If she and the man are found guilty what will happen to them?'

'Arson is a serious charge. If guilty of that alone, even without intention to murder, the punishment would be the gallows.'

'Oh, no!' She turned ashen, her eyes stark, and she put aside her needlework.

'I'm sorry that I have to tell you all this, but I have still more bad news to impart. As the occupant of the cottage, who could have perished in the flames, you will be required to give evidence at the trial.'

She sprang to her feet. 'No! I did not see or hear anything amiss until I woke to find the place alight.'

'But you heard a sound outside. Thornberry said he passed the time drinking gin while he waited in the darkness for your candle to be extinguished. He admitted that the bottle smashed when he tossed it aside and he saw you come to the window and look out to see what it was that you had heard.'

'But why should he betray Martha in such a way when so much time has elapsed since the fire?'

'A while ago he was short of money and tried to blackmail her, but when she refused to pay up he took his revenge by implicating her when his crimes of arson caught up with him.'

She sank down into her chair again. 'How soon is the trial?' she asked tonelessly.

'It is at the end of the month.'

When the day of the court proceedings arrived Robert accompanied Saskia. At the courthouse steps he bought from the flower-sellers two scented posies, one for her and another for himself, which would help to keep the stench of the prisoners at bay. The court was crowded, but seats for the witnesses had been allotted in a side room and she sat next to Ted Robinson, who had been summoned there through having rushed to the scene of the fire, and was accompanied by George as he had been there too. She asked after Kate and promised to visit again soon, for she tried to go as often as she could, their kindness to her never forgotten.

In the courtroom Robert stood with everybody else when the judge in his scarlet robes and grey periwig appeared and took his seat in his high-backed chair, the lawyers in their equally large periwigs bowing respectfully to him with a rustle of their black robes. The judge had his own posy, larger than those being sold outside, which he placed within easy reach. He was to put it to his nose frequently as he judged first three cases of robbery with violence, the prisoners in chains. All three were condemned to the hangman's noose, the judge putting on the black cap as he pronounced their sentence. One of the men wept.

Then Martha and Walter were brought into the dock to be judged together for the cottage crime, both in chains. The charge against them was read out that they did conspire to burn down the cottage with the aim of murdering the sole occupant.

'No! No!' Martha burst out in a choked voice.

The judge glared fiercely at her. 'Remain silent, prisoner in the dock!' he thundered. He considered it to be an open and shut case, wanting no unnecessary time wasted on a pair of arsonists, who had plotted such a foul crime. The fellow had already confessed, but by trying to lay all the blame on the woman he was hoping to escape the rope by appearing to cooperate with the Law. But the woman had mettle in her and was showing no remorse for her crime. Yet there was a terrible fear of the death sentence in her. He knew the signs.

The first witness was Martha's employer at the time of the fire, for Henrietta had dismissed her before that night. The woman's name was Mistress Penn and she was a flamboyant woman, extravagantly begowned and bejewelled, who was clearly of the *nouveau riche*. Robert, remembering all that Saskia had told him, guessed that the woman was not at all the sort of employer whom Martha would have chosen to serve. The woman's resentment at having to come to court was soon very clear. It was also apparent that she had never liked Martha, who had probably looked haughtily down on her for having more money than breeding, and her replies to the lawyer were tinged with malice.

'Yes, she was honest as far as I know, although a pair of my ear-drops went missing for a week. I always found her sullen and disagreeable. Why I kept her on for as long as I did is beyond me.'

'Keep to the point, madam!' the lawyer ordered sternly. 'Did you at any time have any reason to suspect that Martha had carried out the crime of which she and her fellow prisoner have been accused?'

'No, of course I didn't!' the woman snapped. 'But I believe her capable of it. She has a nasty temper!'

The next witness to be called was Ted Robinson, who nervously twisted his hat round and round by its brim in his gnarled hands. He described how he and his two sons had been searching for some errant sheep with the help of some neighbours when they had spotted the flicker of flames in the direction of the cottage and rushed to help. George then went into the witness box after his father, giving more or less the same account. The following witness was Mistress Penn's housekeeper, who identified Walter Thornberry as the man who had called more than once on Martha at the house.

Then Saskia's name was called. She left her seat in the waiting area and entered the courtroom. There she went up the steps into the witness box to take the Bible into her hand and swear the oath. Then she looked across at Martha, who avoided her eyes, straightening her

349

spine and staring ahead defiantly. Yet Saskia was distressed to see the state of the woman who had always been so neat and clean in her appearance. She was in prison-soiled clothes, her hair straggling for want of a comb, but somehow in the squalor of Newgate prison she had managed to wash her cap, making it white enough to almost shine, although it was creased through lack of an iron. The prosecuting lawyer addressed Saskia with respect.

'You were the sole occupant of the cottage, Mistress Harting?' he began.

'Yes. Everybody in the district knew I lived there alone.'

'What was your acquaintanceship with the woman prisoner?'

'We had both been employed as personal maids to different ladies in the same household.'

'But you were not on good terms?'

'People who work together do not always like each other, but we kept to our own spheres and never once was there quarrelling between us.'

The questioning continued. She was asked what she had sold at the cottage and she had to describe the sound she had heard on the night of the fire. Then she was asked why she thought the two prisoners had plotted her murder.

'I do not believe that Martha did!' Saskia declared vehemently, her voice ringing with her conviction. 'Nothing could ever convince me that she intended my death!'

The prosecuting lawyer raised an eyebrow in an actor's show of surprise. 'That is a strange reply, madam. Both the accused knew you were on your own with no help within half a mile. It was sheer chance that the farmer and his sons caught sight of the flames as they searched for some lost sheep. Your cottage was doomed from the moment a burning torch was hurled into the thatch.'

'Martha was not present to see what happened and most surely believed that the smoke would awaken me. It was my shop that she wanted to destroy, knowing what a setback it would be for me, but that is all. I believe that implicitly! May I be allowed to plea for leniency in her case?'

There was no reply to her urgently expressed request and she was told that she could step down from the witness box. She was trembling from the tension of her interrogation as she seated herself beside Robert, who took her hand into both of his. Then the judge was addressing Martha.

'You are fortunate that a reliable witness has spoken so strongly in your defence, seeming to believe that you are not beyond redemption or else you would have been hanged for your crime. I commute the sentence to transportation for life to the American colonies.'

Saskia released a pent-up sigh of intense relief, unaware that she had been holding her breath in suspense and not caring that Martha did not glance in her direction as she was led away down into the cells.

Walter Thornberry was less fortunate. As he had already confessed to the crime the judge took up the black cap and placed it on his periwigged head. Then in a sonorous tone he sentenced the prisoner to be hanged.

'What will it be like for Martha in the colonies?' Saskia asked Robert as they rode home after having a short conversation with Ted before they departed.

'With her skills as a lady's maid she will probably be snapped up by a governor's wife,' he replied. 'She might even get a husband eventually. Women are in short supply.'

Privately he did not believe that the woman had not intended Saskia's demise. There had been cruelty as well as bitterness in the set of her mouth, but he would never express his doubts, wanting his wife to have peace of mind.

Twenty-Six

It was as if a shadow had fallen over the land when Charles II died after a short illness. His nickname of the 'Merry Monarch' had suited him so well, for he had enjoyed life to the full. His brother, James, succeeded him, but clashed with both Parliament and the established Church, his arrogance causing allegiance to him to fall away. The result was a bloodless invasion by William of Orange, for England's army and navy were quick to give him support and James fled the country. Saskia was overjoyed that a Dutchman and his wife, Mary, daughter of the exiled king, were to become joint monarchs to rule together the land that now meant as much to her as her homeland.

'A Dutch king on the Throne!' she exclaimed joyfully.

'And his English queen,' Robert pointed out, amused by her excitement.

Having long since become a respected figure on the London scene Robert received an invitation for Saskia and himself to be present at Whitehall Palace when the oaths of allegiance were to be made to the royal couple. Saskia had a new gown for the occasion in sea-green silk with a pearl-studded ivory underskirt, pearls entwined in her hair.

There were many splendidly dressed people in the great hall when they arrived and they chatted with those whom they knew. Then a fanfare of trumpets announced the arrival of the royal couple.

It was an occasion that Saskia was never to forget. Rubens' beautifully painted ceiling, spread widely overhead, adding to the splendour of the scene as everyone present bowed or curtsied at the diamond-sparkling entrance of the new king and queen in their crowns. It was said that Mary loathed her husband and it was a known fact that she had wept all through the marriage service some years before, but her smile and her dignity matched his impressive presence as they went up the carpeted steps of the dais to sit side by side on thrones of equal height under a canopy of crimson velvet. Saskia was in a trance of happiness.

Saskia had never been back to Holland, for those closest to her had gone, Nurse Bobbins long since and her foster mother struck down a few years later by a sudden illness. Yet she cherished the happy memories of her early years there and was sure that one day she would visit her beloved homeland again.

Her family was growing up. Richard was fourteen, which was the age for intelligent scholars to become students at Oxford University and he was doing well there. The twins would both have been six, but tragically Sarah had died of the sweating sickness in spite of nursing by day and night. Saskia had been devastated, becoming ill herself in her grief, and even after her recovery there was an ache in her heart that could never be erased. Then, as if fate had taken pity on her, she found she was pregnant again.

Elizabeth, now mother to eight children and expecting a ninth, was delighted with the news of her friend's good fortune. Her pride in her own offspring was matched only by her pride in Grinling's successful career. Not only were his wonderful carvings now at Windsor Castle, but also in Hampton Court palace and many great houses, the demand for his work unceasing. He was also working on the carvings for the choir stalls in St Paul's, incorporating the faces of his youngest children. The cathedral itself was beginning to take shape gloriously in a way the clergy had not anticipated but were trying to come to terms with now that it was too late for any change.

Recently Grinling had carved a cover for the

stone font in the Church of All Hallows by the Tower where the Harting children had been christened. It was a dainty mound of flowers and delicate foliage with cherubs reaching up to the dove that seemed to have just alighted at the top of it. His own offspring had been fascinated by it as the cherubs here, as in the St Paul's choir stall carvings, had the likenesses of their younger siblings. It always gave him immense pleasure to see their young faces emerge from under his chisel.

When some premises had become vacant in Bow Street he had transferred his workshop there from *La Belle Sauvage*. It was three times the size of his previous workshop and he was well pleased with it, quite apart from being closer to his home. There he engaged in a new venture by accepting commissions to sculpt marble statues and busts of well-known people, even though wood would always remain his favourite medium.

As Elizabeth had foreseen he did at times trail wood shavings home with him and now there was often marble dust clinging to his clothes from his sculpting too, even though he wore a leather apron in the workshop. Elizabeth was more tolerant now than in the past, for the housekeeper always saw that the trail of his homecoming was swept up immediately.

Royal recognition had come to him when he had been commissioned by the late king to carve what had become known as the Cosimo panel, which was free standing, much as an individual painting was often displayed on an easel-like frame. It had been sent as a gift from King Charles to Cosimo III de' Medici, the Grand Duke of Tuscany, and was extraordinarily magnificent, full of symbolic tributes to the importance of the giver and the receiver. It had taken its rightful place among the glories of Florence.

Soon afterwards Charles II had awarded Grinling a pension of one hundred pounds a year, which was a generous sum, in acknowledgement of his splendid restoration of some valuable old carvings at Windsor Castle. Another important milestone in Grinling's life had been the carving of the reredos for Wren at the newly rebuilt St James' Church in Piccadilly.

Saskia gave birth to another daughter, who was named Prudence. She was a frail little thing, but received such loving care that by the time she was two she had caught up with stronger children of her own age. Mary and Prudence had plenty of playmates at the Gibbons' house. She was always excited to be there with them, for Elizabeth had an 'open house' for children, often playing with them as if she were a child herself until she grew tired and left a nursemaid in charge. Frequent pregnancies had finally taken their toll on her, although the prospect of another new baby always filled her with joy.

There was violent weather one morning when Saskia was ready to take Mary and Prudence to play at the Gibbons' house. During the night there had been wind of almost hurricane force accompanied by a tremendous downfall of rain, which had slashed ceaselessly at the windows.

Robert and the children had slept undisturbed throughout the night, but Saskia had found it impossible to sleep and, when looking out of the nursery window, had seen one of the swaying trees, uprooted by the wind, go crashing down across the lawn.

Now that morning had come Robert had inspected the tree and given orders for the gardeners to saw it up as soon as possible. He also toured the attic, but could not find a leak anywhere. Satisfied, he then went off to his office in his coach, the rain dancing into fountains on its roof.

'It is raining so hard that I think it would be best to stay at home today,' Saskia said to her daughters, but both Mary and Prudence looked so crestfallen that later she relented when the rain seemed to ease, even though the wind did not appear to have lessened.

It whipped their cloaks about them as they darted into the waiting coach. Everywhere people were keeping close to walls, not only for shelter under the overhanging upper stories of houses, but because tiles were flying from roofs and tufts of thatch were whirling about in the air. The central gutters of the streets flowed like rivers, flooding areas where rubbish blocked escape, and the coach wheels threw up fans of spray all the way.

There was a rumble of thunder and a distant flash of lightning as Elizabeth welcomed them with open arms as she always did, and her younger children came running to greet the new arrivals. When all of the young ones had darted upstairs to the nursery playroom Elizabeth drew Saskia into the drawing room.

'What a night!' she exclaimed. 'I was so frightened. To me the whole house seemed to sway with the wind's buffeting, but Grinling just slept through it all.'

'So did Robert,' Saskia replied with a smile.

'We lost some tiles from the roof. I heard them go crashing down in the night and the rain is leaking through into buckets that have been placed in the attic. But no repairs can be done today. A man could be blown away with the tiles in this wind!'

'Yes, indeed,' Saskia agreed.

'We need more than a cup of tea this morning,' Elizabeth declared, letting her hands rise and fall expressively. 'We shall have some sherry-wine.'

A decanter had been placed ready on a side table with two glasses and Elizabeth went across to it. It was so unusual for Elizabeth to touch alcohol, for mostly she only had a little wine when dining, that Saskia realized the extent of how upset her friend had been by the tempest of the night. Then as the sherry-wine was poured into the two glasses Saskia saw how her friend's hands were shaking.

'The worst of the weather is over now, Elizabeth,' she said reassuringly. 'This wind will soon drop.' Then when a glass had been handed to her she raised it. 'Let's drink to sunny days ahead.'

'Oh, yes!' Elizabeth declared, sitting down on the yellow silk-upholstered sofa. 'After last night and today summer cannot come soon

358

enough for me!'

It was at that moment that a tremendous explosion of sound shook the whole house. Elizabeth screamed in alarm. Saskia's immediate thought was that lightning had struck the roof, but a second later she saw to her horror that an enormous crack had appeared in the wall opposite her. She sprang to her feet, Elizabeth doing the same and screaming again when she saw what happened.

'We must all get out of this house! Now!' Saskia cried, giving Elizabeth a push as a shower of plaster descended from the ceiling and cracks flew across it. 'I'll fetch the children!'

Then she was ahead of Elizabeth, who was cumbersome in her pregnancy, and made for the stairs. The panic-stricken servants were already running outside, not stopping to help. Upstairs Saskia was met by the terrified children and the ashen-faced nursemaid, who had appeared at a run with a toddler in her arms.

'Downstairs and outside!' Saskia ordered brusquely. 'At once, children! Hurry!'

Elizabeth had come to the foot of the flight and was on her way up to hasten their descent, calling reassuringly to them. Then Mary realized that one of the children was missing and jerked at the nursemaid's sleeve when she would have rushed past. 'Where's Alan?'

The young woman answered frantically over her shoulder as she hurried on down the stairs. 'I thought he was here! He must still be playing with his wooden farm animals!'

The children were being shepherded out of the

house by some people that had rushed to the rescue. Elizabeth had immediately missed her four-year-old son and, shrieking hysterically, she would have rushed up the stairs to help in the search.

'Get outside!' Saskia ordered fiercely. 'I'm fetching him!'

Alan was a child who was content with his own company and often wandered off from the other children. She found him asleep on the floor in the midst of his farm animals. He opened his eyes wide in surprise as she snatched him up in her arms, but then he smiled, patting her cheek as he recognized her. As she ran with him, making for the stairs, plaster was falling everywhere. A great piece had landed across the flight near the bottom stair, blocking the way, and two of the menservants, who had returned at Elizabeth's screaming plea, attempted to pull it aside with all their strength, intent on making a space to go past. As soon as Saskia was within range she threw Alan into his mother's arms. Then as Elizabeth ran with him out of the house she met Grinling, who had come rushing to the scene, white-faced with shock. Then Saskia saw as if in slow motion a whole wall descending between her and liberty, shutting out the light. Her last thought was one of thankfulness that all the children were safe. Then a brick struck her across the head and blackness melted her far away.

For three days and nights the search went on to find her in the rubble. Robert, haggard with grief and loss of sleep, refused to rest, continuing by

360

lamplight all through the long nights. Grinling searched constantly with him, only taking a break when Robert pushed him away. There were plenty of volunteers assisting, but still Saskia's body could not be found. Now and again Elizabeth came to watch, tears running down her face. Grinling had moved her and the family, including Mary and Prudence for the time being, into temporary accommodation in a furnished house nearby.

It was dawn on the fourth day when Robert, heaving aside a heavy piece of brickwork, saw a gleam of bronze in the dust. It was a strand of Saskia's hair! Grinling, who had come early to help again, saw how frantically Robert had begun hurling rubble aside.

'She's here!' he shouted as Grinling joined him in his task.

It took time to extract her from the ruins, for she had been wedged under part of the collapsed staircase, which had also saved her from being crushed. As she was lifted free there was a spontaneous cheer from volunteers and spectators alike, but when there appeared to be no life left in her a hush fell and several men removed their hats. But Robert had felt a faint pulse in her neck and in a choked voice he gasped, 'She is alive!'

Now cheering did break out as Robert carried her across the street to Grinling's new accommodation where she was laid on a bed. One of the doctors, who also lived on Bow Street, had already arrived to attend her. Both her legs were broken and her face and whole body purple with bruises, but he was most concerned for her dehydration, wanting spoonfuls of water to be given to her constantly.

'I trust that she will pull through,' he said gravely to Robert after her limbs had been set in splints and he was about to depart. 'We have a battle to save her on our hands. I shall call back later.'

Saskia remained unconscious for two more days. Then she opened her eyes just as Grinling, visiting the sickroom, was leaning towards her. A most loving expression suffused her emaciated face as she focused on him.

'My dear Grinling,' she whispered before closing her eyes again.

He withdrew instantly, letting Robert take his place, but the swift look they exchanged shared the knowledge each had never mentioned to the other. It was that Saskia had never given quite all her love to the one who had married her. Robert felt no jealousy, for a youthful dream had no substance and what he shared with Saskia had roots that would be lifelong.

Over twenty years had gone by since the Gibbons' house had collapsed. It was one of several that went down that night, some with fatal casualties, including a passer-by who had been struck down by flying rubble from the Gibbons' house. But Grinling and Elizabeth never moved from Bow Street, he buying a well-built house on the opposite side of the street, for he liked having his workshop close at hand. Now Robert, celebrating his retirement, was taking Saskia on a grand tour of all she had long wanted to see, their family grown and well established, all married with children.

Saskia had been so happy that they had gone first to France, giving her the chance to view Paris, the city that was her mother's birthplace. From there they had gone to Holland where they had visited Grinling's brother, Dinely, and his wife, who were living in his late parents' home. Saskia had found it strange to be in the old house again and her gaze had lingered on the staircase from which she had first seen Robert staring up at her with his fierce, demanding gaze.

'It was at that moment I knew I had found the woman I wanted for my wife,' he had told her once on a wedding anniversary. 'I could not take my eyes from you.'

She remembered so well. 'You were staking your claim to me, although I was too naive to realize it at the time.'

'That is true,' he had replied with a smile.

From Holland they travelled on to Milan, Rome and Pisa, but lingered for three months in Florence where they had taken an apartment. Now at last they were in Venice and had gone first to see Tintoretto's great masterpiece of the Crucifixion in the Scoular Grande di San Rocco that had long ago inspired Grinling's splendid carving. She could imagine how he had stood before it, gazing and gazing as she and Robert had done.

There were other wonderful places to visit, but they had made a return visit to view the master-piece one afternoon before taking a gondola back to the palace on the Grand Canal where

363

they were staying at the invitation of one of Robert's retired clients and his wife. A letter from England was waiting for Robert and he broke the seal to open and read it. Immediately his face became grave. Saskia, who had removed her hat, tossed it aside in alarm and darted to him, her first thought for their children.

'What has happened?'

He lowered the letter and looked at her with great sadness. 'This letter has been sent by a special messenger to tell us that Grinling died four weeks ago.'

She threw herself into his arms and he held her in their shared grief. Elizabeth had borne him twelve children, but two years ago she had died and the zest had gone from his life. In that same year he had been granted the honour of being appointed Master Carpenter of the King's Works. Success and rewards had come to him throughout the reigns of Charles II, William and Mary, then Anne, and lastly from the present King George.

As Saskia stood with Robert's arm still about her shoulders memories swept over her as she reviewed Grinling's life. He, a young Dutchman, had come to England and made it his home, even though he never lost his strong Dutch accent and had continued to write phonetically all his life, letting others decipher his meaning. Throughout his years he had beautified so many of England's great houses and palaces as richly as if he had garlanded them with gold. She and Robert had seen him standing with Wren when in the midst of a great gathering of people they had watched the esteemed architect's son place the Cross at the very top of the great dome of St Paul's Cathedral as the final act in its rebuilding. Then they had gone into the light-filled, gloriously designed cathedral for a service of Thanksgiving and the choir had sung joyously from the stalls that Grinling had carved so magnificently.

'It is time for us to go home,' Saskia said quietly when the letter had been read a second time.

Robert nodded. 'We'll leave tomorrow.'

Later in London, when Saskia had come to terms with the loss that she and Robert both suffered, they went to St Paul's Church in Covent Garden to visit Grinling's last resting place. She had brought with her a small circular wreath of flowers, such as those he had loved to carve, which was like the gift he had given her of a little looking-glass all those years ago. She laid it by his name.

As she came out into the sunshine again, her hand in the crook of Robert's arm, she considered once more how Grinling alone had swept decorative wood carving into the realms of high art. She thought it doubtful that his like would ever come again.